GET THIS FREE DIGITAL BOOK!

For a Limited Time Only

FREE 

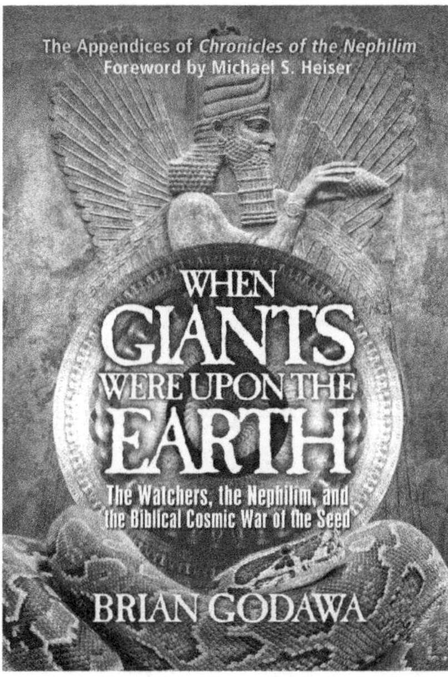

The Biblical Research of All 8 Chronicles of the Nephilim Together in One Book!

By Brian Godawa

Chapters Include:

- The Book of Enoch
- Sons of God
- The Nephilim
- Leviathan
- Cosmic Geography in the Bible
- Gilgamesh and the Bible
- Mythical Monsters in the Bible
- Goliath was Not Alone
- Jesus and the Cosmic War
- AND MORE!

See page 279 for how to get this ebook FREE.

Caleb Vigilant

Chronicles of the Nephilim
Book Six

By Brian Godawa

Dedicated to
The memory of Caleb ben Jephunneh
A man of faith

ACKNOWLEDGMENTS

Special thanks to my Rahab, Kimberly. And to Michael Gavlak for his important story feedback, and his Caleb friendship (Or really, his Joshua friendship since I'm the old man). Thanks to Don Enevoldsen and Blake Samuels for their story feedback and encouragement. Shari Risoff, my sister-in-law did a wonderful job of editing these two volumes.

Thank you, Yahweh Elohim.

NOTE TO THE READER

For those who are new to the series and have not read previous volumes, there is much imagination in this novel and its companion volume, *Joshua Valiant*, that may freak out Christians who are unfamiliar with the ancient Near Eastern worldview and mindset within which the writers of Scripture themselves lived and wrote.

Within these pages one will read of fantasy creatures like Leviathan the sea dragon of chaos, Satyrs with the torso of men and the lower legs of a goat, and other phantasmagorical images. It may shock the reader to discover that all these monsters are mentioned in the Bible in one form or another, often with reference to the paganism of Canaan.

When the Biblical writers engage in this kind of referencing, they are often using well known images and myths of their day to attack with polemical force. Thus, the satyrs that pagans worship are considered goat demons (Lev. 17:7; 2Chron. 11:15; Deut. 32:17). What I decided to do was to literalize the metaphors and bring these demonic creatures to life in all their spiritual imagination, thus embedding historical story with theological meaning. This is just what the Bible writers did for example when describing Yahweh crushing the heads of Leviathan when Moses crossed the Red Sea

(Psa. 74:12-17), or describing the destruction of a nation in terms of the collapse of the universe (Judg. 5:19-20; Isa. 13:10; 24:1-23). So I have shown the actual activity of Yahweh through his angels fighting the sea dragon to put down evil, as well as the true demonic reality behind pagan religion.

In this sense, the Chronicles are not an attempt to reimagine history but rather to imbue it with theological meaning. But despite this use of imagination, everything that occurs in the novels, every monster, every fictional character, is based on real Biblical and ancient historical and mythological research. If the reader has difficulty fully embracing this before reading, perhaps it would be helpful to first read the Appendices I have at the back of each novel before reading the novel. In those Appendices I reveal a bit of the research into the ancient Near Eastern worldview that goes behind the fiction.

I have made up far less material than you may realize.

In these novels you will also see angels that are very physical beings (with extra-physical and preternatural abilities) who fight with swords and cannot fly. It is important to remember that the modern notions of angels as immaterial spirit beings who fly with wings is a medieval construct not a Biblical description.

In the Bible angels may mysteriously appear and disappear, but they never have wings, they are not depicted as flying, and they are very physical creatures who eat food (Gen. 18:8), can have sex with humans (Gen. 6:1-4), and sometimes have swords as weapons (Josh. 5:13). Their flesh is a different kind of flesh than human flesh, but it is physical (1Cor. 15:39-40). I would contend that my view is actually closer to the Biblical picture than the conventional wisdom of winged spirit beings without physicality.

Another element of the storyline is a certain reality to the pagan gods of the world. They exist as supernatural beings with divine powers. But they are not actual gods as the pagans understand them, but rather demonic fallen "Watchers" or "sons of God" from God's heavenly host, who are masquerading as gods in order to draw worship away from Yahweh. This too is not entirely manufactured on my part, but rather an application of Biblical verses that hint at the demonic reality behind Canaanite deities.

Psalm 106:36-38

36 They served their idols, which became a snare to them. 37 They sacrificed their sons and their daughters to the <u>demons</u>; 38 they poured out innocent blood, the blood of their sons and daughters, whom they sacrificed to the <u>idols of Canaan</u>, and the land was polluted with blood.

Deuteronomy 32:16-17

16 They stirred him to jealousy with <u>strange gods</u>; with abominations they provoked him to anger. 17 They sacrificed to <u>demons that were no gods, to gods they had never known</u>, to new gods that had come recently, whom your fathers had never dreaded.

In Genesis 6:1-4 we read that these fallen Sons of Gods or Watchers came to earth and mated with human woman in order to corrupt the human bloodline that would bring forth Messiah. The fruit of that unholy forbidden union were the Nephilim, or giants of old. Though God destroyed this abomination with the Flood, the genetic corruption of the giants continued on into the seedline of

Canaan, so that when Joshua entered Canaan, it was filled with giant clans who traced their descendants back to the Nephilim before the Flood (Num. 13:32-33). Some of these giant clans were the Rephaim, the Anakim, the Emim and Zamzummim (Deut. 2:10-23) and others who show up in the *Chronicles of the Nephilim.*

Then a strange thing happened at the Tower of Babel incident. When God separated the nations in their rebellion, he placed them under the authority of the fallen Sons of God or Watchers. God allotted the territories of nations to those Watchers as their own property (Deut. 32:8-9). God gave them over to their abominations. But then, when Israel would enter into the land of Canaan to claim it for their own, God would disinherit those principalities and powers and give that land to Jacob, the Seed of Abraham.

I have already explained in more detail the Biblical proof of these elements in previous Chronicles, so if the reader wants to understand it more fully, I recommend starting with *Noah Primeval* and read the appendices and the novels from there.

Another element of *Joshua Valiant* and *Caleb Vigilant* that may cause some concern with religious believers in the Bible is my census of about six thousand warriors and seventy thousand Hebrews in the exodus. For those acquainted with the English translations, it seems that the Bible says there were six hundred thousand warriors and by implication, about two and a half to three million Hebrews in the exodus (Num. 1:46). This is not an attempt to deny or change holy writ. The fact of the matter is that the consensus of both liberal and conservative scholarship is that the English translation of "six hundred thousand" warriors cannot possibly be literally accurate.

Most importantly, it would make the Bible contradict itself, because in Deuteronomy 7:1 and 7, God states that the seven nations of Canaan were "more numerous and mightier" than Israel, who were "the fewest of all peoples." But in fact, during this time of the late Bronze Age and early Iron Age, there were less than one million inhabitants of Canaan.[1] That would make Israel more numerous and mightier by a figure of three times the whole of Canaan and as much as ten times the size of any singular people group. Secondly, if there were two and a half million Israelites, then the average Israelite mother would have had about one hundred children each, another absurdity. Worse yet, for the peoples of Canaan to be more numerous and mightier than two or three million Israelites, there would have to be over twenty million Canaanites in the land. That is demonstrably false by archeological and historical evidence.[2]

I do not have the room to explain the details here, but I have included on the ChroniclesoftheNephilim.com website under the "Links" page, several articles that address possible interpretations of the numbers that would maintain the accuracy of Scripture. Scholar David Fouts presents a strong case for the numbers being symbolic, a common technique used throughout the entire Bible. But I have used J.W. Wenham's thesis that the Hebrew word for thousand is *'lep*, which is a word that can mean military units of troops. Since Hebrew numbers were not numerical like ours, but words, the number "six hundred and three thousand" would actually translate as "six hundred and three military units" which would be more like six thousand troops in a population of about seventy thousand Israelites.

---

[1] John H Walton, *Zondervan Illustrated Bible Backgrounds Commentary* (Old Testament): Genesis, Exodus, Leviticus, Numbers, Deuteronomy, vol. 1 (Grand Rapids, MI: Zondervan, 2009), 344.
[2] David M. Fouts, "A Defense Of The Hyperbolic Interpretation Of Large Numbers In The Old Testament," *JETS* 40/3 (September 1997), 378.

One last note of importance: The saga *Chronicles of the Nephilim* employs an ancient technique of changing names of both people and places from novel to novel and sometimes within the same novel. This peculiar technique was universally engaged in by all ancient Near Eastern writing including the Bible because in that world, names were not merely arbitrary sign references. Names reflected the essential purpose, meaning, or achievement of people or places. Thus, when people experienced significant changes in their lives, they might also change their name or the name of a location where it occurred. Or when one nation adopted another nation's deity, it would give it their own name.

Even the God of the Bible uses different names for himself in different instances to communicate his different attributes. While this is not familiar to modern readers and can cause difficulty in keeping all the names and identities straight, I have chosen to employ that peculiar technique as a way of incarnating the ancient worldview and mindset. So reader be warned to watch names carefully and expect them to be changing on you even when you are not looking.

In the interest of aiding the reader in managing the name changes in the series up to this point, and including *Caleb Vigilant*, I have included the following charts that illustrate some of the more significant name changes.

	Creator	Zaqiel	Azazel	Gadreel	Gilgamesh
Enoch Primordial (Sumer)	Elohim	Utu	Inanna	—	—
Noah Primeval (Sumer)	Elohim, Yahweh	Utu	Inanna	—	—
Gilgamesh Immortal (Sumer)	Elohim	Shamash	Ishtar	Ninurta	Gilgamesh
Abraham Allegiant (Babylon)	El Shaddai	Shamash	Ishtar	Marduk	Nimrod
Abraham Allegiant (Canaan)	El Elyon	Chemosh	Ashtart	Ba'al	Amraphel
Caleb Vigilant (Canaan)	Yahweh	Chemosh	Ashtart Ashtoreth	Ba'al	—
Divine attribute	Creator Almighty Most High	Sun god	Goddess of sex & war	God of vegetation & storm	A Nephilim

	Creator God	Nachash	Giant Clans	Sons of God	The World Tree
Other Names	Yahweh Elohim	The Serpent	Nephilim	Bene ha Elohim	Mother Earth Goddess
	Yahweh	The Accuser Adversary	Rephaim	Watchers	Great Goddess
	Elohim	Mastema	Emim	gods	Gaia
	El Shaddai	A Seraphim	Caphtorim	Heavenly Host	
	Angel of Yahweh	Shining One	Zamzummim (Zuzim)	Divine Council	
	Son of Man	Accuser	Anakim	Shining Ones	
	El Elyon	Diablos	Avvim	Holy Ones	
		Belial	Horim	Anunnaki	

	True Heaven	Canaanite Pantheon	Mesopotamian Heavens and Earth
Hierarchy	Yahweh Elohim	El	Yahweh Elohim's throne
	Angel of Yahweh	Ba'al (rises to primacy)	The waters above the heavens
	Seraphim	Asherah (El's wife)	The firmament
	Cherubim	Anat (Ba'al's sister)	The heavens
	Sons of God "Watchers"	Ashtart	Earth
	Archangels	Dagon, Molech, Chemosh	The Abyss
	Angels		Pillars of the earth
			Sheol

This book continues the story begun in *Joshua Valiant*.

Numbers 13:32-33

So they brought to the people of Israel a bad report of the land that they had spied out, saying, "The land, through which we have gone to spy it out, is a land that devours its inhabitants, and all the people that we saw in it are of great height. And there we saw the Nephilim (the sons of Anak, who come from the Nephilim), and we seemed to ourselves like grasshoppers, and so we seemed to them."

Deuteronomy 9:1-2

"Hear, O Israel: you are to cross over the Jordan today, to go in to dispossess nations greater and mightier than you, cities great and fortified up to heaven, a people great and tall, the sons of the Anakim, whom you know, and of whom you have heard it said, 'Who can stand before the sons of Anak?'"

Joshua 15:13-15

According to the commandment of the LORD to Joshua, he gave to Caleb the son of Jephunneh a portion among the people of Judah, Kiriath-arba, that is, Hebron (Arba was the father of Anak). And Caleb drove out from there the three sons of Anak, Sheshai and Ahiman and Talmai, the descendants of Anak.

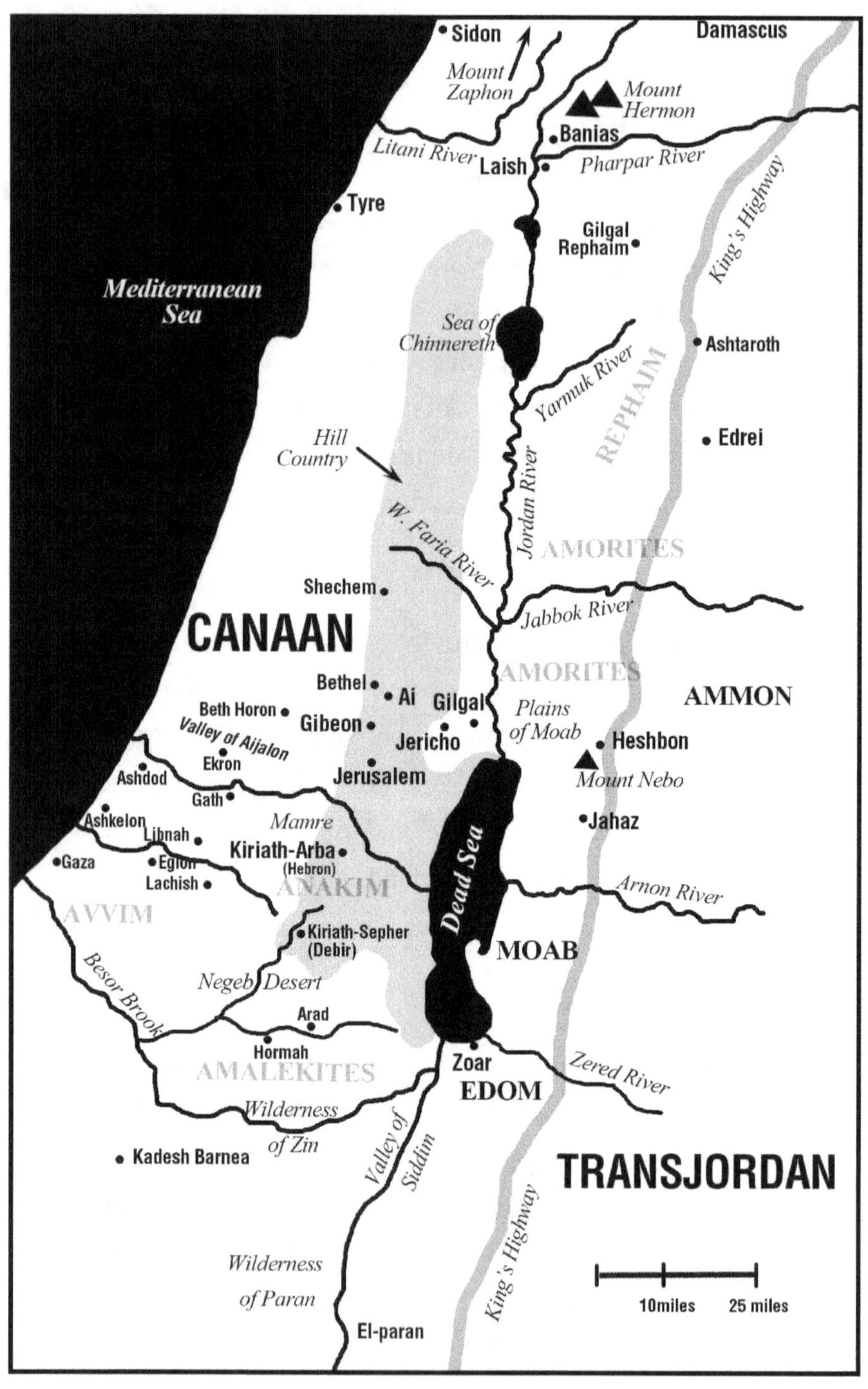
Sidon
Mount Zaphon
Damascus
Mount Hermon
Litani River
Banias
Laish
Pharpar River
Tyre
Gilgal Rephaim
King's Highway
Mediterranean Sea
Ashtaroth
Sea of Chinnereth
Yarmuk River
REPHAIM
Edrei
Hill Country
Jordan River
W. Faria River
AMORITES
Shechem
CANAAN
Jabbok River
AMORITES
AMMON
Bethel
Ai
Gilgal
Plains of Moab
Beth Horon
Gibeon
Heshbon
Valley of Aijalon
Jericho
Ekron
Jerusalem
Mount Nebo
Ashdod
Gath
Jahaz
Ashkelon
Mamre
Libnah
Kiriath-Arba
Gaza
Eglon
(Hebron)
Lachish
ANAKIM
Dead Sea
Arnon River
AVVIM
Kiriath-Sepher
(Debir)
Besor Brook
MOAB
Negeb Desert
Arad
Hormah
AMALEKITES
Zoar
EDOM
Zered River
Wilderness of Zin
Kadesh Barnea
Valley of Siddim
TRANSJORDAN
Wilderness of Paran
King's Highway
El-paran
10miles
25 miles

CHAPTER 30

(Continuing from the last chapter of Joshua Valiant)

Two men entered the tavern to eat their afternoon meal. They looked suspicious to Rahab. She had been an innkeeper in Jericho long enough to be able to spot real danger amidst the rowdies, roughnecks, and rabble-rousers who frequented her establishment.

These two were clearly foreigners. They kept to themselves in the corner and seemed to have the disciplined posture and movements of mercenaries. They were not very good at hiding it.

But they both rather intrigued her.

And she was not very good at hiding her fascination with them. They quickly noticed her and waved her over to them.

She swallowed and patted her dress to make sure her secret dagger was available.

She strode over, with a smooth elegance. It always helped to distract those who might have nefarious intentions. It gave her the advantage—over swine.

The younger more handsome one with a ruddy complexion watched her like a puppy in her hand. But the other one, the older one with intense eyes, glanced away as if he were fighting his attraction. Or maybe he didn't prefer women. That would be more difficult for her to work with.

"How can I help you, travelers?" she said. "Are you looking for some pleasure? Women? Men? I do not do children here, or animals."

The handsome one spoke. Obviously doing the bidding of the older one, the real leader. "Are you Rahab, the innkeeper?"

She looked suspiciously at them. "Who wants to know?"

They looked at each other. The older one nodded.

The younger one spoke, "I am Salmon and this is Caleb. We seek information and were told this was the place for it."

They took a chance. They told her their real names. They knew that if they wanted to gain her trust, they would have to risk being vulnerable.

She looked closely at them. They were telling the truth. She could spot a liar across the room through his eyes. And most men were liars.

Then she said with a touch of surprise, "Semitic names. Are you Habiru, from across the river?"

They both looked around nervously, hoping no one heard her.

Caleb stepped in, "We will pay plenty."

Rahab decided to try for the old one. The ruddy one she already had. This one was a challenge.

She stepped uncomfortably close to Caleb, and dragged her hand across his hair. He was very nervous and would not look her in the eye.

"Well, you know," she said, "You two are not very good spies."

Caleb and Salmon looked at each other. Was it that obvious? Caleb was particularly discouraged because he had earlier chosen the young Salmon for his skilled espionage against the city of Edrei in the Transjordan. Salmon was able to gather intelligence on the city and its army of giants that enabled their victory over Og of Bashan. How was he able to get away when he was now such a poorly disguised spy?

Rahab whispered to Caleb as if she had read his mind, "Actually it is you who is the obvious one. But if you want to do this right, you have to play the game or everyone is going to know why you are here. So, let us go up to my room and give the impression to everyone that you really are just a couple of oblivious reprobates."

She smiled at them.

They had stopped breathing.

She was beauty incarnate.

Caleb turned away again. She took his chin and pulled him back to look into her eyes.

When he did, she shuddered. It was like looking into pools of intense purity. And she suddenly felt very dirty. She had never seen a soul like this before. This one was strangely attractive to her, and strong, even though he was old enough to be her grandfather.

She pulled away from them, grabbing Caleb's hand and leading them both up the stairs into her loft.

They followed her awkwardly, and the patrons of the bar that night were all envious of these two foreigners who were about to discover just how lucky they were to be with Rahab the harlot.

One of those patrons was in disguise that evening in the other corner of the tavern. It was Jebir, the Chief Commander's Right Hand. He watched them closely. He was not sure if he should trust his instincts about them. Or maybe he was just extra sensitive because of his own envy of their privilege of company with the woman to whom he could never reveal that he was secretly in love.

He decided to trust his instincts, and left immediately.

Caleb and Salmon examined Rahab's room. It was on the very roof of the inn with a window on the outer wall of the city as well as access to the rooftop. She had a large beautiful bed with satin sheets.

She sat on those sheets like a goddess. Salmon practically drooled on himself.

But she stared at Caleb.

Salmon said, "How old are you?"

She said, "Are all you Habiru so vulgar? You do not ask a woman such things."

She was only twenty-nine, but her experience made her an old soul far beyond her years.

Caleb could see it behind her ravishing eyes.

She kept staring at Caleb. "Well, what is it you want to know? And how much are you willing to pay?"

Caleb reached in his cloak without a word and tossed a pouch onto her bed with a twinge of disgust.

She opened it and looked inside. Her brows rose with great interest. There was gold in the pouch. A lot of gold.

"You must want me to remain very quiet indeed," she said and gave a flirty glance at Salmon who could not take his eyes off her.

"But before I tell you anything, you never answered my question. Are you Israelite Habiru?"

They looked at each other again to decide if they should tell her.

"Yes," said Caleb. "We come from across the Jordan."

Caleb could see that Rahab's countenance changed almost instantly. She smiled like an excited child.

Salmon kept staring at her.

Caleb continued, attempting to be discreet about his true intentions, "We want to know about the land and the people here.

What is the governance; independent cities or territorial warlords? Would there be a hostile reaction to new settlers?"

Instead, she answered the questions he really wanted to ask. "This is a military post. We only have a thousand soldiers. The Chief Commander of the fort is Alyun-Yarikh. He relies too much on infantry and does not value his archers enough. And we are not due for reinforcements or replacements for another few months. Unfortunately, our walls are strong, and I am not aware of any weaknesses in its defense."

Caleb realized his description as "new settlers" was an obvious deception to her. Their intentions were also transparent.

"Are there any giants?" he asked. "Anakim?"

"Alyun has a bodyguard of five Anakim. Those are the only giants I know of."

Rahab got up and carried the pouch over to Caleb. Salmon watched her like a loyal dog hoping for a piece of food.

Rahab got right up into Caleb's face and handed him the pouch back with an air kiss.

"I do not want your money."

Caleb was confused.

Rahab turned and faced Salmon who finally looked into her eyes instead of every other body part. She recited the words of the secret Habiru poem that she had memorized. She said the words with a loving passionate caress. She even started to sing the words with a slight harmony,

"I will sing to Yahweh, for he has triumphed gloriously;

the horse and his rider he has thrown into the sea.

Yahweh is my strength and my song,

and he has become my salvation;

this is my god, and I will praise him,

my father's god, and I will exalt him.

Then Rahab turned back and faced Caleb again, and recited,

Yahweh is a man of war;

Yahweh is his name."

The men were stunned. They stared at this woman, considered unclean by holiness standards—a Canaanite singing the praises of Yahweh.

Salmon blurted out, "That is the Song of Moses. How did you…?"

She continued, "Amorite traders across the Jordan. I know that Yahweh has given you this land and the fear of Yahweh has fallen upon Canaan. I have read how Yahweh brought you out of Egypt and dried up the Red Sea before you. I have heard of how you defeated the Amorite kings of the Transjordan, Og of Bashan and Sihon of Heshbon. How you devoted them to destruction. As soon as I heard this, my heart melted within me. Your god Yahweh is god of the heavens and the earth and I want to join you. I want to become an Israelite."

Caleb was no longer surprised with her bluntness. "We cannot take you with us. It would be too dangerous."

"I do not need to go with you. Just swear to me by Yahweh that as I have dealt kindly with you, so you will deal kindly with me and will not put me to the sword."

Caleb said, "I swear it."

Rahab said, "And my family as well."

Caleb nodded.

"My mother and father, and sisters and brothers."

Caleb raised his brow.

"And all that belong to them. Promise me."

Caleb repeated, "And all that belong to them."

"Oh, and that you will not enslave us."

Caleb was about to respond.

"Or leave us in the desert to die."

"Rahab," said Caleb, trying to interrupt.

"And also if you change your mind, or fail to fulfill your vow, that Yahweh would curse you."

"Rahab, I am the Right Hand of the Commander of Israel. I promise you on my life that we will deal kindly and faithfully with you."

"Good," said Rahab, "Then you are the perfect person to sign this."

She walked over to a trunk and pulled out a piece of parchment. She brought it over to Caleb and handed it to him.

He looked at it. "What is this, a treaty?"

"I made it, hoping for this very day. I have been planning for a long time."

Caleb read some of it. He looked up at her, impressed with her determination and thoroughness.

She said, "I *am* the owner of a business."

Caleb shook his head and said, "Let me look this over in my room. Salmon?"

"Uh, I will stay here," said Salmon with a guilty look. "I would like to talk some more to our kind host."

Caleb turned and glared at his compatriot. "Salmon, your weakness is unbecoming a soldier of Yahweh."

"I am sorry, Caleb, but we cannot all be paragons of holiness like you and Joshua."

Caleb said with contempt, "suffer your own consequences," and left them.

It was one of those sins that the men of Israel too often turned a blind eye toward.

Rahab watched Caleb leave, offended by his self-righteousness. She had never met a man who could turn away from her like Caleb did. She was not going to capture that one after all. But she knew she had better increase her chances of favor by endearing herself to Salmon.

He was the better-looking one anyway.

She turned and gave him a seductive look. "Well, Salmon, what did you want to talk about?"

CHAPTER 31

Mastema strode pompously before the divine council of holy ones. In the heavenly court he was called *the satan*, which meant "adversary" or "accuser." It was his duty to prosecute legal accusations against Yahweh Elohim and his people. He would go to and fro amidst the earth seeking ways to challenge the Law of God or manipulate it to unjust ends.

One of those unjust ends was currently in process. The Accuser had filed a temporary restraining order against Israel to keep them from entering the land of Canaan. And he was following through on a class action lawsuit on behalf of the people and gods of Canaan. He now stood before the court presenting his evidence that Yahweh had made an illegitimate claim of eminent domain on Canaan, and that Israel was engaged in war crimes against humanity.

Behind him were the divine claimants, the gods of Canaan, represented by Ba'al, Chemosh, Molech, Dagon, and Asherah. Of course, in the divine council, their real names would be used: The Watchers Gadreel, Zaqiel, Neqael, Kestarel, and Turiel. Ashtart, or Azazel the Watcher, would not be involved in this covenant lawsuit as she was currently indisposed—had her hands tied—in the depths of Tartarus under the watch of the Rephaim of Sheol.

Ten thousands of the heavenly host surrounded the throne chariot of Yahweh Elohim with the burning brilliance of ten million lamps. The sphinx-like Cherubim held his chariot below and the serpentine Seraphim guarded his holiness from above. A flame of fire was at his right hand, and a stream of fire poured out before his throne.

The defense team included the Son of Man and Enoch ben Methuselah, who stood by the other defendant Mikael, the representative prince of Israel. Enoch was the righteous one who had been translated in antediluvian days before he could see death. He too shined with the luminescence of his heavenly habitation.

Enoch had been here before. In the days leading up to the Deluge, the Accuser had filed another class action lawsuit against Yahweh Elohim in order to distract his heavenly host from being available to defend against a surprise attack on the Garden of Eden. He had charged Yahweh Elohim with breach of covenant against Adam and Eve and the human race. Enoch had become one of the defense lawyers but did not have the experience to face his adversary, as he would have preferred. Yahweh liked to use weak vessels. Yahweh liked irony.

However, the Son of Man was primary counsel and would determine who would present what and when. He was an enigmatic presence whose identity Enoch could not quite get his mind wrapped around. He was not particularly striking, had no form or majesty that anyone would give him a second look, and no handsomeness that anyone would desire. He was extraordinarily plain looking, considering the position he held before the presence of Yahweh Elohim. And yet, he exuded the very presence of Yahweh Elohim. He was an embodiment of Yahweh himself, a second power in heaven.

Mikael was angered at having to be present at this circus trial. The Accuser loved class action lawsuits because they were a way of exploiting a multitude of others for his own despicable purposes. As if he cared one whit for the lives of these Canaanites he enslaved to demons. The Israelites were on the threshold of entering the Promised Land to take possession, and this slippery little serpent could derail it all with his diabolical mastery of legal loopholes and technicalities.

It was forensic protocol for the two disputants to stand before the Judge and present their cases, whereupon the Judge would render his declaration of righteousness unto one of the disputants. This was called justification.

Enoch stood in the bar and listened to the Accuser, that master of theatrical oration, pace back and forth delivering his scathing legal attack on the Creator. His lanky features and less than impressive voice hid his intellectual brilliance—and his spiritual malevolence. He was a seraph with bright burnished bronze skin of subtle scales, and serpentine eyes.

"Regarding my first charge against Yahweh Elohim, I consider his command for this—this moral atrocity he calls "dispossession" of the Canaanites—to be the most wanton act of tyranny and imperialism in the history of the creation."

The Accuser huffed and continued. "I bring into evidence, Yahweh Elohim's own covenant, agreed to by him, under blood oath, with the *Bene ha Elohim*, his own Sons of God. And I quote, 'El Elyon the Most High gives to the nations their inheritance, at the division of mankind with the confusion of tongues. He fixes the borders of the peoples according to the number of the Sons of God. But Yahweh's portion is his people, Jacob his allotted heritage.'"

He paused. "Is there any need for cross examination or for this trial to even continue? It is right there—in blood. We were all there, all of us, at the Tower of Babel division. We were all called as witnesses to the covenant of inheritance."

He pointed to the tens of thousands around the throne who were those very witnesses.

"Yahweh has allotted the seventy nations and their land under the authority of those of us on earth." He pointed to the Watchers on his side. "And now he seeks to take it away as if he has the right. That is not eminent domain, that is colonialism! All these poor innocent Canaanites will be slaughtered in mass ethnic cleansing, and their cities burned to the ground in a holocaust of flames to make room for the expansionist policies of a greedy land-grabbing god who claims 'divine exceptionalism' as justification for genocide."

The Accuser then raised his hands in mocking worship.

"'The incomparability of Yahweh.' Well, let me just say right now, *all* the gods consider themselves exceptional. He is not the only one. But I would say, he is surely the most angry, bitter, and wrathful one that I have ever seen. What kind of a loving god would be so cruel as to kill non-combatants and cast them into Sheol? Not only that, but also every last woman and child, as they are declared as *herem*, or devoted to destruction. I ask, who would want to worship a god like that, a god who gets his jollies punishing innocent human beings forever with eternal torture?"

Enoch rolled his eyes. Here he went again with his "what kind of a god" hateful ad hominem attacks. He made plenty of them back in the Eden lawsuit, and he would never stop reaching for an opportunity to unfairly impugn Yahweh's character.

Enoch burst out, "I object. These are ad hominem attacks without material force."

"I beg to differ, counsel," said the Accuser. "They are quite material as to the credibility of the accused to fulfill his covenants."

"Overruled," said Yahweh Elohim to Enoch.

The Accuser grinned with pride. "May I also remind the court that this is exactly what I predicted in the Eden trial. And now I say the chickens have come home to roost."

Enoch thought the Accuser looked like a chicken strutting around with his chin thrust out and his nose in the air.

"Now, regarding those innocent and peaceful indigenous peoples, the Canaanites—who were in the land first—long before Israel ever got here. I would also like to charge the Israelites as well as Yahweh with racial discrimination against a protected minority. They are singling out Canaanites from all the races on the earth as the victims of their hate crimes. These racists and their xenophobic religion foster an 'Us versus Them' mentality that lashes out in fear and violence against 'the Other.' Why should these innocent Canaanites be targeted with such violence and wrath? They were simply victims of their birth and geography. They were born and raised in Canaan, and they were taught the religion of Canaan. If they were born in Babylon, they would believe Babylonian religion, if in Egypt, Egyptian religion. What kind of a god would punish and destroy a people for an accident of birth? And why should these foreign Habiru be considered 'chosen ones' when they are no better than the Canaanites? You have seen for yourself how they played the harlot with Ba'al, Chemosh, and Molech when they got the chance."

Those three named Watcher gods felt offended by the reference, but they knew it was all just rhetoric to try to use Yahweh's own religious morals against him.

The Accuser wound it up, "The Israelites are simply not a righteous people and therefore have no right to 'dispossess' the Canaanites from their land just because they are the putzes of Yahweh."

He wasted no opportunity to attack his human enemies with verbal arson. The fact was, the Accuser would like to burn all of the Israelites in the flaming ovens of Molech if he got the chance.

He gave his concluding statement, "I warn you, if you follow through with these Yahweh Wars, as you call them, you will be giving permission to every religion known to man, from now until the end of history, to do the same thing in the name of their god. And all the innocent blood of those hundreds of millions of victims will be on your hands. I rest my case."

CHAPTER 32

Caleb was having a difficult time reading Rahab's treaty because he could not get the image of her out of his mind. He had tried not to look at her because of his desire to be pure in his heart before Yahweh. But the few looks that he did get of her were burned into his mind like a branding iron.

And it was not just her looks either. When she was close to him, he could smell her scent, and when she turned, her hair brushed over him. He felt a shudder go through his body at the touch of her hand returning the pouch. She was like a heavenly vision that made him come alive. And it had been some time since that had happened. He had hardly noticed women since his wife had died so many years ago.

As he read over Rahab's scrupulously detailed and enumerated rights, he smiled at her industriousness. But he also felt himself strongly attracted to her like a moth to a flaming torch and he felt stupid for it—weak. Was he just like every other man in that establishment, crumbling in complete vulnerability to such a woman? Was he too, just a prisoner of his desires?

Yet there was something different about her. Something strangely pure. He could not put his finger on it because it seemed so counter-intuitive. But when she had looked into his eyes, he saw a passionate soul like his own. A zest for life and a strong will in submission to Yahweh. He considered himself unclean for thinking of it but he almost felt that she had submitted herself to him at that very moment.

He shook it out of his head. It was probably because she was an abused woman, a destroyed soul.

He was interrupted in his thoughts by Rahab's arrival in his room.

"Caleb, come quickly."

He followed her into her room where he found a smiling Salmon. A jealousy swept over Caleb.

But he could not bother with such silliness in this moment.

She rushed them over to the balcony.

"The Commander's men are on their way here. They are looking for you."

"How did they know?" asked Caleb.

She said, "They have spies in the tavern looking out for spies."

Salmon said with a smirk, "Did they spy us spies?"

Caleb shot him a dirty look. "Now is not the time for frivolity."

"Sorry."

Then, Caleb added with a glance at Rahab, "or to gloat in your sin."

Rahab looked back at Caleb with anger. She had a lot to figure out about these Habiru and their peculiar ways.

She led them up to the roof where she had stored a pile of flax for cloth making.

"Here," she said. "Hide under these. I will tell the men you have already gone."

Caleb grabbed her arm. "How can we trust you will not give us up?"

She returned, "How can *I* trust that you will not give *me* up?"

He pulled out her treaty and handed it to her. She looked at it. It was signed. She grinned.

Salmon was still watching her like a loyal puppy.

"Now hide yourselves. There is not much time."

She left them and rushed downstairs to settle herself in the tavern as if she had been there all along.

Salmon watched her go.

Caleb said, "Hurry up, Salmon."

He turned to Caleb. "Is she not amazing?"

Caleb rolled his eyes.

When Jebir left Rahab's tavern, he had intended to make his way directly to the Commander Alyun's quarters and alert him to the presence of spies. But because of his lust for Rahab, he was conflicted, so he walked through the streets of the city reevaluating his options. It was the law that an innkeeper who harbored or aided spies would be executed. It happened too often in these lands.

But he could not bring himself to be the messenger of death for the most arrestingly beautiful woman on the face of the earth. He desired her with much pain. Until he realized that he would lose his own head if the Commander ever found out. So self-preservation won out over self-gratification and Jebir found himself just before dark giving Alyun the news.

When Jebir arrived at the tavern with his company of ten soldiers, he found Rahab cleaning up at the counter where she poured the beer and wine.

"Rahab, where are the travelers with whom you spoke earlier this evening? Bring them out to me."

"Which travelers?" she asked with an impatient look. "I have had twenty new travelers today, as I do every day from all over the land."

"The Habiru," he said. And then with jealous grit, he added, "The ones you brought upstairs."

"So those were Habiru?" she said with feigned shock. "They never told me. They were very private. Would not tell me anything."

She was taunting him.

"Which rooms are they in?"

"Oh, they have already left through the city gate before it closed at dark. I do not know where they went. But I can tell you one thing I know about them: they treated me with respect. Like a lady."

She threw in that last line just to distract Jebir with more anger. She knew he had a crush on her and she knew she could use that to her advantage one day. That day had finally arrived.

"It was not but an hour ago. If you hurry, you might catch them. If they are Habiru as you say, then would they not be going to cross the Jordan?"

Jebir looked hard into Rahab's eyes. He wanted to see if she was lying, but he could not tell.

He turned to his men. "Check all the rooms before we leave." And then added as an afterthought, "And the roof."

A pang of fear rushed over Rahab. She tried to hide it.

The men checked the rooms. Jebir ended up with two of them on the roof of Rahab's inn.

There was nothing there but a big pile of flax.

Jebir looked at the stalks lying in order. It was too orderly.

He nodded to the two soldiers.

They pulled their swords and walked over to the stalks.

And then both of them thrust their swords into the piles to seek out anyone hiding underneath. They jabbed around the whole stacks to make sure they did not miss any possible fugitive hiding out.

But there was no one there.

"Let us go," said Jebir. We will follow the path to the Jordan."

And they left.

In their focus on the flax stalks, they had failed to consider checking the edge of the roof, where Caleb and Salmon hung by their fingertips over the edge fifty feet up in the air.

They had originally been hiding under the flax. But Caleb made a last second change of plans and they slid over the side of the building.

They pulled themselves up.

They met Rahab back in her room.

"Thank Yahweh they did not find you," she said.

Caleb said, "Can we go through the gate?"

She said, "No, It is closed for the evening. Besides, everyone would see you. I have a better idea."

She moved over to a basket by her window and opened it. She pulled out a long rope died scarlet red.

"What is that for?" asked Caleb.

She said, "Well, as you now know, I am always well prepared for contingencies. I have had to be in my life."

She took the rope and hung it outside the window against the wall.

"Why is it red?" asked Salmon.

"To throw off suspicion. If anyone should come upon it for any reason, they would consider it some kind of decoration, similar to the red banner that marks this tavern as a house of indulgence."

"You are cunning," said Caleb.

"If you only knew what I have been through," she said.

Caleb said, "When we arrive at the city, tie this cord outside your window so the troops will know where you are and will pass over your household."

"You are cunning yourself," she replied.

He said, "But if any of your household venture out of this building, their blood will be on their own heads."

She countered, "And if any of your men lay a hand on any of my household within this building, our blood will be on *your* heads."

"Fair enough," he said. But he would not be outdone. "But if you reveal our plans to anyone, then we are released from this treaty on all counts."

She deferred, "According to your words, so be it. Now make sure you go into the hills for three days until they return before you set off for the Jordan."

Salmon said, "I will be back for you, Rahab."

She rolled her eyes and said, "That is what they all say, Salmon. Now get going."

CHAPTER 33

The Son of Man stood before the throne of witnesses and began his legal defense of Yahweh's War. Mikael waited impatiently in his place, knowing that he was needed by Israel as soon as they could get this ridiculous restraining order thrown out of court.

Unlike the Accuser, the Son of Man would follow protocol and properly give honor to the Judge of all things.

"Let the heavens praise your wonders, O Yahweh, your faithfulness in the assembly of the holy ones! For who in the skies can be compared to Yahweh? Who among the gods is like Yahweh, a God greatly to be feared in the council of the holy ones, and awesome above all who are around him? O Yahweh Elohim of hosts, the heavens are yours; the earth also is yours; the world and all that is in it, you have founded them. You have taken your place in the divine council; in the midst of the gods you hold judgment."

The Accuser muttered under his breath to his fellow litigants, "Brown-nosed godlicker."

The Son of Man then took his own turn around the dais to give his delivery some movement. But he was careful not to take the bait and respond to the Accuser's pompous bloviating with his own in kind. Enoch had learned this lesson at the Eden trial where his pride got the better of him and he almost lost the case, had it not been for the Son of Man who came and rescued the verdict with victory.

The Son of Man's delivery was passionate yet professional. He decided to begin with restating the charges that were lost in the emotional vomit of manipulative rhetoric used by the Accuser.

"Do the Israelites have the right to dispossess the land of Canaan from its inhabitants? Are the Wars of Yahweh just or unjust? That is the question before us today in this court. And we will prove that the plaintiff's charges are prejudicial and frivolous; his arguments fallacious and without legal or moral merit."

Mikael could hear the reaction of the litigants' scoffing mockery and ridicule under their breaths. They were Sons of God, divine heavenly beings, and yet in this courtroom they acted like snide sophomoric juveniles. It was despicable.

The Son of Man continued, "First, regarding the prosecutor's accusation of imperialism, I think a definition of terms is in order here. Imperialism is defined as an act of empire asserting authority over dependent states. You have no argument from the defense on that count, since Yahweh Elohim is the emperor of the heavens and the earth and he does as he pleases. So, yes, he is the imperial authority and his acts are indeed imperial and all humanity are his subjects. Duly noted. And without moral condemnation.

"Which brings us to the only charge with legal merit in this case: The covenant documented between our sovereign emperor and the *Bene ha Elohim*. Did Yahweh break his covenant promise to the Sons of God? I submit to you that if you consider the wording of the document you will notice that at no time did Yahweh forfeit his absolute ownership and therefore authority over any land. The earth is Yahweh's and the fullness thereof. The world and those who dwell therein. In his allotment of the nations and their boundaries to the Sons of God he did not sign over the deed of absolute ownership. He is a landlord who has loaned the inhabitants the land. Simply put, the Sons of God and those under their authority are renters, not owners. The land has always remained Yahweh's to distribute as he wills, when he wills. He is after all, as we already established, the emperor."

He paused to change course. "But even so, his dispossession is not an arbitrary act of power. It is rooted in a moral and legal failure of the gods to fulfill their responsibility to the covenant, thus rendering the covenant null and void."

The Watcher gods huffed again with contempt.

The Son of Man turned to them and prophesied, "How long will you judge unjustly, O gods, and show partiality to the wicked? Give justice to the weak and the fatherless; maintain the right of the afflicted and the destitute. Rescue the weak and the needy; deliver them from the hand of the wicked. You have neither knowledge nor understanding, you walk about in darkness; all the foundations of the earth are shaken. I said, 'You are gods, sons of El Elyon the Most High, all of you; nevertheless, like men you shall die, and fall like any prince. Arise, O God, judge the earth; for you shall inherit all the nations!'"

Again, the plaintiffs rolled their eyes, muttered curses under their breaths, and made theatrical faces of disgust that made Mikael wonder how great was the gracious patience of Yahweh that he did not simply annihilate them in his presence.

The Son of Man continued, "What does the claim of victimhood, the protest of grievance, and the accusation of oppression tell us of the litigants, when they are made against the Creator and owner of the universe? Very simply, that they define everything against their own wills as oppressive and unfair, because they are the oppressors, they are the despots, they are the tyrants—every last one of them."

The hubbub grew loud now from the plaintiff's corner. The Accuser spoke up, "I object. Counsel has complained about me engaging in ad hominem attacks and yet that is exactly what he is doing now."

The Son of Man addressed Yahweh, "Your honor, I am merely proving that the plaintiff's claims are actually expressions of his own guilt."

Yahweh Elohim said to the Accuser, "Overruled."

The Accuser sat down, but not without grumbling, "I am outraged and personally offended."

The Son of Man moved on. "Now regarding the accusations of anger and wrath unbefitting the Creator and Judge, let me just say this: It is not the god who punishes that is cruel and wicked, but the god who does not. Because the so-called "god of love" who does not pay recompense on the evildoer multiplies and extends the suffering of the victim which multiplies and extends injustice. Compassion to the guilty is cruelty to the innocent. The god who does not punish evil is the god who inflicts evil."

The Son of Man took a pause to prepare mentally for his next launch. "Now in reference to that punishment of 'innocent' Canaanites and the law of *herem,* or devotion to destruction, I have a series of points to address.

"First, Yahweh is the creator and sustainer of every living thing. He gives life and he takes it away, blessed is the name of Yahweh. He owes no man, woman, or child anything. So who can complain when something they do not own is taken from them by the one who owns it? And he takes it when he wills.

But I find it a bit of an oddity that the Accuser would argue that the actions of Yahweh toward women and children are cruel, when the Canaanites themselves kill women and children, and the gods of Canaan enslave women as property and sacrifice their children on altars of blood."

"I object!" interrupted the Accuser. "The Canaanite gods are not on trial, Yahweh is!"

The Son of Man said, "Yes, the Canaanite gods are not on trial, because they have already been judged as unjust idols worthy of execution, and their land to be confiscated as criminal property. But since the prosecution is charging the Creator with crimes against humanity, it is only fitting that their witness be disclosed as not credible in light of their own criminal behavior."

Yahweh announced to the Accuser, "Objection overruled. My Law states that a plaintiff may not be guilty of the crime of which they are a witness against a defendant."

"But your honor," said the Accuser with a slithering sarcasm, "We do not kill *every* man, woman, and child like you do."

The Son of Man said, "You know full well the *herem* is standard military hyperbole used by all Near Eastern nations."

The concept of *herem* meant complete spiritual victory or triumph over the opponent. Most non-combatants who lived around cities were not generally touched and were allowed to escape to other towns not under the *herem*. Only those who stayed in solidarity with the city were under its judgment and were annihilated.

The Son of Man added, "But regarding women's innocence, we have already seen with the Midianite seduction, women may act in ways unlike warriors, but just as evil."

The Son of Man moved on again. "And this brings me to the fallacy of innocence asserted over and over again by the prosecution. Are the Canaanites really innocent? Is Israel a barbaric xenophobic oppressor who is engaging in racist hate crimes against innocent victims? Or is that just another manipulation of emotional hate rhetoric from a barbaric xenophobic oppressor himself who seeks to engage in racist hate crimes against Israel?

"The fact of the matter is the Canaanites are *not* innocent. The wrath of Yahweh falls justly on them because they suppress the truth in unrighteousness. For Yahweh has made himself known through his creation and in the consciences of all men, so that they are without excuse. For even though the Canaanites knew Yahweh, they did not honor him as their Creator nor did they give him thanks, but their wicked and foolish hearts were darkened with evil and they exchanged the truth of Yahweh for their lies. They turned and worshiped creation in place of the Creator. So Yahweh gave them up to their depravity to dishonor their bodies and defile themselves with shameless unnatural acts of sexuality, idolatry and rebellion that they engage in to this day. And even though they know the law of God and that such things are punishable by death, they nevertheless rejoice in their evil and heartily encourage others to do so as well."

The Son of Man paused again for a conclusive punch. "So you see, the devotion to destruction of *herem* is not based on racial prejudice at all. It is based on criminal religious behavior and immorality. This is not ethnic cleansing, it is evil cleansing. But even then, Yahweh offers grace. If anyone repents from their idolatry, they will be accepted into the congregation of Israel. Yahweh has even provided laws protecting the alien and the sojourner who live amidst his people.

"Yahweh's holiness is not a double standard. For Israel too will be judged if and when she engages in the abominations of the Canaanites, as we have already seen with the judgment on those seduced by the Moabites and Midianites. God is not partial, he extends his justice to all who commit evil, Canaanite or Israelite, and he extends his loving-kindness to all who repent, Canaanite or Israelite. And one day, he will bring all the earth under the dominion of his kingdom."

The Accuser jumped up again, "I object! If the Israelites are no different than Canaanites, if they are no more holy, then why do *they* get to be the instruments of Yahweh's wrath? Why would he not choose Egyptians or Hittites or Babylonians? That is not fair! In fact, why does he not choose the Canaanites to dispossess the Israelites?"

Mikael was holding back his righteous indignation. He wanted to smite the snake. The Accuser was objecting to every petty little detail he could to try to derail the defense line of argument.

But this tactic did not faze the Son of Man. He responded to detailed attacks with detailed counterpoint truth. "Yahweh Elohim has chosen Israel to be a people for his treasured possession out of all the peoples who are on the face of the earth, not because of their righteousness or the uprightness of their hearts. They will be given possession of the land because of the wickedness of the nations. That is why Yahweh Elohim is driving them out of Canaan, that he may confirm his promise he swore to their fathers, Abraham, Isaac, and Jacob."

"That does not answer the question!" snapped the Accuser.

The Son of Man countered, "Yahweh Elohim chooses his elect, based not upon human will or deeds, but based upon Yahweh who has mercy. He has mercy on whom he has mercy, and he hardens whom he desires."

The Accuser became desperate. "Then why does he condemn anyone, for who resists his will?"

"On the contrary," said the Son of Man. "Who are you to answer back to Yahweh? Does the potter not have the right over the clay to fashion what he desires? The potter takes one lump of clay and makes some vessels of mercy prepared beforehand for honor, and glory, and makes other vessels of wrath prepared beforehand for destruction to make known his power. Such is the folly of that which is molded demanding an answer from the molder, 'Why did you make me like this?'

"Lastly, the notion that other religions will use the dispossession of the Promised Land as a justification for their own land grabs and 'holy wars' is moot. The Yahweh Wars are restricted to establishing his ownership of Canaan alone and cannot be extended to normal warfare or other nations. This is a one-time historical event that cannot be repeated. Only Yahweh is the Creator who owns all the cattle on a thousand hills as well as the hills on which those cattle stand. Only Yahweh owns the land to distribute it as he wills. All claims by other gods that mimic the Wars of Yahweh are illegitimate forgeries and therefore null and void. They are mere rationalizations of tyranny. And so I rest my case."

Yahweh Elohim retreated with his divine council to deliberate the verdict. When he returned, he announced to the lawyers at the bar, "I declare the defense righteous in standing. The Accuser has failed to provide proof of his charges against Yahweh's right to eminent domain, and his use of Israel as his instruments of justice."

"Your honor," spouted the Accuser, "I demand a court order for a stay of execution. This is a capital trial and I think we need to reexamine the evidence in light of the extreme sentence."

"Motion denied," said Yahweh Elohim. "The iniquity of the Amorites is complete. Canaan has filled up the measure of its guilt. Israel shall commence its possession of the land immediately. Court is dismissed."

CHAPTER 34

Caleb and Salmon had waited three days in the hills outside of Jericho before returning to the camp of Israel on the east side of the river Jordan. They relayed their intelligence to Joshua, and told him of the harlot Rahab and how she helped them. Joshua accepted the sparing of her life and her family's lives. He would alert the entire army of this provision.

But today was a holy day that Joshua and Caleb had been anticipating for forty years. They stood side by side with the people of Israel behind them. They followed Yahweh's very specific directions in how they would cross the river and enter into Canaan.

They watched the priests carry the Ark of the Covenant to the water's edge and step their feet just into the bank, waiting for a miracle. The miracle would have to deal with the fact that this was the springtime, when the river was flooded with a stronger current. At this location it was about one hundred and fifty feet wide and about twelve feet deep. Crossing thousands of people in riverboats would take many days.

But Yahweh had promised a sign that he would be true to his word that he would not fail to drive out the inhabitants of the land before them.

That sign began seventeen miles north of their location near the city of Adam. An earthquake shook the earth mounds around the river and a large landslide of debris tumbled down causing a temporary damming of the Jordan river.

The water stopped flowing southward and dried up the riverbed where the Israelites were standing with the Ark.

The people buzzed with excitement and were amazed.

Caleb watched it all with his poetic eye. He had seen how Yahweh was establishing Joshua as a new Moses to lead the people. This water crossing was reminiscent of the crossing of the Red Sea during the exodus under Moses. Joshua's coronation occurred after coming down from the mountain much like Moses came down Sinai with the tablets of the Law. And now Yahweh talked to Joshua almost as he had talked to Moses.

The priests carrying the Ark now walked out onto the dried up riverbed and stood with it in the middle as the people crossed over in procession.

According to Yahweh's own commands, twelve chosen men, one from each of the twelve tribes, pulled twelve large stones out of the riverbed from around the priests. They carried them to where they would be camping that night and placed them in a pile as a memorial of this day. At the same time, twelve others gathered a stone each and placed a pile of those stones in the center of the riverbed where the priests were standing.

After the people had hastily crossed over, the priests took up the Ark and left the pile of stones in the riverbed. As soon as they had made their way onto the dry land, the waters of the Jordan began to flow again and the river renewed its course to the Dead Sea.

The people made camp at a location they called Gilgal. They set up metal forges to immediately begin manufacturing more weapons for the Yahweh Wars before them.

Forty troop units came over for battle with the people. But not all of Israel came over with them that day. The Reubenites, the Gadites, and the half tribe of Manasseh had begged Moses before he died to give them the land east of the Jordan as their inheritance. It was where they had conquered Sihon and Og, and it was a rich fertile area that the tribes desired. He had granted it to them on the condition that they would send their warriors across the Jordan to fight with the rest of the tribes in Canaan. Only after they had secured their victories would they be allowed to go back and build their lives with their tribes in the Transjordan.

But the ceremonial preparations were not yet finished. Ever since the exodus, the Israelites had failed to perform the sign of the Abrahamic covenant on their sons: circumcision. Circumcision was the act of cutting off the foreskin of the male generative organ of Israelite boys at the eighth day after birth. It was the badge of covenant that marked the Israelite commitment to Yahweh. Some believed it was a physical picture of spiritual cleansing from a sheath of corruption. Others believed it was a symbol of Yahweh's blessing upon Abraham's fathering of a multitude of nations.

Yahweh never explained. But explanation was not required for obedience. And obedience was not a badge of the grumbling and complaining exodus generation. By the time that generation had died out, no one was circumcised in the entire nation of Israel.

Joshua had the priests make flint knives and they circumcised every male in Israel. There was much pain and crying by men throughout the camp, but they had healed within a week and were ready for battle.

One last element remained for the consecration of the Children of Israel. On the fourteenth day of the first month of Nisan the people all kept the Passover meal in their new base of operations at Gilgal on the plains of Jericho.

The Passover was a feast that commemorated God's tenth and final plague on Egypt, the death of the first-born. Before their exodus from Egyptian slavery the Israelites were commanded by Yahweh to slaughter a lamb and brush its blood over the doorposts of their homes. The Destroyer then came to kill the first-born of every family in Egypt, but passed over those with the blood on their lintels.

It was the last plague that Yahweh sent on Pharaoh to bend his will. When Pharaoh's own son succumbed to the Angel of Death, it did not merely bend Pharaoh, it broke him, and he let Moses and his people leave the land of the Nile.

How appropriate that their entrance into the Promised Land of Yahweh be accompanied by the first of their Feasts that marked their exodus, an event that would forever be etched into their souls like the permanent markings on the monuments of Egypt.

From Gilgal they would launch their campaign of military conquest of the land. On that day, they ate of the produce of the land of Canaan, their unleavened cakes and their parched grain. And on that very day, the manna ceased from heaven.

They were now in the land of milk and honey.

ie Israelite icampment

of Numbers describes the layout of the encampment
ael's 40 years of wilderness wanderings (2:1–34).
encamped around the tabernacle, both in order to
to the tent of meeting and to defend it during attack.
ides were surrounded by four groups, led by Judah,
Ephraim, and Dan. The Levites—specially chosen to
o God—camped around all sides of the tabernacle.

Joshua called the congregation of Israel to gather in the open areas and aisles around the tabernacle. They crunched in to be able to hear him, and he spoke to them as Moses used to. He stood beside the high priest, the three prophets of Israel, and Caleb, who was now his Right Hand, as Joshua had been Moses' Right Hand.

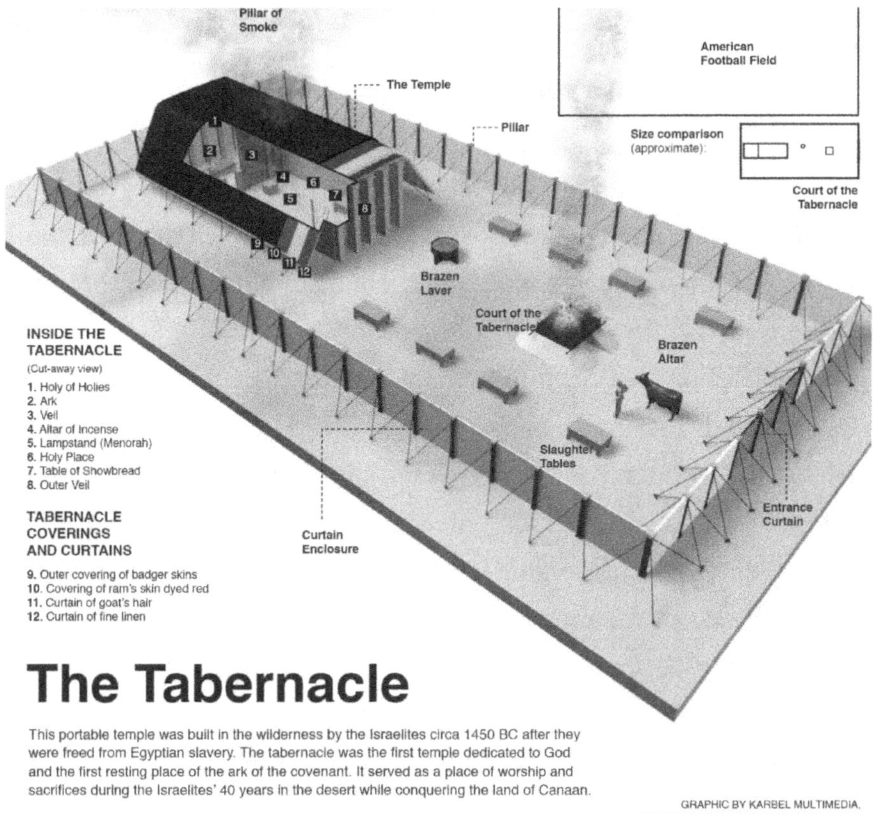

The Tabernacle

This portable temple was built in the wilderness by the Israelites circa 1450 BC after they were freed from Egyptian slavery. The tabernacle was the first temple dedicated to God and the first resting place of the ark of the covenant. It served as a place of worship and sacrifices during the Israelites' 40 years in the desert while conquering the land of Canaan.

Yahweh has spoken to me and has told me to be strong and courageous, for we will inherit this land that Yahweh had sworn to our forefathers! But we must be careful to do according to all the law that Moses commanded us! We must not turn from it to the right or to the left, and only then will we have success wherever we go! The book of the Law shall not depart from our mouths, but we shall meditate on it day and night, for Yahweh our Elohim is with us wherever we go!"

The people applauded. Caleb beamed with honor. They had been through so much. They had survived thirst and starvation in a desert land, the death of loved ones, rebellion, plagues, famines, and wars. And now, finally, *finally* they were about to gain their inheritance.

Their eternal wandering would be over.

It was overwhelming to Caleb. To be a part of history, to be the instrument of Yahweh's choosing, to see his mighty wonders displayed in the heavens above and the earth below, was more than anyone could ask for.

But the pang that hit him hardest was the fact that he could not share that with his long dead wife, Nathifa. He loved his daughter Achsah with all his heart, but it was not the same as sharing life with a beloved spouse. He remembered that when Nathifa was alive, nothing seemed of much value unless he could share it with her. And now, it was one of the moments he had prayed for all his life, and he had no beloved to share it with, to make it—*real*. It was a deep and abiding ache in his soul he could not shake.

Joshua finished his charge to the people, "We are about to face a land of people more numerous than us, a land of giants, of cities with walls that reach up to heaven! But again, I say, be strong and courageous and fear not! For we battle not against flesh and blood, but against principalities and powers in high places! But we are surrounded by an army of Yahweh's heavenly host, ten thousand times ten thousand strong! We will triumph! Our god will triumph!"

The congregation burst out in applause again. This time, it must have been heard across the plains in the very first city targeted for destruction: Jericho.

CHAPTER 35

Joshua led his forces to within striking distance of Jericho. The city had known they were coming and had all shut up within their walls, prepared for a siege of great length. The surrounding villages had all fled, leaving a howling wilderness before them.

Joshua stood at a distance with Caleb looking out upon the plains and the city. Even from afar, Jericho's walls looked menacing.

"I have no idea how we are going to breach those walls. We have no siege experience like the Hittites or Mittani. All those who may have aided us from their knowledge of Egyptian sieges are dead. And the prophets have had nothing to say."

The three prophets of Israel would often accompany Joshua in his war tent as he considered strategies. They would sometimes have counsel from Yahweh. But sometimes Yahweh made Joshua figure it out on his own. In this case, the prophets had told him the first target but not a strategy. To Joshua, it was like receiving half of a crucial communication.

Caleb stared at the gigantic fortification standing before them in the distance. It was impressive. As a first target, it could well be the hardest. Normal strategy was for the first target to be an easy win. It built courage in the soldiers by setting a victorious momentum.

Caleb said, "If we fail in our very first battle, or take too long with heavy losses, untold damage will be done to the morale of the forces. It could devastate us."

Joshua said, "Or if our first battle is an impossible victory that can only be attributed to Yahweh, then it is all downhill from there. We will have an army full of faith required to subdue the rest of Canaan."

Caleb could not deny it. Joshua was crazy. But he was right. And crazy faith is precisely what they would need to face the giants of this land.

He said, "Yahweh gave this target, did he?"

"Through the prophets."

"I would not want to argue with him."

Suddenly a single cloaked figure appeared as if out of the waves of heat that distorted their view of the distant landscape.

Their senses piqued. It was a messenger.

He seemed to make vast jumps of space with the distorting effect of the heat waves on their vision.

One moment, he seemed to disappear. Joshua and Caleb squinted to see if it was just a mirage, an apparition of the desert heat.

They saw nothing and mounted their horses to return to their men.

But Caleb called out before Joshua could mount his steed.

"Commander."

Joshua stopped and turned.

The figure was suddenly right upon them as if he jumped time and space.

Joshua grabbed his sword.

The figure already had his drawn sword in his hand. And he was wearing strange-looking armor Joshua had never seen before.

No, wait, he *had* seen it before.

"Are you for us or for our adversaries?" he asked.

"No," said the figure.

Caleb said, "No, you are not for us, or no, you are not for our adversaries?"

The figure said, "Neither. I am the commander of the army of Yahweh."

Joshua whispered under his breath, "The Angel of Yahweh."

He was the Son of Man in an earthly presence.

Joshua and Caleb dropped to their knees and worshipped the Angel, who said, "Take off your sandals, for the place where you are is holy."

Joshua and Caleb obeyed. Caleb knew in his heart this was another connection to Moses who had removed his sandals before the burning bush of Yahweh's presence.

The Angel spoke with a calm assurance, "I would wager you are wondering how in the world you are going to assault the mighty walls of Jericho."

Joshua said, "The thought had crossed our minds, my Lord. You would not happen to have any secrets about its weaknesses that might help us?"

"No," said the Angel. "But be strong and courageous this day, for I will tell you how you will conquer the city by the power of Yahweh."

Joshua and Caleb had returned to their men and were standing before their commanders of thousands and hundreds.

Othniel, Caleb's younger brother, was one of them and stood dutifully by him.

Salmon, the spy who had traveled with Caleb was one of the commanders. He blurted out what everyone was thinking, but was too afraid to say.

"We what? Walk around the city seven times in seven days and blow our trumpets? Forgive me, my Commander, but what is that going to do, kill them with laughter?"

The other commanders snickered.

Joshua chose not to be angry. He thought it was rather silly himself. "Our god has quite a sense of humor, does he not? But nevertheless, he did tell me that is what we should do. So, unless you have a better idea than Yahweh, Salmon, I suggest we obey him and see his salvation."

Salmon was duly chastised. "Forgive my offense, commander."

Joshua said with a smile, "You are forgiven, Salmon. You are too good of a spy."

Caleb was impressed with Joshua's temperament. His sense of holiness would normally be offended at remarks like that. Perhaps he was beginning to appreciate Yahweh's sense of humor after all.

Joshua ended his remarks, "And remember, Commanders, avoid the home with the scarlet rope. Caleb and Salmon, you will be responsible for Rahab's deliverance."

CHAPTER 36

Rahab was packing her few most precious items into a small sack when her youngest sister, twenty-three year old Yasha, broke into her room. "Rahab! There are soldiers outside! Look!"

She set her sack down and went to the window from which the scarlet rope hung. She tugged at it to make sure it was tied tightly to the bronze bar embedded in her wall. It held firm.

She looked out the window and saw an army of four thousand strong surrounding the city walls. She gasped.

The Israelites.

She heard the sound of her own city's battle horns announcing positions on the wall. The gate would be heavily fortified with double reinforcements and their pathetically few archers would ready themselves for launching their darts when the melee began.

But a melee did not appear to begin. The Israelites marched quietly in line about five soldiers wide. They circled the city in some kind of ritual procession to the sound of constant ram's horns creating a kind of marching order.

Then she saw in the middle of the train a group of seven priestly looking men dressed in white garments. They blew the ram's horns whose sound seemed to penetrate the city walls and into her very bones. Behind those seven were another four priests carrying a strange looking gold box on poles like a kingly carriage. Behind those were three monkish men who looked like they may be prophets.

She could see the box's golden surface glinting in the sun, and could only surmise that it was some kind of graven image of Yahweh, their deity—now, her deity.

A shiver went down her spine. She had become so absorbed in the sight before her that she had forgotten her sister was still with her. When Yasha spoke, Rahab jumped with fright.

"Who do you think they are? Are they bad men come to hurt us?"

"No," said Rahab. "They are not bad men, Yasha. Go get mother and father and your siblings. I am calling a family meeting in the tavern."

• • • • •

Salmon and Caleb had reached the northern wall in their parade around the city. They saw the scarlet rope hanging from the window and looked at each other with foreboding. They did not need to speak to one another. They knew theirs would be a dangerous task to rescue the harlot and her family.

Salmon could not help but remember the time he had spent with Rahab. She was like a goddess to him.

Caleb was thinking of her as well. But his thoughts were of the heathen woman who had rejected her past with an open heart toward Yahweh. It had reminded him of his own spiritual awakening all those years ago. He was a member of an Edomite tribe of Kenizzites living in the Negeb when he first heard of Israel. He was from the lineage of Eliphaz, the eldest son of Esau. Stories of their forefather

Abraham were passed down to them through the sages. But they were not hopeful stories.

Esau and Jacob had been twins, but Yahweh favored Jacob the youngest over Esau the eldest. Through Jacob's line Yahweh would bring forth his Seed of Promise. This was not the normal way of the world, where the eldest, as first-born, would usually inherit the birthright. It had made Esau bitter and he had mingled with the Canaanites in rebellion. There was a phrase that Caleb had heard that haunted him all his life. The sages whispered it but no one would speak openly of it. It was a phrase attributed to Yahweh himself.

"Jacob I loved, Esau I hated."

It marked their souls for all time and separated the brothers into two nations at enmity. But Jephunneh, Caleb's father, was one of the patriarchal elders of the tribe, and he had convinced his people that Yahweh would undo the curse upon them if they converted and became a part of the Israelite tribes in the wilderness.

Because Caleb had the talisman of Rahab, the whip sword handed down to him, he always felt like he did not belong with the Edomites. It had been used by Lamech, the father of Noah and passed to Abraham through Shem, Noah's son. Caleb had always wanted to be an Israelite. So it was easy for him to embrace his tribe's conversion when it happened.

And now, here he was, an Israelite, the Right Hand of Joshua the leader of Israel, but he still did not feel like he was a true blooded Israelite. He still felt haunted by his past identity. He still felt like he had to have something to make him feel more secure. He hoped that owning the very land of his forefather Abraham's burial would solve that. And that is what drove him on toward his goal.

• • • • •

Inside the city walls, Alyun-Yarikh, the commander of Jericho, was frantic. His Anakim bodyguard, five of them, guarded his war room outside. Jebir deliberated with Alyun and his two other counselors.

"What does it mean? What does it all mean?"

"I do not know, my lord," said Jebir.

Alyun kept talking as if he did not even hear Jebir's response. "They march around the city, blowing horns, carrying their holy idol, and then they retire to their camp. Is it some sort of curse?"

Jebir interjected, "We have our sorcerers and enchanters countering any curse with our own rituals. The astrologers have given us good reports from the stars."

One of the counselors added, "The gods favor us. Yarikh is a strong deliverer."

Alyun was not accepting any of the encouragement. "Are we sure of the walls? Will they hold? We have not paid for reinforcements in years."

"That is because the walls are impenetrable, sire," said the other counselor, "We do not need reinforcements."

"What are they up to?" Alyun exclaimed.

Then it came to him. His eyes lit up. "Bring me the harlot, Rahab."

• • • • •

Rahab had gathered her family around her in the tavern room. Her mother and father sat on a chair, her brothers and sisters stood expectantly.

"I did not tell you this before for fear of discovery should it slip out from any one of you. These Habiru who are about to attack the city have made a secret covenant with me."

The family members looked around in surprise at each other.

"I cannot explain it all now. I just know that they will not enter this house to kill any of us. But you must stay in the house. If you stray outside, you will be killed. Stay together. Get a small sack of clothes or valuables, nothing more, and be ready to leave. Some Habiru will come to the house, not to kill us, but to save us and guide us safely out of the city."

A knock on the barricaded front door frightened them all. She said to the family. "Go, prepare! And not a word to anyone."

She went to the door as they left for their respective rooms.

She lifted the bar on the door and opened it to see Jebir with two Anakim guards.

"Rahab," he said. "The king wants you."

When Rahab followed Jebir into the war room, Alyun was alone. She looked around seeing no others, and knew something was amiss.

"My lord called for me?" said Rahab.

"Rahab," said Alyun. He looked disheveled and distraught. He had not slept in two days. "What do you know about these Habiru? What did the two men say who visited your inn?"

"I told your Right Hand everything I knew, my lord. They did not say anything. I did not even know they were Habiru until Jebir told me."

Alyun looked at Jebir, who nodded.

"They ate and drank—and paid for their pleasure. Just as all men do. They left out of the gate before it was closed for the night."

Alyun was dead serious. "You do know, Rahab, that harboring spies is punishable by death."

Rahab protested, "I did not know they were spies, Alyun." She switched to more personal language as a way to throw him off her scent. "Surely, my love, if they said anything that endangered this city and with it, my family, I would have immediately contacted you."

"Hmmm, yes," he agreed.

"I will ask my servants and harlots," she said. "Maybe they saw something I did not."

But then Jebir broke in, "I have heard that you have expressed an interest in the god of these Habiru, who is he, Yahwo, Yahwa?"

He was trying to get her to say the name correctly and indict herself. But she did not take the bait.

Instead, she said, "So now you are spying on *me*?"

"No," said Jebir. "It is no secret that you are one of the most gossiped about persons in the fort, Rahab. One cannot help but run into such tales."

Jebir did not have the guts to tell her he only found out about it because of his own obsession with stalking her just to watch her. He was still harboring the tiny little hope in his heart that if he could survive this battle, and maybe if Alyun would be killed, then he would rise to leadership and he might have a chance to finally have her all to himself.

Alyun said, "But you *do* have interest in this god?"

Rahab decided to tell as much of the truth as she could so that it would not sound like the lie it would be.

"My lord, in all the years you have had me as your consort, have you ever asked me about my past?"

Alyun hesitated. "No, I guess I have not."

"Well, if you had, you would have discovered that I have endured the greatest of hardships under a variety of deities that has caused me to have less than faithful trust in *any* gods."

Alyun's face turned sorry. He had actually taken his mind off his own troubles as his heart turned toward Rahab's painful reminiscences.

"I was a priestess for the goat demons of Panias." She spoke the insulting word *demons* with spite while remembering Izbaxl. "Are you aware of the responsibilities of a nymph of satyrs?"

Alyun and Jebir were both drawn into the story with empathy.

"They serve the god Azazel, an antediluvian deity most known for his violent passions. And then there is the goddess Lilith who guards Gaia, the Mother Earth Goddess who cannibalizes her own worshippers. I escaped from there to Gilgal Rephaim, the Serpent Clan, who sought to use me as a womb for breeding Nephilim from the god Mastema."

Alyun and Jebir could not believe what they were hearing. Jebir was even tearing up.

"While I was there, I was introduced to the gods Ba'al, the bully Ashtart, and Molech. Molech, as you know consumes little children, as he did my first brother and sister that I never told you about."

She never told him about them because it was not true. But they knew the violence of Ba'al, the extraordinary wickedness of Ashtart, and the lusts of Molech.

Alyun broke in, "Rahab, I am so sorry you have had to experience all this. It has only been my desire to bring you comfort."

"And for that, I am grateful, Alyun. But as you can see, the gods have not done me well. My only interest in them is in protecting myself from their atrocious behavior and violations of my person.

What benefit would another foreign male divinity of war be for me?"

She did not give the answer that the benefit of that divinity was that he was out to destroy all the other divinities who had hurt her. And that he was in fact a loving father and shepherd that Rahab had never experienced. Just the little she memorized about Yahweh from her couple scraps of poetry brought more truth and love into her soul than anything she had ever encountered. She could not wait to meet this god on the heap of carcasses of the soldiers in this fort.

"Jebir," said Alyun, "return Rahab to her tavern."

CHAPTER 37

By the sixth day of Israel's siege of Jericho, the inhabitants had gone back to their normal daily lives, and soldier duty had reduced to minimal shifts of observation on the walls. Alyun had become convinced that these Habiru were completely ignorant of what was required for a siege. They built no siege towers, no battering rams. They did not even seem to build ladders for climbing the walls. He toyed with the possible notion that they may very well be the most ignorant foreigners he had ever encountered.

The reason for this was that the Habiru did the same thing every day without change. They marched in procession around the walls with their golden idol on poles and blew their ram's horns. After they completed one circuit, they would remove themselves to their camp a short distance away.

The soldiers on the walls would laugh and make jokes at the Habiru, pulling up their battle skirts to flash their private parts at the morons.

It was ridiculous. What were they doing? They must surely have no idea what to do, so they walked around in circles like a mad child chanting delusions to themselves, thinking that their repetition would be the necessary magic to make Jericho surrender to them. Or maybe it was just their silly religious ritual of waiting for the city to run out of supplies.

Let them try to wait this out, thought Alyun. *We are rationing and we have enough supplies to last two years.*

Alyun thought they might just pick up their weapons and go home like a little child who cannot win at a game.

• • • • •

That night, Joshua and Caleb ate their meal with the Commanders. Even they were becoming a bit impatient and embarrassed with what they were doing. Commanders had asked Joshua how long they were going to do this, and what were his plans for besieging the city. He had told them they would get an answer tonight.

Caleb took a bite of mutton and washed it down with some wine from his goatskin flask. He was sitting with Salmon and his brother Othniel at the commanders' fires with the other commanders of thousands and of hundreds.

Salmon was in midstride detailing in hushed tone his time with Rahab to those closest to him. He had their attention—and their imaginations.

Joshua overheard him and cut him off, "Salmon, that is enough of your whispers. You should shame in your weakness, not glory in it."

"But sir," replied Salmon, "I want to marry Rahab. I am in love with her."

The commanders groaned teasingly.

Suddenly, Othniel who had quietly listened this whole time burst out of his silence.

"You are not in love, captain," said Othniel. "You are in lust."

"What is the difference?" said Salmon, and everyone laughed. They were all men. They really did not know the difference.

Othniel said, "Lust is gratification, love is sacrifice."

Caleb was amazed to hear his brother, a man who was too fearful of revealing his own interest in Caleb's daughter Achsah, speak so eloquently of love. Perhaps he was maturing after all. Something Caleb dreaded.

Salmon said, "I would sacrifice my life for Rahab. I do not lie. I am in love with her."

Joshua said, "You are a loyal warrior, Salmon, I will grant you that. But love without holiness creates lawlessness and chaos. God has made us to obey him, and when we do not, we sow the seeds of our own destruction."

Salmon and the commanders remained silent, chastised.

Then Caleb finally spoke up, "And what does holiness without love create, Commander?"

Caleb and Joshua had had this discussion many times in private. Of course Caleb did not condone immorality. But he often felt that Joshua had lost his love when he lost Hasina. He had become hard and bitter. His dedication to discipline, rules, and order had become almost intolerable after his loss.

Hasina had been an influence of grace on him. She had softened his rough edges and had calmed his cantankerous spirit. It was not that she made him soft or less of a warrior, but rather that she made him a whole human being. Without that influence, he had become a cruel taskmaster, a warrior who only knew force and judgment without persuasion and grace.

Joshua ignored Caleb's question and told them, "Tomorrow will be our victory." He gave an angry look at Caleb and added, "But it will be a holy victory. For Yahweh has declared that the city and all that is within is *herem*, devoted to Yahweh for destruction."

The men gave each other somber looks. Joshua continued, "Only Rahab and all her family with her in her house shall be spared because she has helped Israel. All items of silver and gold, bronze, and iron are to be brought to the tabernacle. They shall be cleansed and placed in the treasury of Yahweh. But every living thing, men and women, young and old, as well as the oxen, sheep, and donkeys shall be put to the sword. There can be no compromise in this *herem*.

It was a solemn moment. The commanders were silent. They had not understood how they were going to attack the city, but they could see in Joshua's fiery eyes that he was certain of Yahweh's course.

Then Joshua said, "I want to tell you exactly what Yahweh has told us to do tomorrow."

CHAPTER 38

Early the next day, the Israelites arose and circled the city again as they had been doing for the past six days. Their actions went almost unnoticed as they blew their ram's horns and paraded around the city one more time.

But today would be different. Today they circled the city seven times instead of one.

It started to draw a crowd of onlookers on the walls around the fifth time. They jeered and yelled insults at the Habiru. They thought that the Israelites had truly gone insane.

Even Alyun had mounted the inner wall to see what was going on. He stood with his five Anakim towering around him, and Jebir by his side.

The seventh time around, the Israelites stopped in their procession near the south walls of the city.

The priests stopped blowing their horns.

The priests toted the Ark away back to camp, followed by the prophets. The soldiers closed in the gap.

Joshua then rode out on his horse and yelled at the top of his lungs, "SHOUT, FOR THE LORD HAS GIVEN YOU THE CITY!"

With that, the sound of several thousand Israelites yelling a war cry reverberated all the way up to the Commander's post. It was also accompanied by the ram's horns again. But this time it was a long blow that lasted the length of the battle cry.

And then all was silent.

Alyun waited for something to happen. But nothing did.

He turned to Jebir and remarked, "Well this really takes the dessert for the most mentally deranged people I have ever seen."

The Jericho defenders began to laugh.

Others began to dance silly dances like children or insane people.

Jebir enjoyed the mockery.

But then a rumble in the earth stopped him.

It stopped all of them.

It started low at first, as if only a sound.

But it increased to the point of causing wooden structures all around the city to shake.

Then it became an enduring quake of large magnitude.

The very walls they were standing on began to shake back and forth with such force that the soldiers could barely steady themselves.

And then the ground in the center of the city split in half and a massive wave of energy swept over the city.

Large portions of the outer walls of Jericho just crumbled to the ground like sandcastles in a desert wind.

The inner wall was the second to fall under the wave. A large part of it tumbled over and crushed houses and inhabitants.

Alyun, Jebir, and their guards were on part of that tumbling wall. They fell to the ground thirty feet below in a pile of dust and rubble.

• • • • •

The Israelites were as shocked as the inhabitants of the city. They did not anticipate such a spectacular act of their god. Their faith was amazingly weak.

But the commanders sallied forth with charges and the forces stormed the fort.

They climbed over the rocky rubble and broke into the city fighting the stunned soldiers that had not been crushed in the earthquake.

It would be over quickly.

Caleb and Salmon swiftly made their way to the north of the city where Rahab's house was. They had prayed that hers was not a part of the wall that had collapsed.

Othniel, who had distinguished himself at the battle of Jahaz by killing King Sihon, had a penchant for taking out leaders, so he led a platoon of men toward the crumbled palace walls to seek out the commander of the fort.

• • • • •

Jebir had landed on top of one of the Anakim in the fall of their wall. The giant had cushioned his fall and had left him miraculously unscathed. The Anakite however was barely alive from being bashed on sharp rock edges.

Jebir searched through the dust coughing, trying to find his king. There were a couple other of the Anakim bodyguards unhurt in the fall, as they had tumbled free of the crushing rocks.

And then he found Alyun. He was alive, but he was badly wounded. His legs were under a boulder and he was covered in debris.

He crouched to his side.

"Alyun, my commander."

Alyun was delirious. Jebir could see immediately that he would not be of any help to the defense of the fort. So he did what he was prepared to do in such a fortuitous situation; he looked around to make sure no one was looking. Then he picked up a large rock and finished off the commander with one swift blow.

Jebir got up and brushed himself off. He found his weapon and turned to see the two Anakim guards that had survived approach him.

"Alyun has died under the rubble. I am the new commander of the fort."

They bowed in respect as Jebir looked out onto the devastation below. The Israelites were pouring in like water through a broken dam, killing everything in their wake.

Jebir knew it was all over.

He even noticed a band of Israelites heading straight for their position. He didn't know this was Othniel, the king killer. But he knew enough to get the Sheol out of there.

He had one last concern before escaping the city. He turned to the Anakim and ordered them, "Follow me to the red district!"

He had considered the fact that if Rahab was alive, she would no doubt be spared as spoils for the plunderers. But his obsession with her had become so all-consuming, that he could not think of losing her any longer. A tragedy had granted him the authority he wanted to attain his desire. But he would probably never be allowed to enjoy it because of these evil Habiru.

He concluded that if he could not have Rahab, then no one would.

• • • • •

Caleb and Salmon found their way through the rubble and various skirmishes to the north quarter of the city. They brought along several other soldiers to help them.

When they got there, they saw that the sections of the wall that held did indeed include Rahab's inn. Yahweh's providential care should not have surprised him. Her scarlet rope was now hanging out the front window marking her location like the blood of Passover on the doorposts.

They rushed in and found Rahab with her family waiting with their sacks to leave.

Caleb said, "Let us get out of here."

"Wait!" said Rahab. "Where is Yasha? Has anyone seen Yasha?"

Everyone shook their heads.

"Did anyone check her room?"

Baraket barked, "We all rushed down here like you said."

Rahab rushed back up the broken down stairwell. The inn did not fall under the earthquake, but it had been shaken apart badly.

Caleb told one of the soldiers, "Bring these family members out to safety beyond the walls. We will meet you."

He turned to Salmon, "Keep watch," and he bolted after Rahab to help her find her little sister.

He found Yasha's room where Rahab was nursing an unconscious Yasha.

"She was knocked out by falling debris in the earthquake. I think she is okay."

Yasha came to.

Rahab looked at Caleb, "Did Yahweh do this? Did he collapse the walls?"

Caleb smiled, "With the snap of his fingers."

Rahab said, "I guess I chose the right god to follow after all."

"No, I think he chose you, Rahab."

The look in his eyes shook her to her core. *What kind of a god would choose me?*

Rahab looked at Yasha in her arms. "Come, little sister, it is time we go home."

They were interrupted by a shout from below, "CALEB!"

Caleb rushed out to find Salmon at the bottom of the stairs with his back against a wall—and two Anakim soldiers, about nine feet tall each, with swords drawn, facing him. At the doorway was Jebir who recognized Caleb and Salmon with a satisfied look.

Caleb leapt off the balcony and grabbed the decorative drapery hanging against the wall. He judged correctly. The drapery could not hold his weight and it ripped, dropping him easily to the ground next to Salmon.

The Anakim attacked.

Their huge weapons came down simultaneously with massive power.

Caleb and Salmon rolled out of the way.

The counter was crushed into splinters.

The Anakite that went after Caleb had an iron war hammer. He was furious and relentless. He was too fast for Caleb to get his whip sword out and extend it for a strike. Caleb was too busy ducking and dodging and rolling out of the way of the monstrous pounding hammer shattering everything in its path into fragments.

The Anakite that went after Salmon had a sword. Fortunately for Salmon, he had confiscated an iron sword from the battle at Edrei; otherwise his old bronze sickle sword would have been broken in half by now under the force of the Anakite's flurry of blows.

Salmon was an excellent swordsman. He had won plenty of contests in the Israelite camp sparring with his fellow warriors. But this was no friendly Israelite. This was a screaming mad Anakite that was one and a half times his height and twice his weight.

But he was not as good of a swordsman. Salmon immediately found his weakness. He was left-handed and he repeated the same crisscross slash pattern as he hacked at his small foe. Salmon could predict his behavior.

Caleb rolled out of the way as a hammer blow broke a hole in the floor. It took a second for the Anakite to wrest the hammer from the splintered floorboards, which was all the time Caleb needed to roll out his whip sword, Rahab.

But it was not quite enough time, because the giant pulled it out and without even looking, immediately swung around expecting Caleb to be there. The hammer came in contact with a main pole holding the building. Caleb was next to that pole. He hit the floor tumbling. His sword was no longer in his hands. It was by the pole. The wood and debris fell down upon them all.

Salmon found his opportunity and followed his opponent's swing until he knew his moment to strike. And he did, piercing his opponent through the stomach. The giant screamed and backed up.

Salmon did not anticipate that his strike, since it did not kill his enemy, would only make him angrier. The Anakite unleashed a fury of blows that Salmon could barely keep up with. His arm could not hold up. The hits wore him down.

At last the sword flew from his hands and he was up against the wall again, but this time unarmed before his towering menace.

The Anakite smirked with satisfaction and swung his blade to cut Salmon in half.

But before he could, a serpent wrapped around his arm—that is, a serpent blade—and sliced his arm off. The sword fell to the ground in a clatter.

Salmon rolled, picked up his blade, and jumped upon the monster, jamming it through its heart. No mistakes this time.

The Anakite was dead.

Salmon looked up to see Caleb with his whip sword in one hand and the head of the hammer Anakite in his other.

They were trying to catch their breaths. Their fight had exhausted them both.

Rahab's scream drew their attention to the bottom of the staircase.

Jebir held Rahab from behind with his sword to her throat.

He would have killed her immediately, but then he would have to fight his way through the two warriors who just bested his Anakim, which was not a hopeful possibility. If he could just get to the doorway he could escape.

"Back away!" he yelled.

Caleb and Salmon did not move.

"I said back away!"

They started to move backward, but slowly.

Rahab had one hand free. She slipped it beneath her own robe to pull the secret dagger she kept.

But before she could do anything with it, Jebir saw it and knocked it out of her hands to the floor.

He inched his way toward the door, watching the Israelites like a hawk.

A few more feet, and he would cut her throat and run into the streets.

Caleb stepped forward.

Jebir tightened his grip on Rahab and stopped.

Caleb's hand tensed on his blade. The son of perdition was too far away. His blade would not reach.

Salmon could not throw his sword because Rahab was in front of Jebir.

They were not going to be able to stop him.

And they did not realize that he was going to kill her anyway.

He reached the doorway and smiled.

But instead of cutting Rahab's throat, he gritted his teeth in pain, released Rahab, and dropped his sword, trying to reach behind his back.

Behind him was the small and stealthy young Yasha, Rahab's sister. Jebir had completely forgotten about her. She had picked up Rahab's dagger and slipped behind Jebir to the doorway, so that when he got there, she jammed the blade into his rib cage, puncturing his liver and lung from behind.

Jebir fell to his knees.

Yasha cried in horror at what she had done.

Salmon and Caleb ran to help Rahab.

But Rahab was fast enough. She pulled the dagger out of his back and heard a gush of wind collapse his lung. He gasped for air.

She pulled his head back by his hair so he could see her face.

She said, "I should have known you would try, you Canaanite piece of filth," and cut through his throat.

But she had surprised herself. She had called him a Canaanite, as if she were not one. She had already begun to see herself as one of these Habiru.

Salmon reached her and they hugged with desperation for her safety.

Yasha was frozen in horror at what she had done. She did not believe she could do such a thing. But when her beloved sister was in danger, she just reacted without thinking.

Caleb held Yasha. She burst out in tears into his shoulder. She shook like another earthquake was hitting her, but Caleb held her tight until she calmed in his strong arms.

He led her gently outside.

They could see that the battle was already over. The Israelites had captured the city and were marching throughout the streets.

The commander's palace was already in flames. They would burn the entire place to the ground.

Salmon held Rahab. "Fear not, Rahab. Your family is safe outside the walls."

"Thank you," she said to Caleb. "Thank you so much for keeping your promise."

Caleb just nodded silently. He envied Salmon for his close attendance to Rahab.

He saw Rahab look up at Salmon with a tenderness that disclosed their intimacy, and he knew he could never have her as his wife.

"Salmon," said Rahab, "I bear your child."

CHAPTER 39

Jericho was a smoldering pile of ashes and ruins. The Israelite soldiers celebrated the victory of Yahweh throughout the camp, with much wine and beer. They took the spoils of war back to Gilgal where they would be purified and given to the treasury.

Salmon and Caleb led Rahab and her family toward the Commander's tent to meet Joshua.

Rahab trembled with anxiety. She knew he would hold her fate in his hands. And she knew he was the one who communed with the god Yahweh. What would he say? Would he see through her and into her damaged soul so full of evil? She prayed silently to Yahweh to be merciful to her family if not to her.

But on the way, they passed a small group of refugees herded into their own area.

She said, "Salmon, wait."

Caleb and Salmon stopped to watch Rahab walk over to the group.

Caleb said, "We best not keep the Commander waiting."

Salmon went to see what Rahab was doing.

He noticed a young girl about thirteen years old standing out from the crowd staring at Rahab. She looked unkempt, dressed in rags from traveling. Salmon thought of a little wild jackrabbit at her sight.

Rahab said, "Donatiya? Donatiya, is that you?"

The girl cried and nodded her head.

Rahab ran and embraced her. They hugged desperately and Rahab crouched down to her height.

"I am so happy to see you again," said Rahab. "How did you arrive here?"

A lot of traveling around Canaan," she replied.

Salmon stepped up to them.

Rahab said, "Salmon, this is Donatiya. I met her months ago after Israel had taken the Transjordan. She was with a group of refugees who passed through Jericho."

Of course, Rahab would never mention the other part of that experience: the sorceress who recognized her and recalled the prophecy about her— the old woman killed by Rahab.

"Hello, Donatiya," said Salmon.

She looked away without response.

Salmon smiled. "Shy, are you?"

Rahab said, "I want to take her with me. I want her to be my maidservant. Would you like that, Donatiya? Would you like to live with me?"

Donatiya's eyes lit up.

"I do not know," said Salmon. "We cannot just assimilate foreigners beyond your family."

"I will adopt her."

Salmon sighed.

Donatiya said, "I heard the sorceress that night."

Salmon's ears perked up.

Donatiya continued, "The night you visited us outside the city walls."

Rahab tried to avoid what was coming, "That was a long time ago, dear."

"What did the sorceress say?" said Salmon, jumping in.

Rahab said, "Just some babbling craziness."

Donatiya would not stop. "She said that your womb would birth a great and mighty warrior, whose kingdom would overthrow all kingdoms."

"That is not right, Donatiya," said Rahab. "You misheard her."

Donatiya would not fight back. She hung her head in submission. "I am sorry."

Salmon however was intrigued. "You said she was a sorceress?"

Rahab said in a hushed tone to Donatiya, "Do not speak of this again."

Salmon said, "Was it a prophecy?"

She stood up and pulled Salmon out of her earshot. "Salmon, think about it. I am a harlot. I am a vile and corrupted vessel. Do you really think Yahweh would choose my womb to birth anything noble? I do not want to speak any more of this nonsense."

Salmon stared into her eyes. He was heartbroken. She really did feel that she was worthless.

"Rahab," he said, "marry me."

She kept staring into his bold courageous eyes. Her own filled with tears. She felt weak. Salmon held her.

Rahab whispered to him, "I am unclean. You do not want me."

"I will be the judge of what I want, woman. And you can be made clean."

She could not speak.

He added, "You carry my child, and according to Yahweh's law, I am required to marry you, so try to get out of that one."

He gave her a big loving smile.

She finally smiled back.

They kissed deeply.

Donatiya scrunched her face, closed tight her eyes, and muttered, "Ewwwwww."

• • • • •

Joshua was consulting with his war counselors when Caleb's voice brought him to attention.

He turned to see Caleb and Salmon in the tent. And between them was the most beautiful woman he had ever seen. It actually stirred within him something he had not felt in many years since the loss of his beloved Hasina.

Caleb said, "Commander Joshua ben Nun, I introduce you to Rahab of Jericho."

Rahab blurted out, "No longer of Jericho."

Joshua smiled at her anxiousness. "Indeed."

He stepped closer to them, within a few feet. "I understand that it was you who hid my spies, and provided intelligence of the city."

"Yes, my lord," she said with shaking voice. She felt so unworthy.

"Well then, I believe gratitude is in order."

She would not look Joshua in the eye.

"Rahab," said Joshua. "Look at me."

She looked up, expecting wrath, but found only peace and strength.

"I want to thank you on behalf of Israel and Israel's god, Yahweh. What you did was a righteous deed, and it will not be forgotten. I will send guards to accompany you and your family to any village you desire."

"My lord," said Salmon, "She will not need to go anywhere. She wants to become an Israelite."

Joshua was shocked. He was not prepared for this. Few were prepared for this. It was a rarity.

Joshua did not like the idea. He scowled.

"Is there a problem, sir?" asked Caleb. He knew Joshua's sense of holiness was so overwrought, he could not conceive of such unclean persons becoming a part of the holy people of Yahweh. But it was part of Yahweh's word and his law to allow for repentance and forgiveness. Only the most self-righteous would not see their own faults when compared against the standard.

"Well," said Joshua, "I am not sure what appreciation you may have of our ways, Rahab, but—" He paused. "There is no room for the traditions of the Canaanites. Yahweh detests them."

"So do I," she blurted out hastily. Then remembered whose presence she was in. "My lord, Commander."

Joshua sighed. It was too much for him to consider. He said, "Prostitution is not allowed in Israel."

Rahab was too humble, so Salmon said it for her, "She is no longer a harlot, sir. She has repented from her sins."

Joshua appeared incredulous, "I am concerned about the morale and trust of the congregation. If we enter Canaanite cities and devote all their inhabitants to destruction, it would create a disastrous contradiction if I allow this entire Canaanite family in our midst. I would not be upholding the holiness of Yahweh."

Rahab wiped the tears that lagged down her cheek. She was crushed.

Then Caleb spoke up, "Commander, did Moses uphold the holiness of Yahweh by accepting repentant Midianites into your midst after the exodus? Did he uphold the holiness of Yahweh by accepting my Canaanite tribe into your midst? If not, then I should leave right now because I am no different than this woman."

Joshua was cornered and he knew he was wrong. His pride would not let him admit it.

Salmon threw on the final sack that broke the camel's back. "She carries my child. I will marry her according to Yahweh's Law."

Joshua looked at Salmon with more shock. But so did Caleb.

After an uncomfortable moment of thought, Joshua turned and said dismissively, "Very well. But not until after our next battle."

"I can wait, my lord," said Salmon.

Joshua added, "And she must shave her head and mourn for a month outside the camp. According to Yahweh's Law." He would stick that back in Salmon's face.

Rahab and Salmon hugged each other with joy.

Caleb smiled. "Thank you, Commander. I knew you would affirm Yahweh's gracious provision for converts. Faith is the beauty of holiness."

A couple of Israelite spies entered the tent. One of them said, "Commander. We have reconnaissance on the city of Ai."

Joshua became distracted again and barked, "Everyone is dismissed. My commanders, prepare for counsel."

CHAPTER 40

"The city of Ai is a couple miles into the hills," said the captain of the spies. "As its name suggests, it is a fortress of ruins that is being rebuilt by citizens of nearby Bethel. There are few inhabitants. We will not need but a couple company units of men to take it."

Othniel asked, "Then why bother? If it is already in ruins."

Joshua and Caleb were surrounded by a dozen of their highest commanders of thousands and hundreds.

The three prophets of Israel were not with them as they usually were. Joshua had not bothered to call on them because it seemed such a minor skirmish.

Caleb answered Othniel first, "Ai is the northernmost fortress for the southern Canaanite city-state coalition. It is the connection to our southern campaign."

Joshua added, "Our goal is to capture the hill country, the spine of Canaan. If we control the hills and valleys, we control access to the entire region. But just as importantly, the Canaanites are masters of chariot warfare. They are made of iron and are too formidable to face on open fields and plains. But chariots and heavy armor cannot be used in the hills."

Othniel smiled now. He followed completely.

Joshua finished, "Because of our small numbers, light armor, and complete lack of chariot forces, our best strategy is to control the hill country to our advantage. We make the spine of the land our spine."

The spy captain asked, "What are your orders, sir?"

"Take three companies and secure Ai. We can take Bethel from there."

Caleb interrupted, "Excuse me, Commander, but should we not be more cautious and send a larger force? Just to be sure."

"Three units should be plenty," said Joshua. "That is seven hundred men for a barely inhabited city of ruins."

"What say the prophets?"

Joshua answered, "They are in prayer. I did not want to bother them with such a trivial need."

Caleb thought it was unwise to take the advice of spies who were only trained in gathering information, not in field tactics. But he could see Joshua had made up his mind. He prayed that his Commander had not become overconfident with pride.

• • • • •

Caleb led the forces toward Ai. Othniel accompanied Caleb, and Salmon joined him as one of the commanders of hundreds.

When they arrived in sight of the city, Caleb could see why the spies had reported Ai to be an easy target. The area of the city was several acres. Its walls were mostly reduced to rubble and the interior of the city was just as ruinous and in need of rebuilding.

But the Bethelites from nearby were rebuilding it. Caleb could see the builders working on the stone wall of the exterior, and laying bricks and timber for the interior structures.

The armed force looked small. They would not populate the fortress until it would be restored to its former strength.

Caleb waited until night to attack. He led his men against the most open part of the wall so their entry would be the easiest.

They easily breached the low stone rubble and entered the city. But when they began the raid, the soldiers of Ai did not fight. They rather ran back into the city and hid amidst the wreckage and ruins. Another sign that they were too few.

The Israelite warriors broke up into several units to chase down the fleeing Bethelites. Othniel took one of them. This was turning into a troublesome search and destroy mission that Caleb did not relish.

Caleb was with Salmon as they led a unit of a hundred that chased some soldiers down a dark street into a large square that appeared to house the governmental structures at one time. They were large stone edifices crumbling and vacant.

They had lost the band of soldiers. And then Caleb realized they were out in the open, surrounded by too many dark and unlit buildings. There was too little light in this city to see well.

Moments in advance, he discerned what had happened.

But it was moments too late. They had been tricked into an ambush.

They were suddenly surrounded by hundreds of warriors who came at them from everywhere. The Bethelites were using the ruins of the city as a cover to engage in guerrilla warfare tactics.

The Israelites instinctively withdrew into a circle of defense. Caleb knew enough to have his hornsman blow the sound of retreat. If the other units had not been trapped yet, they might avoid a catastrophe.

Salmon drew his sword and stood near Caleb. His experience with him as both spies and deliverers in Jericho had endeared him to his commanding officer. He saw himself as a bodyguard for Caleb.

"MOVE TOWARD THE EXIT!" yelled Caleb to his men.

The Bethelites were already upon them, slashing, hacking and thrusting.

But the Israelites were seasoned fighters. And they had learned to move as one. They began to defend themselves in their circle, but moved back toward the way which they had entered.

They were being pounded on all sides. Shields were starting to weaken. They were outnumbered three to one. But they kept moving and pushing, until they fought their way back to the broken wall where they had entered.

Caleb saw Othniel's unit under the same kind of fire. But they too were able to make it back to the wall to escape.

But as they launched themselves over the rubble to break from their ambush, an arrow struck Salmon through his back.

He had just stepped behind Caleb. A second later or a second earlier, and it would have been Caleb now on the ground.

Caleb picked Salmon up with the help of another soldier and they made it out of the city walls to regroup with the other units.

Now, as one, they found more strength and were able to hold off the Bethelite forces long enough to make their retreat back down the hill.

The Bethelites stopped chasing them and the Israelite forces paused to count their losses and gather their breath. It had been a frightful hour of the most heated battle they had seen since Edrei.

They had lost about thirty-six men.

Salmon would be one of them. He was dying in Caleb's arms.

The arrow had pierced his back and lodged in his heart. Caleb could not pull it out. He could only try to make Salmon as comfortable as possible.

Salmon was sputtering, trying to get his words out to Caleb. "Commander – I am – honored – to serve – with you."

"And I with you—gibbor."

It was a compliment of the highest order to call a man a gibbor, as it meant they were a mighty man, the equal of a giant.

"Please – please take care – of Rahab – for me."

"She and her family will be safe. I will not allow them to be cast out of Israel."

"Tell Rahab to call our child—Boaz."

"I promise you, soldier," said Caleb.

Then he added, "Friend."

And Salmon breathed his last.

CHAPTER 41

Joshua was prostrate with his face on the ground before the Holy of Holies. Outside the Tent of Meeting, the elders lay on the ground, their clothes torn in anguish, and dust thrown over their heads in despair. The judges and prophets were beside them in the same posture.

Joshua cried out, "Adonai Yahweh, why? Why have you brought us over the Jordan at all, if you are only going to give us into the hands of the Amorites to destroy us? If only we had dwelled beyond the Jordan. Do you not care that all the inhabitants of Canaan will hear of this defeat and will surround us and cut off your name from the face of the earth? Do you not care for the reputation of your own name? Is this not what Moses himself had begged from you?"

Suddenly, the voice of Yahweh broke Joshua out of his weeping. "Get up, Joshua. You sound more like the pathetic Israelites wishing they could go back to Egypt than their leader Moses in pleading for them."

Joshua was terrified. He did not get up.

"Joshua, get up, will you."

Joshua got up.

"Israel has sinned. They have violated my covenant and taken some of the devoted things of *herem* from Jericho. They have lied and taken them for their own possession. Therefore the people of Israel have become *herem*, and devoted to destruction. I will be with you no more unless you destroy the devoted things in your midst."

"Who, my lord and god?" said Joshua. "Who is it who has taken these devoted items?"

• • • • •

Caleb entered Rahab's tent. She and all her family were bald shaven and in their thirty day period of lamenting. Her mother and father were there, as well as her sisters and brothers. They had been in bed for a short time already, but few were sleeping. And certainly not Rahab.

When she saw Caleb at the tent entrance, she instantly knew the fate of her betrothed Salmon.

She rose from her bed, approached Caleb and embraced him with trembling.

Then she stepped outside and bowed low to the ground and began to wail. It was the tradition of women's response to tragedy. She also threw dirt upon her head and tore her bedclothes. But it was her wailing that would be heard throughout the camp, blending into the wailing of the dozens of other women who had lost their husbands, fathers, and brothers.

Caleb noticed Donatiya, her head also shaven, get out of her bedroll and make her way out to the side of Rahab.

She knelt with her, tore her bedclothes, and threw dirt on herself as well. Donatiya did not fully understand the Israelite ways, but she sought to be beside her mistress.

• • • • •

The next morning, Joshua had called all Israel to meet just outside the camp in a large open area.

He shouted to the masses, "Thus says Yahweh Elohim of Israel! You cannot stand before your enemies unless you rid yourselves of the devoted things in your midst!"

The people murmured with anxiety, not knowing whom amongst them had done so.

He then proceeded to call before him each tribe by name and drew lots. Yahweh would show him, by means of the lots, which household, in which clan, in which tribe was the offender.

When he had come to Judah, and the clan of the Zerahites, the lot fell to Achan, son of Zabdi.

Joshua said, "My son, give glory to Yahweh Elohim and tell me what you have done."

Achan was a simple man, stout with full beard, and mostly kept to himself. His wife, three sons and two daughters stood behind him trembling with fear.

Achan fell to his knees and spoke with a shaking voice, "I have sinned against Yahweh, Elohim of Israel. I saw some spoils that I coveted, and I took them and hid them in the earth in my tent."

"What did you take, Achan?"

"A cloak. A beautiful cloak of Shinar, two hundred shekels of silver and a bar of gold. But that is all. I have nothing else. I will return them."

"There is no need for that," said Joshua.

A group of men were sent to his tent to dig them up.

Joshua turned to Caleb and said, "Take them to the Valley of Achor, stone the entire family and burn them with all his possessions and animals."

"But my Commander," said Achan. "Please have mercy."

"We are to have no mercy on the *herem*. By disobeying Yahweh's holy commands, you have made all of Israel *herem*. You have endangered all of Israel by your selfish action. *You* are *herem*. Yahweh has spoken."

Achan screamed and his family begged for their lives as they were dragged away.

• • • • •

Caleb stood before Achan and his family, tied to poles in the Valley of Achor. Thousands of Israelites came to the stoning. Hundreds participated. It was a gruesome affair. Caleb could barely watch the family crying out, and ultimately dying under the crushing blows of hundreds of stones hitting them all over their bodies. They became bloody pulps surrounded by a pile of rocks.

And then wood was stacked around their dead bodies to burn them along with all their sheep and oxen.

They were burning the evil from their midst.

Caleb's mind wandered to the cloak of Shinar that Achan had stolen and was one of the causes of this entire tragic scene before him. Shinar was in Mesopotamia, the land of Babel. The cloak had been traded or stolen as war spoils and found its way all this distance to Canaan. Caleb had seen it spread out when the men brought it from Achan's tent. It was a truly beautiful cloak.

The image haunted his mind. It was a colorful tapestry dominated by lapis lazuli blue, like the bricks on the walls of Babylon. It had golden thread interwoven through it with expert craftsmanship. It was a depiction from the scene of the Babylonian creation epic, the Enuma Elish. A glorious kingly figure in bright colors, the god Marduk, carried his weapons of bow and mace. He stood on the neck of the fleeing sea dragon of chaos, the goddess Tiamat, ready to cut her in two to create the heavens and the earth.

Caleb was captivated by its beauty. He had never seen anything so colorful and artistic since he left Egypt so many years ago. Desert living was not conducive to the fragility of beauty.

And yet, in this somber justice before him, that beauty became hideously ugly. It was like a smooth and graceful serpent that reared its head to bare its fangs and bite. A flood of terror came over him and he understood, like he had never before, the true nature of beauty without holiness.

It was the seduction of the gods.

It was the lie of the Garden.

And it was evil. Monstrous evil.

The meaning of the tragedy before him became clear. The judgment Achan received was not an extreme punishment for a minor misdemeanor. It was not the significance of the criminal act that warranted the consequences. It was the significance of the one against whom the act was committed that made it so serious. This puny created man defied the everlasting Creator of the heavens and earth, and threatened the lives of thousands of his countrymen, and the existence of his nation.

The final thought that struck Caleb was that humanity does not consist of isolated autonomous individuals unconnected to others. We are all connected to our communities in inextricable consequences. Our choices and actions affect not only ourselves but also all those around us.

It was time to get back to camp. Joshua had planned an immediate second attack on Ai.

CHAPTER 42

As it turned out, the city of Bethel must have heard about Israel's victory over Jericho and had fortified the ruins of Ai with their forces as a buffer from the approaching Israelites.

Joshua had made a mistake he would never make again. He had let his pride blind him into trusting in his own military strength. This time, he would use his full force. But this time, he would also inquire of Yahweh before moving ahead with his human plans.

He called upon the high priest and used the Urim and Thummim to discern Yahweh's response to his strategy. The unearthly glow of the Lights and Perfections fell upon Joshua's form like lightning.

Yahweh approved.

In the dark of night, an advance force of thirty units of warriors, several thousand strong, were sent ahead to lie in wait at the rear of the city of Ai in a wooded valley. Another five troop units were sent in between Bethel and Ai in case more forces would arrive from that city.

The morning of the attack, Othniel led about a thousand warriors out onto the open plain before the elevated city on the hill. It drew the Commander of Ai out from the protection of the ruins. He had a few thousand soldiers and led two thousand of them out onto the field to smite the Israelites.

Seemingly overwhelmed, the Israelites retreated and the Bethelites chased after them, followed by the thousand other soldiers from the ruins. They had seen this as the opportunity to end the Israelite invasion of their land with one swift tidal wave.

But it had all been a ruse, because when Othniel had drawn them far enough away, Joshua signaled from a hilltop with his javelin to the ambush forces behind Ai. They entered the city and torched it to the ground.

The flames and smoke rose high enough for the Bethelites to see that they had been fooled. But it was too late, for they were already in the steep gorge of a wadi before they realized that Joshua had the rest of his forces waiting there.

Othniel's forces turned around, joined by their fellow warriors in wait, and fought the Bethelites. They pushed them back toward the other Israelite forces that had burned the city and were now attacking them from the rear.

The Bethelites were surrounded on both sides by the Israelites and were crushed by the ambush.

They struck everyone in Ai with the edge of the sword and hung the Commander of Ai on a tree until morning because of Yahweh's own words that anyone who was hung on a tree was cursed. Joshua took his body from the tree and threw it at the entrance gate of the city, another defilement by not burying the body properly. Then he piled a great heap of stones upon it as a memorial sign of its devoted destruction.

The Israelites returned to their home base in Gilgal.

CHAPTER 43

The funeral of Salmon ben Nahshon was a somber affair. Salmon had been a positive beacon of faith in his family, and a faithful warrior of Israel who had fought heroically beside Caleb ben Jephunneh, the Right Hand of Joshua.

He had many mourners for his ceremony in the desert, more than all the others who had been killed in the fight against Ai. Joshua and Caleb even showed up to pay their respects and honor to this fallen warrior.

Rahab wore sackcloth and covered herself with ashes. For seven days she mourned. According to custom, Caleb paid some female mourners to accompany her grief with wailing and their own sackcloth.

Because the Israelites were not settled in the land and could not engage in proper burial, they improvised by digging simple shafts in the ground to bury the individual soldiers near the cities where they died in battle. It was a way to honor them and to plant their hope as a seed of victory in the land. Their deaths were not in vain.

But at this moment, Rahab could not see it that way. It was the seventh day, the end of her grieving process, and she could not but fear what her future would be with Israel, now that her covering was gone. Salmon was her redemption. His marriage to her would have legitimized her as an Israelite according to their laws. Her days of isolation from the camp would soon be over, but she would no longer have that hope for inclusion. Would she remain forever at the periphery of the very people with whom she had chosen to identify? She had finally found the first real man who would have taken care of her instead of using her, and he too had abandoned her. She had finally found the god she could trust and worship, and he too would keep her at arm's length like a leper.

It was too much to face. She began to contemplate her options of running away yet again. It was her way of avoiding the pain of a life of rejection and abuse at the hands of others. She wondered if she should find a sorceress to get rid of the life in her womb through forced miscarriage. She had done it before plenty of times. Why not again to protect herself? It was a battle of confusing voices within her heart and soul.

She decided instead to end it all. She would stop her endless wandering of unfulfilled hopes and dreams. She would stop the pain that she could not seem to escape in every moment of her existence. Despite all the suffering she had experienced, she had maintained the hope that there was a love that could redeem her, that could set her free. But she now gave up all hope of ever finding it.

She left the small mourning tent and entered her own tent to find her personal dagger within her belongings.

She grabbed it in her fist. She looked at her belly, just barely beginning to show. She had stopped her flow weeks ago. She felt bloated, and was having morning sickness.

She put the point of the dagger to her belly.

She said goodbye to her child within her.

She started to cry.

But she could not do it.

She dropped the knife.

And she left the tent with a new plan.

There was a ridge not far from her location outside the camp, with a deep ravine of about fifty feet that she had often visited to be alone. She would spend hours there looking out onto the Israelite camp below and wondering about this god Yahweh who had changed her life.

When she found herself looking down at the rocks below, she felt dizzy. Her breathing got shallow. She was going to cast herself to her death, but it was harder than she thought it would be. She had lived with such hunger for life. It was almost impossible to deny that zeal right now.

But she had to. There was no other option left to her.

And then a voice interrupted her thoughts. "Rahab."

It was such a shock that she slipped a bit on the rocks but caught herself.

Was that the voice of Yahweh?

No, she knew exactly whose voice it was. She turned to face Caleb, standing a mere ten feet away with Donatiya by his side. She must have led him to her.

"Are you praying out here or are you just getting away?"

Of course he meant it innocently as in getting away from everyone to have some time alone. But it had so much more meaning to her right now.

"What do you want, Caleb?" she said. She sounded almost scolding to him.

"I want to talk to you."

Donatiya began her descent back to the camp to leave them alone.

He approached her. But she noticed him looking away. It annoyed her.

"Caleb, why can you not look me in the eye?"

He gestured to her chest.

She looked down and noticed that her torn sackcloth had been inadvertently uncovering some of her modesty. She covered herself up.

But the thought had struck her that this man had such integrity. Any other man would have stared at her like a gawking child. But not Caleb. He treated her with such honor. Honor she did not deserve.

"What do you want to talk about?" she said, softening.

"I am sorry for your loss, Rahab. Salmon was an honorable man and a mighty warrior of Yahweh."

"Yes. Yes, he was. But not anymore. And my family must suffer."

"No," he said. "You do not have to suffer."

"What do you mean?"

"You were going to marry him. You carry his child."

"Yes. So?"

"Well, in our law, we have what is called 'levirate marriage.'"

"What is that?"

"When a woman's husband dies, if she has not borne him children, his next of kin is obligated to marry her so as to provide for her the safety of the tribe, that she would not suffer exclusion from the community."

"What are you saying?" she asked.

"Salmon has brothers," he said.

"So you are saying that I could marry one of them because of this 'levirate' rule?"

"Yes."

"But I am already with Salmon's child."

"The first born would be considered the son of the deceased brother."

"I do not like any of his brothers."

Caleb smiled. "Me neither. And the law is only a provision, not a requirement. The brothers can legally choose not to do so. And that is another complication."

"What do you mean?"

"Well, I have spoken with his brothers, all three of them, and…" he paused sadly. "None of them wants to marry you."

Her head swirled. She started to consider casting herself to her death right in front of this man mocking her very existence.

"But that is actually good news." He continued.

"How can that be 'good news'?"

"Because that allows anyone within his tribe to step up and take his place."

"So? His whole tribe is going to reject me and exile me into the desert wilderness?"

"No. That is not what it means."

"It might just as well," she said, looking back down the cliff.

Caleb stepped forward closer to her. It was as if he began to understand her true intentions of being here.

"Rahab, his tribe is Judah."

"So?"

"I am in the tribe of Judah."

Her entire body flooded with a tingling shock. Her eyes filled instantly with wetness. She knew what he was going to say, but still it shocked her.

"Marry me, Rahab. I know I am an old man more than twice your age. But I am one of the mightiest of warriors in Israel. And I will love you. I will take care of you and be a husband to you. I will treat you as the precious treasure that you are. You deserve a lifetime of adoration because you…"

She interrupted him. "No! I cannot."

She tried to get away from him. To leave his presence that burned in her soul like a bonfire.

He went after her.

"What do you mean, you cannot?" he said. "Am I unsightly?"

"No!" she yelled.

He grabbed her arm to stop her. She pulled away and kept going.

"Am I undesirable to you? Am I too harsh?"

"No, no, no!" She collapsed and wept with deep sobbing that made Caleb's heart melt with pain for her.

He held her. "Tell me Rahab. I want to know. I am not afraid. Am I undeserving of you?"

She stopped her sobbing, and looked up into his eyes. He was serious. She could not believe what she was hearing.

"Are *you* undeserving of *me*?" she said with incredulity. "No. A thousand times no." And she broke into tears again.

She managed to get it out through her sobs. "It is I who am undeserving of you. I am an abomination."

He said sternly, "No, you are not."

"You do not know what I have done. You do not know the evil."

"Rahab!" He gripped her tight in his hands.

She suddenly felt safe. It was strange to her. Like all her fears melted in his strong grasp of concern.

She looked into his eyes. She could see his heart was torn in two for her.

And finally, she told him.

"I was born in the caves of Panias at the foot of Mount Hermon."

"I am familiar with the area," he said.

"They are ruled by the goat demons of Azazel. Satyrs who took me when I was but a child and groomed me to be a nymph."

She looked into his eyes for a sign of rejection that would justify her feelings. But she could see none.

"When I was of age, I was initiated." She stopped. It was starting to rise up in her again. The pain that she had kept so suppressed. It was all coming back.

Caleb's heart was stabbed with a giant's dagger. He knew what initiation of nymphs required.

"As soon as I was well, I ran away and never went back. But I discovered I was pregnant. I stumbled upon Gilgal Rephaim and I was taken in and cared for. But eventually I had to do something about the fruit of the crime that was growing in my womb. The sorcerers of Gilgal Rephaim gave me herbal potions to drink and I aborted the baby."

Caleb would still not show an ounce of rejection in his look.

"When it came out, I saw that it had six fingers on each hand and six toes on each foot. It was a son of Anak."

Caleb closed his eyes tight and held her with all his strength. He pulled her away to look at her again.

He said, "Is this why you think you are unworthy? Is this why you were considering ending your life and your baby's life?"

He had figured out why she was there. This man was in tune with her like no one had ever been before.

"How can you marry someone so unclean, so stained by such— evil? Yahweh is a holy god who detests abominations."

"Yahweh is a god who atones," he replied. "Whatever was done to you is not your sin. And whatever you have done can be removed from you as far as the east is from the west. If righteousness were based on our own goodness, none of us would stand. None of us are worthy of his presence. We are all stained by evil. We are made clean by blood atonement."

She protested, "But I am not of Abraham's seed. I was born under the cursed flesh of Edom."

"So am I. I was born a Kenizzite, a descendant of Edom as well. But Yahweh accepts those of any nation who turn from their idols to the living God of all flesh. It is faith that Yahweh wants, Rahab, not flesh."

A sudden silence penetrated their conversation. Rahab felt as if a great weight had lifted from her soul. The dark cloud that had followed her ever since she became a follower of Yahweh was dissolved in the cleansing of a spring rain.

She smiled and said softly, tenderly, "Yes, I will marry you, Caleb ben Jephunneh."

He smiled broadly and kissed her.

Her heart came alive. It had taken her by surprise. She had only known Caleb to be prudish and judgmental of her. Even moments earlier, he had avoided a look at her. How could this passionate sensual kiss come from such a being?

He released her. She almost fainted at his gallantry.

"You are surprised?" he said. "Woman, there is a lot more passion where that came from. I suggest we get married immediately or I am going to feint from desire."

You? She thought. *I am already feinting.*

"Now comes the hard part," he said: "Persuading Joshua."

CHAPTER 44

"Absolutely not!" yelled Joshua. He was in his war tent surrounded by the three prophets counseling on spiritual matters. Caleb and Rahab stood before him with Othniel, Achsah, and Rahab's father and mother and maidservant Donatiya, behind them. Caleb had just asked Joshua for his blessing in marrying Rahab.

"Commander," said Caleb, "It fulfills the levirate marriage. She was betrothed to Salmon. I am in the line of Judah."

"She is a Canaanite," said Joshua. "Her family is Canaanite. I already caused endless debates with the scribes and elders when I accepted her marriage to Salmon. If you do this, and I support it publically, we could do more damage to the faith of this congregation than the defeat at Ai."

Caleb countered, "But is it not faith that accepts me, a Kenizzite, into the congregation? Is it not faith that accepted Judah's Canaanite wife into the congregation, or our patriarch Joseph's Egyptian wife Asenath into the congregation, or Moses' Midianite wife Zipporah, and Cushite wife Neferhetep into the congregation?"

"Okay, okay." Joshua turned away.

"We have gone over this before, Caleb. You are my Right Hand. If you do this, if you marry this Canaanite, no matter how 'acceptable' it is as an exception, it may jeopardize the solidarity of my forces to engage in their campaign of *herem*. For Yahweh's sake, you just burned Achan and his family, born Israelites every one of them, out of our midst for violating *herem*."

"Then burn me with Rahab and her entire family if it is the same thing," said Caleb.

Rahab and her parents looked at him with shock. But they remained wisely silent.

"It is not the same thing," admitted Joshua, "But you are pushing me into a corner, Caleb. I must reinforce holiness in Israel."

Caleb would not back down. "And is holiness a matter of flesh or faith?"

Joshua would not back down. "Are you going to marry this Canaanite, Caleb?"

"I am going to marry this convert to the Israelite faith," he said.

"Then I have no other choice but to demote you in rank to a commander of fifty and pull you from service for an indeterminate amount of time."

"What would it take, my commander, to get you to change your mind?"

In the course of their heated debate, the two men did not notice the three prophets had slowly stepped forward, staring at Rahab. As they approached her, she felt a chill go down her spine and she drew near to Caleb, holding his arm for protection.

Donatiya and her parents stepped back in fear.

Achsah was more courageous like her father. She stood her ground. Othniel stayed beside her like a loyal guard dog.

Caleb and Joshua stopped and watched the prophets.

The three of them were staring at Rahab as if they saw something in her that they did not quite understand.

Then a shudder and a gasp of breath seemed to flow from one to the other. Everyone in the room saw it. It was like a rushing wind that penetrated their bodies, but only *their* bodies, no one else's.

It was the Spirit of the living God.

One of the prophets spoke up, "Thus saith Yahweh, behold this woman before you will bear a child in the line of Judah."

The second spoke as if continuing the sentence like they were all three connected in spirit.

"It will be a royal bloodline from which a king of Israel shall arise. A gibborim warrior."

And the last one finished, "The Seed of Promise shall issue forth who will crush the Seed of the Serpent."

A strange peace came over Rahab. It was as if Yahweh's spirit rested upon her as well. It was as if he were comforting her, clearing away all her doubt, and all her years of pain and anguish in search of one true love. And now she had found it.

She kept clinging to Caleb.

The prophets then lost their breath and looked at one another. The Spirit that had come over them was now gone.

Caleb looked up at Joshua, whose face was frozen stupefied. He said, "Commander, I never heard your answer to my question."

• • • • •

Caleb and Rahab had a small wedding for their two families alone. The feast would only last one day instead of seven. Caleb did not want to draw too much attention to the affair out of respect for Joshua's wishes to avoid controversy. It was a sad fact that even though Yahweh had clearly spoken through the prophets, many in Israel did not trust the prophets as they had Moses and would continue to cause problems if it was made public.

They kept the prophecy hidden. They emphasized the levirate nature of the marriage in order to stress its legal side. It would be hard for the scribes to argue with the Torah, the revealed law of Yahweh.

The first order of business was business. Caleb signed a contract, called a *ketubbah*, with Rahab's father. This was the transfer of authority from father to husband and was the legal foundation of the marriage. Caleb then paid a dowry to her father of fifty shekels, according to their law. This was the customary money held in faith by the father should a wife's husband forsake her through divorce or death.

The next order of business was for the wife to give an inventory accounting of her assets that would be transferred to her husband's estate. Since Rahab had left everything behind but her family when Jericho was destroyed, she had nothing. To Caleb that sacrifice was more than he could ever offer her.

Then the families gathered in Caleb's tent. Wine and oil were distributed among the participants, and nuts for the children. A small band of minstrels played on flutes and lyres.

Since Joshua had not followed through on Caleb's demotion, Caleb was dressed in his military officer's garb. He wore a pure polished copper breastplate and shin greaves, and he carried a pure copper sword in his sheath. It was all ceremonial dress and weapons and it made him shine like the heavenly host. He had a royal purple cape made from the Philistine coast, and a fine cloth headpiece whose three corners lay down his back, reminiscent of their Egyptian past.

He walked around greeting people and making small talk with the several commanders who had been invited.

Caleb's daughter Achsah accompanied him, dressed in a fine white linen celebration garment with flowers in her hair.

Othniel watched Achsah with longing. She had grown into a beautiful young woman of seventeen years old. He had shriveled up into a coward who could not reveal his desires to her or to Caleb. But now was his brother's day. He would not want to distract from that in any way.

At least that is what he told himself.

Caleb stepped up to Joshua, also dressed in military ceremonial garb like Caleb.

"General," said Caleb. "I am honored with your presence."

"You deserve it, Caleb," said Joshua. "I do not want any of the men doubting my support—or Yahweh's support—of this union."

Caleb grabbed wrists with Joshua and gave him a look of solidarity.

At one point, Caleb looked at Achsah and leaned in to whisper to her, "You are as lovely as a bride, my child. One day, this will be your joy as well."

"Thank you, father," she said, hiding the painful resignation of her own despair.

Achsah was a bit afraid of this enigmatic new stepmother and her Canaanite family. But she trusted her father because his wisdom and valor were impeccable. Ever since her mother had died, her father had always made decisions with a careful concern for how they affected her.

The crowd went hush. The bride was coming.

Rahab had walked along the pathways of the camp, accompanied by her companions carrying flowers and lamps. Others joined in the procession until she arrived at the bridegroom's tent with her entourage.

When Rahab arrived at the tent opening, Caleb's breath was taken away. The afternoon sun glared behind her, creating an angelic presence to her astounding beauty. Her hair had been growing back in, but it was still rather short, so she wore an elaborate headdress and translucent veil.

Her eyes were the most gorgeous intense and penetrating eyes Caleb had ever seen. The elaborate makeup accentuated them even more and hypnotized him.

She wore a multi-colored gown covered with flowers. She was a Garden of Eden to him. White was reserved for maidens. But as far as Caleb was concerned, Rahab was a clean and pure soul.

She saw him and her own legs went weak. His uniform and confidence made him so strong and dignified that she never saw his age. He was a tower of strength to her. He was a gallant, virtuous, and mighty man who would protect her from the monsters of her past and the monsters of the future. She never thought she would ever be worthy of such grace. She fought back the tears.

They met in the middle and were crowned with garland. He led her to the priest who waited to make a benediction over them, and announce the celebration of their newfound life together.

As the people feasted, Caleb and Rahab left their guests to go to her family's tent for their consummation.

Everyone had been cleared out for them to be alone that night.

Caleb and Rahab bathed themselves in separate tents. Caleb made his way to Rahab's tent and found the marriage bed. He had a surprise for her. He had brought a bag of white rose petals picked by Achsah. He spread out the petals on the floor all around the bed as a symbolic gesture of purity. He sat down on the bed and waited for her to finish her preparations.

When she appeared from behind her partition, he lost his breath a second time this day.

He saw her eyes first. They were the most beautiful eyes in the heavens and earth and her dark eyeliner only accentuated their loveliness. She had switched headdresses to a more exotic one than at the ceremony. This one was laden with gems and had strings hanging down, touching her body.

She wore a very expensive looking translucent garment. He could see she had tattoos all over her body. They were marks of her past life that she would not be able to erase. She was forgiven now, and would never display them for any other man than him.

She moved toward him with sublime sensuality.

He was entranced with her.

But then she saw the white petals on the floor.

She knew what they meant.

And it was too much for her to handle.

She broke down weeping.

"I cannot do this, I cannot do this," she cried.

Caleb was up in a flash and was holding her, comforting her.

"What is wrong, my lovely bride?"

She would not answer.

He pulled her gently over to the bed and they sat down. He continued to hold her in his strong arms.

"I will not hurt you, Rahab. I will not treat you as other men have. I will not let anything hurt you ever again."

"I know. I know you will not."

"Then what is it?"

"I do not know how to be. Please forgive me, Caleb. Please do not divorce me. I want to love you. I just do not know how."

She had lived a life so entrenched in abuse by bad men, that she had no idea of how to behave with a good man. Memories of past experiences haunted her and spoiled the holiness of this moment.

And then she felt this strong man in whose arms she felt safe, tremble. But he spoke with a voice that was strong and true. "It is all right, Rahab. Do not fear. I will never divorce you. I will show you how to love. And I will start tonight. This is love."

He helped her to stand up. He pulled back the linen bed sheets. He lifted her and laid her in the bed, and pulled the sheets back over her.

Then he lay down beside her, outside the sheets, and held her in his arms.

"Sleep my dove. You are safe now. Sleep."

She sighed deeply and realized how drowsy she was. It was like a magic spell on her—a spell of peace and rest. And she soon discovered she had never slept before in her entire life until this very moment.

She drifted off into a deep slumber.

CHAPTER 45

Rahab awoke the next afternoon. It was late already, and Caleb was gone. She became anxious and looked around.

"Caleb? Caleb?"

Caleb stuck his head into the tent, "Just a moment."

She felt like she had awakened from a year of sleep.

Caleb entered with a smile.

"Hello, sleepyhead," he said.

"What time is it?"

"Late afternoon."

"Late afternoon?"

"Yes," he said, "You slept about eighteen hours."

She plopped back into bed exhausted by the thought of it, and called out, "I am starving."

She heard servants come inside. They were carrying trays of food: Pomegranates, dates, bread cakes and honey, fresh goat's milk. They set them up for her to access from her bedroll.

Caleb jumped onto the cushion next to her with a smile.

"Food for my queen."

She gave him a wry smile, and hungrily grabbed a couple dates to munch on them. "You are too good to me, Caleb ben Jephunneh."

"Yahweh has been too good to me," he said. "Although I will now have to change the name of my whip sword." She knew which one he was talking about. She had seen him use it in Jericho. He was a master, wielding the strange flexible blade like a whip with frightening accuracy. And he had saved her life with it.

"What do you mean?" she said.

"My sword's nickname is the same as yours—'Rahab.' That might be confusing."

"You named your sword after me?"

"No, silly," he said, "It was named by my ancestor, Lamech ben Methuselah, who was the father of Noah. He named it after the sea dragon of chaos. The sword was handed down to me through the family line."

"I chose that name for the same reason," she said.

"Now you really have me curious," he said. "What was your birth name?"

"I do not want to speak of my past, husband. It only brings back memories of pain."

"Then speak of it no more," he said.

"Keep the name. I like it. But if you ever betray me, I will be like your whip sword. I will bite like a cobra."

Caleb was suddenly somber, "Rahab, my precious garden, you have only known indignity and betrayal. And for that I do not blame you. I will earn your love."

She looked into his deep blue eyes, as if she could see his soul.

She leaned over and kissed him.

"You already have."

He was so grateful, just for the moment. But when he pulled away, she pulled his chin back and kissed him again.

But then she stopped. Something had intruded on her mind. She realized something had been missing.

"Where is Donatiya?"

"I do not know," he said.

"She was not with the servants. She should have been. She would have been."

"I have not seen her anywhere," he said.

She jumped up and began to get her clothes on. "Something is wrong, Caleb. Donatiya would not do this. I know her."

He said, "Check the tents. Get the family to help. I will mount my horse and scout the perimeter of the camp."

• • • • •

It was nightfall and they had still not found Donatiya. She had vanished. They spent the entire day inquiring of neighbors, but no one had noticed anything strange.

Back at Caleb's tent, Rahab felt sick.

Caleb tried to comfort her. But Rahab could only think the worst. "I just know she was kidnapped. But who could have entered the camp unnoticed?"

Caleb said, "Is it possible she ran away?"

"I thought she was content with us."

"I am sorry, Rahab. I have alerted the outer tribes. If she is spotted near camp, we will be notified."

"What more can I do?" She looked at him with tearful eyes of dread. She knew the barbaric things that would be done to a young innocent girl by desert criminals and brigands—Amorites and Canaanites—once they got ahold of her.

He said, "We have done all we can do for now."

She said, "I will never forgive myself."

They both knew that if Donatiya had run away, they would not find her because there was a hundred possible directions she could have gone.

She would not last two days in the hostile desert. She was gone and there was nothing more they could do about it.

At that moment, a servant announced a messenger from Joshua waited outside the tent. Caleb found the messenger on a horse.

"The Commander wants to see both of you."

Caleb did not understand, "Rahab too?"

"Yes, sir."

Caleb shook his head. Why Rahab? Had Joshua changed his mind on supporting Caleb now that he was married? This could not be good.

"Tell him we will follow you shortly."

When Caleb and Rahab met in the war tent, Joshua was alone and seated pensively in his chair.

When they approached him, Joshua stared at Rahab with his troubled look.

Caleb said, "My Commander, we hurried over as soon as we could. We have spent the day in a frantic look for Rahab's maidservant. She disappeared after last night, and we could not find her."

Joshua turned to concern, but still kept his eyes on Rahab. "I am sorry to hear that. I can see you are distraught, Rahab. I will not keep the both of you long."

"You cause us no inconvenience," said Caleb.

Rahab added, "We are your servants, my lord."

Joshua rubbed his hand around his face. "Yes, well, we are all servants of Yahweh. Unfortunately, I just happen to be one of his more rock headed servants."

Caleb and Rahab were surprised at Joshua's self-deprecation.

"I owe the both of you an apology. My temper and lack of wisdom was a display of foolishness and spiritual ignorance that are unworthy of my position as leader of this people."

Caleb said, "Joshua, there is no need to…"

"No," interrupted Joshua. "I do have need of confession and repentance. To you, my dear friend, and most trusted warrior of Yahweh, I was a proud and faithless man."

He shifted his gaze to Rahab and a chill went down her spine. "And to you, precious woman of Israel, I was a heartless hypocrite."

"My lord," she protested. She could not believe it. He had called her a woman of Israel. It was another redemption for her to be called such an honor by the very leader of Israel himself.

But he continued, with his eyes set on her, "It took the Spirit of Yahweh to chastise me, and I beg your forgiveness."

Joshua kept his look on Rahab. She demurred, "We are all sinners in need of atonement."

Joshua would not release her with his eyes. "Do you forgive me, Rahab?"

She said with humility, "I do, my lord."

Joshua looked at Caleb, "And you, Caleb?"

"All is forgiven, Joshua."

Unfortunately, for Joshua, all was not confessed. For within his heart, he felt an irresistible attraction to Rahab. At the wedding, he had seen her as he had never before. She was the incarnation of feminine beauty that he had lacked for so long. Caleb was right. When he lost his wife and children to the Canaanites, he had become a hardened man. He felt like he had no love in his soul left. But seeing Rahab resurrected those feelings. And now he felt more terrible for having them.

He was not sure if he had called them here to confess or just as an excuse to see her again. He had been forgiven of his sin of pride, only to fill the hole with a new sin of covetousness.

The uncomfortable silence was punctuated by the sound of a ram's horn. It was a military alert coming from the north end of the camp.

Caleb said to Rahab, "Get back to the tent. Quickly."

Joshua and Caleb sprinted out of the war tent to mount their horses and gallop to the sound of the horn.

Joshua and Caleb arrived at the north end of camp. It was not the discovery of Donatiya as Rahab had hoped. Donatiya was never to be found.

Instead, a company of about a hundred Israelite warriors stood guard around what appeared to be a diplomatic coterie of foreign emissaries. There were four of them accompanied by twenty guards.

Joshua and Caleb strode up to them to look them over. They looked ragged and weary. They wore Mesopotamian clothing, not Canaanite.

Joshua said, "Who are you? Where are you from?"

One of the diplomats stepped forward and bowed to Joshua. He said, "My lord, my name is Lidunnamu, We four are ambassadors for the four cities of the nation of Shukura on the Euphrates in Mesopotamia."

"What is your intent?" said Joshua.

"Quite simply," said Lidunnamu, "to make a treaty with you."

"Indeed," said Joshua. "And why?"

"We have travelled a great distance from the Land between the Rivers because we had heard of your infamy in the land of Canaan. We had heard reports of what your god did in Egypt, and how he delivered you with great judgment upon Pharaoh. And a little while later, we heard how you overcame the Amorite kings, Sihon of Heshbon, and Og of Bashan. We are no fools, mighty Joshua. We seek alliance, not conflict. So our elders appointed this delegation, and laden us with many supplies to travel this great distance so as to covenant with you. We are your servants."

And the four diplomats all bowed.

But Joshua was skeptical. "Shukura? I have never heard of that nation before."

"It is near the ruins of Mari, my lord," said Lidunnamu.

"What do you offer us in return?" said Joshua.

"Unrestricted trade in Mesopotamia."

That was tempting to Joshua.

"We are on good economic terms with the Hittites and the Mittani. We traffic in gold, silver, fine fabrics, grains, beer. But also weapons."

"I thought you said you seek alliance, not conflict," said Joshua.

"We sell weapons for profit, my lord, we do not use them."

Joshua gestured for Caleb to turn their backs to the envoy in counsel. Their horses ambled a short distance away as the guards watched over the entourage.

Joshua said, "What say you, Caleb?"

Caleb said, "Their clothes are clearly not Canaanite. They are quite worn, as well as their sandals."

"I noticed that too," said Joshua. "The sacks on their donkeys are empty and full of patches, as well as their wineskins. They appear to have come from the great distance they claim."

"They mentioned elders as their rulers, not kings," said Caleb. "That is Mesopotamian not Canaanite. They are outside the boundaries of the Promise Land, so they are not under *herem*."

Joshua said, "We could use all the allies we can get. And weapons."

Caleb said, "But we do not know anything about them, Commander. I would recommend you consult the prophets or use the Urim and Thummim to inquire of Yahweh."

Joshua sighed. "I do not want to be running to Eleazer and the prophets for every minor decision like a child for his mother's teat. Yahweh made me leader after all, not a juvenile."

Caleb could see Joshua was not going to listen.

"I would be cautious," said Caleb as his last advice.

Joshua turned back and strode over to Lidunnamu, followed by Caleb. "We will covenant with your nation. But I will demand that our alliance be made known to the Hittites and Mittani for our sake."

"Of course," said Lidunnamu.

Joshua said, "Come with us to my tent and we will finalize negotiations. Tomorrow we will give you supplies for your return to Mesopotamia."

CHAPTER 46

King Hoham sat on his throne of carved stone. Under both armrests were the engraved bodies of Sphinxes: Lions with wings and human heads. The backrest was a large span of the remains of previous Anakim kings fused together in a mass of bones that projected both death and power.

Hoham stroked his red beard in contemplation of the scene before him. On his sides were the Brothers Arba: Ahiman, Sheshai, and Talmai. In the darkness of the pillars behind him were the shadow forms of the gods Ba'al and Molech. It was not readily apparent whether they were alive or graven images.

Before Hoham, was the small frail form of the thirteen-year-old Canaanite girl Donatiya.

She had just given him the intelligence she was commissioned with months earlier when the Anakim had captured her people fleeing from Jericho. Because of her encounter with the prophesy of the sorceress, she was chosen to be a spy under the threat of annihilating her entire tribe if she did not return.

She was to find out who was the Chosen Seed of Israel. Sheshai had read the oracles of Balaam in Ammon, and had discovered that it would be from the line of Judah. But he never imagined that the

Chosen Seed would be a woman, much less a prostitute of such insignificance.

This Yahweh seemed like a toothless moron to all of them.

The little girl trembled with fear. She was so small before these towering massive giants, that she had to crane her neck up to look at them. They were godlike to her. They could crush her with one of their thumbs.

"Are you sure that it was confirmed by their prophets?" Hoham asked the little waif.

"Yes, my lord," said Donatiya. "Three of them. They said a warrior king would arise from her royal bloodline and his Seed would crush the Seed of the Serpent."

Sheshai whispered to Hoham, "That is corroboration with the sorceress from Bashan." He was referring to the sorceress that Donatiya saw prophesy over Rahab outside Jericho. Two sources of completely alien seers prophesying the same identity could not be more persuasive evidence of confirmation.

But Hoham was confused. "Why is it not the king who arises who will conquer, but his Seed? And is this Seed plural or singular?"

Ba'al whispered to Sheshai from behind the pillar. The gods had the ability to throw their whispers at a distance.

Sheshai then said, "Either way, my king, we kill the woman, we choke the Seed."

Hoham asked Donatiya, "What is the name of this whore's husband?"

"Caleb ben Jephunneh."

"We must kill him as well."

She cautioned him, "He is the Right Hand of the leader of Israel. He is a mighty gibborim."

"We will have to target him in battle then."

Hoham could see her fear and became soft in his expression. "My sweet little girl, you have nothing to fear. You have accomplished your task with more effect than one of my warriors. Your tribe is safe. In fact, I graciously reward such service."

Donatiya calmed a little. But not a lot. These Anakim were imposing looking monsters no matter how appreciative they were.

They were interrupted by a herald, "My lord, the king, mighty ruler of the Anakim, a messenger from King Adonizedek has arrived."

He bowed low and Hoham gestured to bring him in. He then waved one of the guards to move Donatiya aside in waiting.

His huge six-fingered hands seemed to swallow up Donatiya's back as he gently moved her to the side of the throne out of the way.

The messenger entered the room and stopped short when he saw the gargantuan Ahiman beside the throne. He knew who he was and was clearly apprehensive as he approached Hoham and knelt before him.

The messenger held out a sealed dispatch and said, "King Adonizedek of Jerusalem gives his greetings and prays that all goes well with the king of Kiriath-arba."

It was a clay envelope with a seal on it. Hoham read the letter as everyone waited.

Talmai became fidgety waiting. He could not stand court politics. He wanted to kill someone.

Sheshai knew this had something to do with Israel. They were making headway into Canaan with their full destruction of the cities of Jericho, Ai and Bethel. It was only a matter of days before they would turn their full force to the south to capture Jerusalem and its surrounding cities.

Ahiman was haunted by his desire to sit on the throne of power. It made him hate Hoham to see him in his entire regal splendor where Ahiman should be sitting. And Ahiman should be reading the private dispatch of kings, not this unworthy wretch.

Hoham called out, "Scribe!"

A sniveling little human monk ran forward with a small table that held a blank clay tablet. He readied his blunt reed stylus and looked to the king for commands.

Hoham dictated. The scribe followed with frantic pressings to keep up, "Say to Adonizedek, king of Jerusalem, thus says Hoham, king of Kiriath-arba. For you and your mighty city may all go well. For me and my city all goes well. I have received your urgent request for our support in a military coalition. I agree that the Habiru jeopardize our very existence in this land."

Sheshai smirked. He was right. Just as Ba'al had told them, the War of the Seed was upon them.

Hoham continued, "You say the city of Gibeon has tricked Israel into a treaty to protect herself. If this treaty is as you say, then we can afford no delay. Gibeon is a city of mighty warriors and their act is treachery to all of us in Canaan. We will meet with your forces, and those of the other three kings of the area in three days hence. May the gods be with you and with your kingdom."

The scribe finished and prepared to bring the clay for a quick firing in the ovens before it was sent back to Adonizedek.

Sheshai asked, "What are the other three cities that Adonizedek has allied with?"

Hoham said, "Jarmuth, Lachish, and Eglon."

Ahiman interjected, "We have not much time. I will prepare some of our forces to aid them."

"Hold our elite corps back home," said Hoham. "I do not want to waste our best forces on someone else's campaign."

"Wise choice, my king," said Sheshai.

Talmai butted in, "Can I join them, my lord? I am itching to kill."

"No," said Hoham. "I have a more important task for you and Sheshai."

That got Sheshai's attention.

"If we battle Gibeon, the Habiru will be obligated to protect them. That means they will leave their own camp at Gilgal wide open. So, while the Habiru are busy battling us, I want you two to find your way to Gilgal, hunt down this Rahab of Israel and kill her."

Talmai smiled. This Rahab was no doubt heavily protected, which would result in him killing Israelite scum after all.

Sheshai leaned in and cautioned Hoham, "My king, the girl spy."

"Oh, yes," said Hoham. And he gave a wave to the soldier behind Donatiya. He stepped aside and the dark form of Molech appeared from between the columns. He grabbed her entire face from behind with his large monstrous hands and lifted her off her feet, with muffled cries, back into the shadows.

Sheshai was repulsed at the unspeakable things Molech did with children. But he had to begin planning his strategy for assassinating the Seed of Eve.

• • • • •

Molech met with Ba'al in his temple. Molech paced nervously. Ba'al watched him with contempt. He despised the creature.

Molech said, "I do not think I will be of much help to you, here. I had better go back to Ammon."

Stinking cowardly dog, thought Ba'al. *He would be the weak link that would bring about my downfall anyway.*

"Yes, you should leave as soon as possible."

"Good idea," said Molech. "I will leave now. And I will spread word among the others. I only wish I could see the looks on those wretched Israelite faces when Elyon Ba'al, the Most High, exterminates them like ants in a flood from the power of his mighty storm."

Filthy conniving flatterer, thought Ba'al. *I'd like to rip out your tongue.*

If only Ashtart were still here. They would have been able to put up a powerful united front against these Habiru and their archangels.

But she was not here, and Ba'al would have to do this on his own. He had heard that it had taken three of the archons to successfully imprison Ashtart in Tartarus. He did not know how many were coming for him, but he would be ready for them. He had been preparing for this for a long time. They would not know what they were walking into.

CHAPTER 47

It was the Feast of Weeks for Israel in Gilgal. The time of year when all the people celebrated the giving of the law to Moses on Sinai, and presented offerings of new grain and bread to Yahweh. These were mixed by the priests with the burnt offerings of seven unblemished lambs, one bull, and two rams. Then a peace offering was made of one male goat and two male lambs, all one year old.

All the offerings had been made and the people settled in to various parties all over the camp.

Joshua had a special gathering for the families of the commanders of thousands and hundreds around the war tent. A feast of the finest foods that could be gathered was lavished on them. There was beef as well as fish caught from the Jordan, a rare delicacy. All kinds of fruit and vegetables adorned the tables along with pitchers of milk and honey for the bread cakes. It was Joshua's way of saying thank you to his commanders for their fearless leading in the first battles of their conquest of Canaan.

It was also a way of getting to see Rahab again. He felt guilty, but he could not deny it. He could not stop thinking of her. She was invading his mind, keeping him awake at night.

And now she stood before him next to her husband Caleb at the festivities. She was gorgeous. Her hair was growing in more and she seemed to dress in the most exquisite of outfits. She had not yet fully embraced the more modest clothing of her new Israelite sisters. This evening, she wore a kind of Hittite looking colorful dress that laid on her body with such elegance that Joshua could not keep his eyes off her.

Caleb was busy telling stories with a couple other commanders and their wives. So he did not notice Joshua's stare. Neither did Rahab.

Joshua would steal as many casual glances her way as he could during the night. He took a sip of some wine and it went down his throat and numbed his conscience.

He began to dream of being with her in a spring meadow beside the rushing waters of the Jordan. He imagined kissing her large pulpy lips.

The thought followed that he was the mighty leader of Israel, who had strongly and courageously led his forces in powerful victories over the Canaanites. He was a gibbor, a mighty man of valor. He lived at a level beyond the normal man in intensity and adventure. And as the mighty leader of Israel, he also had needs that were beyond that of normal men as well. Everything was more intense for him. And did not Yahweh make him this way?

He was the leader of Israel. Almost a king. He could take her if he wanted.

Joshua's fantasy was broken by the sound of Caleb raising a toast.

"And I for one, would give my very life to protect the man who has led us on this journey of faith and victory in the Promised Land. He is an example to me of the kind of discipline and holiness that I lack in my own spiritual journey. Here is to our Commander, Joshua ben Nun!"

Everyone toasted Joshua with a loud, "Amen! Amen!"

And Joshua felt like a complete and utter hypocrite. Here he was, coveting his neighbor's wife, while everyone was praising him for his "holy" character.

I am a fraud, he thought. *There is only one thing I can do to rip this evil from my heart.*

Joshua proclaimed, "Grab the ram's horns. Announce to Israel a gathering around the tabernacle, for a reading of the Torah!"

It had taken some hours, but Joshua had read through all the Law that Moses had written after Sinai. And he did so before all the congregation of Israel at the Tent of Meeting.

His throat was hoarse by the end, but his soul had been scrubbed clean. At first, he could barely keep his mind on the words he was reading, because of the depression about his own sinfulness. But as he read on through the stories of his ancestors, Abraham, Isaac, and Jacob, he felt in the company of great men with greater flaws and weakness of character whom Yahweh nevertheless chose for his purposes.

As he recounted the Egyptian slavery, the exodus, and the wilderness journeys, his memories of Yahweh's goodness and care became alive again. And as he read through the Levitical laws, he received a vision of Yahweh's holiness so pure and intense, it was like a blinding light that pierced his soul. Israel was a royal priesthood of Yahweh's perfection. And he understood again that Yahweh's laws were not restrictive, but freeing. They were the boundaries for experiencing the best that the creator offered to humanity.

And then the reading of the civil laws affirmed to him that Israel was a chosen nation to receive the laws that would make all nations seek such justice.

It was a cathartic experience for him. It had saved him, pulled him from the cliff's edge. He silently prayed to Yahweh that he would never entertain such covetous thoughts ever again.

He wept bitterly that night alone in his tent.

• • • • •

Joshua was awakened in the early hours of the morning by the blast of the ram's horn. It was another envoy visiting the camp.

When Joshua rushed out to the west side of the camp, he discovered Lidunnamu with a small guard of five men surrounded by a band of one hundred Israelite warriors and Caleb. But he noticed that the emissary was wearing Canaanite clothing, and the guards as well. Strange.

"Lidunnamu. How did you come back? Where is the rest of your entourage?"

"My lord," said Lidunnamu, "I need to speak with you."

Joshua brought him to his war tent with Caleb and his seven commanders of thousands.

"My name is not Lidunnamu, and I am not from Mesopotamia. My name is Yassib. I am the king of Gibeon."

Joshua's head spun. Caleb swallowed. They knew Gibeon was a city of Hivvites a few miles away from Ai over the hill. They had been tricked into a covenant with this liar, and now he was back to flaunt it in their faces.

Caleb grabbed Yassib by the scruff of his neck and said, "Shall I execute him, Commander?"

Yassib whimpered.

Joshua said, "No. We cut a covenant with them, and swore before Yahweh, the Elohim of Israel. I will not violate my word made under oath." He turned to Yassib, "What were the other cities of your accomplices?"

"Chephirah, Beeroth, and Kiriath-jearim, all Gibeonite sister cities."

Caleb huffed audibly. "That is just great. We are making treaties with half the cities in Canaan we are supposed to be destroying."

Yassib said, "We feared for our lives. We are in your hands to do with us as you please."

Joshua clenched his teeth. But he had no idea what was coming next. He made a decision, "You will give us your mightiest warriors to fight with us. Do you have any Hittite citizens with a knowledge of siege warfare?"

"We do, my lord."

"Good. They will help us with these Canaanite walled cities. And lastly, inhabitants from every one of your cities will become cutters of wood and drawers of water for the congregation of Israel and for the altar of Yahweh. Perpetually."

"Yes, my lord," said Yassib. "It is all appropriate."

Yassib paused with a guilty look. "But I must confess. I am here to press for our rights under the covenant."

Caleb rolled his eyes. "What have you not told us now?"

He quivered with fear as he told them, "King Adonizedek has heard of our treaty with you and how you are on a campaign to conquer the land. So he has sent a five-coalition army of Amorites to make war with Gibeon in revenge against us. He has surrounded the city walls as we speak."

Caleb said, "First, you deceive us into a treaty, then you drag us into a fight with terrible odds. Is there any other surprise you would like to impair us with?"

Joshua said, "Who are the other cities in alliance?"

"Jarmuth, Lachish, Eglon, and Kiriath-arba." Cities of herem.

"You are being too hasty with your judgment," said Joshua to Caleb. "Those are all cities in our campaign anyway. If we defeat their kings away from their cities without their full armies or city defenses, then we kill five rats with one sling shot."

Caleb began to follow him. "And all five cities will then be without their leadership and their strongest forces. *That* is why I am proud to serve you, Commander."

Joshua said, "We will travel through the night to Gibeon with our full forces. But first, we will inquire of Yahweh."

CHAPTER 48

Sheshai and Talmai hugged the mountain ridge a half-mile out from the plains of Jericho where the Habiru camped at Gilgal. They had a small section unit of six other Anakim warriors with them. They had to be as stealthy as possible because their dangerous plan necessitated the element of surprise.

But the small number was sufficient for their goal because they watched below them the full army of Israel marching away into the mountains toward Gibeon. There would only be a minimal guard left at Gilgal to protect the civilians—to protect Rahab.

It would be an easy slaughter for these giant warriors. Like a group of vipers entering a hutch of rabbits.

They waited until late in the night to make their move. Donatiya had provided them with a rough layout of the entire camp and the specific location of Caleb's family tents where Rahab would be. She also described Rahab and the number of family members. Donatiya's intimate experience with the family would be their bane of doom.

The Anakim split up into two groups of four. Sheshai and Talmai took two warriors with them to find Rahab. The other four were to create a diversion by attacking on the opposite side of the camp. It was to be a speedily executed seek and destroy mission.

Assassinate the harlot wench, do some destruction to create terror, and get back to Kiriath-arba.

The tabernacle's gates faced southwest toward Jerusalem. Caleb's tribe of Judah was at that southwest edge of the camp just past the priests' tents. So the squad of four Anakim saboteurs circled around to the far northeastern edge of the camp by Ephraim and Benjamin to make their surprise attack.

They did not know how many soldiers were left to guard the camp, but there appeared to be a couple hundred around the entire camp holding watch, spread out in posts a few hundred feet apart. No doubt there were reserves of several hundred others sleeping lightly in their own tents ready for mustering.

Sheshai and Talmai would take out their post with stealth so as not to draw attention, while the other team would create a loud ruckus with their battle on the opposite side. This would draw other watchmen to join their fray. Once the brothers Arba had accomplished their mission, they were free to wreak a little death and destruction on the rest of the camp just to strike terror into their hearts. No one messes with the Anakim and walks away unscathed.

Sheshai and Talmai crawled up to the Judah post. They saw half a dozen sleepy watchmen with another twenty asleep behind them.

They were fifty feet out.

All four of them drew their bows and targeted four of the most awake watchmen. They released simultaneously and the four dropped to the ground.

They immediately dropped their bows and ran full force toward the other two who were nodding off in the soft moonlight. By the time the watchmen realized what was happening and shook themselves awake, Sheshai and Talmai had pounced and killed them with socket axes.

The four of them proceeded to move around the sleeping men, finishing them off before they could awake.

Success.

At just that moment, as planned, they heard an Anakim war cry followed by an Israelite ram's horn on the opposite side of the camp. It ripped apart the quiet night with alarm, but the war horn choked and went dead too quickly. The other Anakim squad had launched.

Sheshai and Talmai made their way to Caleb's tents.

· · · · ·

The other team of four had carried shields and ran at their watchmen with spears, skewering them. The Israelite soldiers had awakened and tried to engage the enemy, but they were simply not ready. The Anakim slaughtered them with ease.

Their challenge would be the several hundred other soldiers, newly awakened and rushing to the aid of their comrades.

· · · · ·

Sheshai entered Rahab's tent and approached the sleeping form. He ripped off the covers—only to discover Rahab's mother and father in wide-eyed fear.

So, the cunning little bastard child was not entirely forthright, he thought. Donatiya's misinformation to the Anakim would give Rahab a few moments of warning to escape from her real location. It was the little girl's way of trying to amend for her betrayal.

Well, it is not going to work, thought Sheshai as he cut the parents down.

Talmai's half-whispered, half-yelling voice came from a couple tents away, "Sheshai!"

Sheshai ran over to find Talmai outside another tent holding Rahab by her newly grown-in hair like a fish from a line. She grimaced with pain.

"So that little twat got the best of you, I see," jabbed Talmai.

Sheshai ignored the insult about Donatiya's lie and walked up to Rahab.

• • • • •

The other squad had jettisoned their spears and was now using their shields, swords, and battle-axes to annihilate their Israelite enemies.

They had set tents afire with wild torches.

One swing of a battle-axe would cut down three soldiers.

An iron Anakite sword would chop right through an Israelite shield.

The numbers were increasing against the giants. But this was an elite team of gibborim. They were mincing the Israelites into pieces.

They started to back away toward the perimeter, so as not to get surrounded.

• • • • •

The other Anakim dragged Rahab's brothers and sisters out into the opening. He had completely missed Achsah, who had been hiding when he entered. She had heard the commotion in the camp and had slid beneath a pile of blankets.

As soon as she was alone in the tent, she rushed to grab her bow and arrows. Caleb had taught her how to use a bow after she had almost been killed by the marauding Aradians years ago.

And she had been practicing. She was the best marksman of all the women in the camp. She could hit a pomegranate at fifty yards.

Now would be her first chance at a giant's head, which according to her calculations was about twenty times the size of a pomegranate. It should be easy.

What she had not anticipated was how different it would be aiming at a living person's head.

She stepped out of the tent.

She heard Sheshai say, "There should be one more."

The giant turned back to her tent to get her.

Achsah aimed at the giant's eye.

But she froze.

Even though he was an evil giant, she had never killed anything before and it made her shiver.

The monster kept coming.

She dropped her aim. She couldn't do it.

But she accidentally released the arrow and hit him in the leg.

He cursed in pain and limped the rest of the way to her.

She looked up into his eyes. He was red with rage.

Behind him, Sheshai yelled, "Do not harm her, Dragol! Or you die!"

The giant had his hand around her neck. She could feel the six fingers ready to snap her in two.

Instead he took the bow and snapped it in half. He pulled out the arrow from his leg with a wince, and carried her over to the rest of the captives.

Sheshai pulled his dagger. He stepped in close to get a good look at Rahab.

She could smell his hot putrid breath on her.

"I can see why Caleb chose this slut for his own. She is rather comely. Though I still do not understand why their god chose a harlot."

Rahab spit into his face.

He smiled. "On the other hand, such beauty and defiance does make for a better game."

Sheshai looked around. The others were holding Baraket and Baxilet, Shiba and Yasha, and Achsah in their arms.

"Bind them and bag them. We are taking them back to Kiriath-arba."

"What?" said Talmai. "The king said…"

"I know what the king said. But I have a far better offer for his majesty."

"What are you talking about?"

"These Israelites are the descendants of Abraham, our blood enemies. Killing the seedline is not enough satisfaction. If we use them as hostages we can cause a multiplication of Israel's pain beyond imagination."

Talmai smiled with agreement. That would be more fun.

Sheshai finished, "They become a human shield for our interests—before we wipe them from the face of the earth. Now let us get these pups out of here. We are wasting time."

They tied them up and were about to carry them out in sacks when a contingent of twenty Israelite warriors noticed them and shouted for attack.

But twenty warriors was not a sufficient number to threaten these elite Anakim gibborim.

It would take much more than that.

· · · · ·

Across the camp, the other four Anakim heard the horn announcing the getaway of their commander.

The Anakim immediately withdrew to escape out into the night. They would lead the Israelites away from the camp and into the wilderness, which would also aid Sheshai's escape.

They melted into the forest of the night. The Israelites would never find them.

They had massacred over two hundred men.

• • • • •

Sheshai put away his horn. His team had wiped out the twenty Israelites who had discovered them.

They retreated for the woods to make their rendezvous with the others.

The giant that Achsah had hit with an arrow was limping. It was not serious, but it slowed him down. So Talmai swung his sword and decapitated his weakened comrade.

The warriors kept running.

They could not afford to slow down, no matter how minor the inconvenience.

They were well on their way into the hills with their sacks full of hostages by the time a second force of Israelite searchers chased after them on horses.

Anakim could run as fast as horses.

CHAPTER 49

Joshua had marched his forces all night to reach Gibeon. It was a full moon which gave them light enough for their speedy journey over eight miles. But a storm had been brewing on the horizon and began to release just as the Israelites arrived. When they broke through in the early morning mists, they appeared like phantoms of a storm god attacking the fivefold force of Amorite kings. The Gibeonite army exited the city and joined the Israelites in a two-pronged attack.

The impact was like a tsunami hitting the Amorite coalition. Though they outnumbered the Israelites and Gibeonites three to one, Yahweh struck fear into the hearts of Adonizedek and the other kings.

The Anakim warriors of Hoham were the only flies in the ointment. They held their ground fearlessly. These were not the mightiest gibborim giants of Kiriath-arba, but they were mighty enough. They pounded the Gibeonites backward.

The Anakim would have been the rallying call for a turn in the battle, had it not been for the fact that the other four armies withdrew in panic at the order of their kings. This left the bulk of the Anakim numbers alone and surrounded by fighting mad Israelites and vengeful Gibeonites.

Lightning flashed and thunder cracked overhead. And then it began to rain, which slowed down their skills and stuck them in the slippery muck. The Anakim did great damage on their enemies that day, killing several hundred Israelites and Gibeonites. But they were now the outnumbered and eventually succumbed to the wave of fury.

This served to strike even more fear into the Amorite armies. They retreated toward the plateau of Beth-horon not far away. The Israelite allies chased them, but when they arrived at the plateau they stopped in awe at the miracle that played out before them.

The rain and wind whipped about with ferocity. The clouds overhead had darkened the sky.

As the Amorite coalition descended the plateau of Beth-horon, a sudden hailstorm began to hit the slopes. Joshua and his army backed off to stay out of the danger zone of the falling ice. They were at the very edge of the storm.

At first the hail was normal frozen pebble-like pieces of ice. But then Joshua noticed that they were followed by massive blocks of hail, some the size of a man.

Yahweh was throwing rocks from heaven upon Joshua's enemies. It was a massive slaughter. Amorites were killed by the droves under the crushing weight of the huge hailstones.

And then it all stopped.

The forces had been decimated. The Amorites had lost half of their men. More had been killed by the hailstones than by battle with Israel.

There were only a couple thousand survivors left. They had stopped their flight to tend to the wounded at the bottom of the plateau.

But that was only the beginning of Yahweh's war with them.

Caleb approached Joshua on his horse. "You know, these Amorites worship the sun and moon as the gods Shemesh and Yarikh. They follow omens of the heavenly host."

"So?"

"Today is the fifteenth of the month, and if the sun and moon stand waiting in the sky in opposition they believe that is favorable to their enemies."

It was part of the Canaanite celestial study of omens. At mid-month of the full moon, the sun and moon would be visible in the early morning, standing in opposition on the east and west horizons. If the moon did not set before the sun rose, it was considered to "wait" or "stand," and the sun was considered as "not hurrying to set." If this standing of opposition occurred on the fourteenth of the month, it was a good omen for the Amorites and marked a full-length day, which was favorable. If it occurred on the fifteenth instead, it was a bad omen that indicated a less than full-length day. Unfortunately, the previous day had been cloudy so no one knew what celestial event had occurred yesterday morning.

"What are you suggesting?" asked Joshua.

"This storm is fast moving. If you pray to Yahweh to clear the clouds and make this the omen of disadvantage, they will be further demoralized by their own superstitions. There is nothing more easy to conquer than an army that has lost its hope."

Joshua smiled widely. "*That* is why you are my Right Hand, Caleb."

Joshua got off his horse and knelt in prayer before Yahweh.

After he stood back up, he had an idea.

He got up and walked to the edge of the plateau. The Amorites below saw him raise his javelin in the air and shout with a mighty voice that echoed through the valley, "O SUN, WAIT OVER GIBEON, AND MOON, OVER THE VALLEY OF AIJALON!"

Then the clouds cleared.

Everyone could see the moon was indeed visible in the lower western horizon opposing the sun in the east.

The Amorites stood like stunned deer in the aim of a crossbow. This Habiru foreigner just commanded their gods and they obeyed.

In fact, what had happened was that Yahweh had heeded the voice of a man, and there would never be another day like it.

The Israelites blew their ram's horns, gave a mighty war cry, and descended the plateau to smite the Amorites to the last man. It was a massacre of carnage and destruction. Yahweh fought for Israel.

In the midst of the slaughter, Joshua saw the five kings departing with a remnant to guard them on their way back to their cities.

After they had completed their victory over the Amorites, Joshua sent Caleb and Othniel with a company of several hundred men to pursue the fleeing kings as Joshua led his forces on a warpath south through the lowlands of the Shephelah.

•••••

On his way to Libnah, Joshua received word from Caleb that he and Othniel had found the five kings hiding in the caves of Makkedah on the way to Kiriath-arba and Kiriath-sepher. They rolled a large stone over the caves to trap them until Joshua could arrive.

When Joshua finally arrived at Makkedah, they rolled the stone back from the cave and brought out the five Amorite kings who had led their forces against Israel at Gibeon.

Of particular interest to Joshua was Hoham, the giant king of Kiriath-arba. He knew that city would be the most formidable of all to defeat. It had been those Anakim who had captured Joshua and Caleb many years ago when they had spied out the land for conquest.

These were the mighty giants as tall as cedars who had been nurturing a vengeance for centuries against the Seed of Abraham. Joshua was concerned about the might of these people and was putting off that city to the very end of the southern campaign, hoping that his own soldiers would be far more experienced and battle-hardened by then to be able to take on the fearsome Anakim warriors.

But now, with the king of that city in his hands, he had just achieved an advantage that could only be attributed to Yahweh's gift.

They hog-tied the kings and threw them to the ground at Joshua's feet. He called forth the five commanders of thousands and another eight of the commanders of hundreds.

Then he told them, "Put your feet on the necks of these kings."

They obeyed. Each king had several feet on his neck. Their faces pressed into the ground.

Joshua said, "Do not be afraid or dismayed. Be strong and courageous. For thus will Yahweh do to all your enemies in this land."

The kings seemed pathetic shadows of the soldiers they commanded. The kings of Lachish and Debir wept. Piram, the king of Jarmuth had actually soiled his robe out of fear. And Adonizedek begged hysterically for mercy, "Please do not kill me. Please do not kill me. I do not want to die!"

The only ruler who was not in tears was Hoham of Kiriath-arba. He was laughing.

Caleb looked around fearing an ambush or trap of some kind. He alerted his men to keep an eye out for any sign of subterfuge.

Joshua then ordered every one of the commanders whose feet were upon the necks to execute them.

All of them were executed, except Hoham, whom Joshua kept alive. He wanted Hoham to face his destiny a little longer for effect.

But Hoham kept laughing.

Joshua knelt down and looked challengingly into Hoham's face.

The commanders let Hoham raise his grime-filled face from the dirt. He looked up at Joshua with broken teeth and a bloody nose. But he was still chuckling as if he were getting the last laugh.

"Do you have a funny joke you would like to share with us before you meet your maker in judgment?"

Hoham spit out some dirt and pebbles and said, "You think you have won. But you have not. You have lost. More importantly your god has lost."

"What do you mean?"

"While you have been chasing us out here in the lowlands, I sent my finest warriors, Sheshai and Talmai, with an elite squad of assassins to your camp at Gilgal."

Joshua's face dropped.

Caleb's whole body charged with shock. He knew those brothers. All of Canaan knew those brothers as the most fearsome of all the Anakim giants.

Othniel had felt the same shock as Caleb had. All he could think of was Achsah and her safety.

Hoham continued to sputter, "Right now, they are feasting on the flesh and bones of your Chosen Seed, Rahab and her family."

Caleb's knees almost buckled.

Othniel clenched in fear.

"You will kill me. But I killed your coming king. And ate him."

Caleb trampled over to Hoham and pushed the commanders away. He turned Hoham over onto his back.

He jumped on top of his chest and grabbed Hoham's head. The monster was still laughing as he glared into Caleb's eyes. Caleb grabbed the head of the ten-foot tall giant in his hands, and squeezed with all his might.

His sweat dripped down onto Hoham's face that turned from a cackling grin into a painful grimace under the pressure.

Then Hoham began to growl. His eyeballs bulged, and his growl turned into a squeal, that was stopped short by the death grip of Caleb ben Jephunneh.

Caleb got off the dead body of Hoham and stumbled back to his horse in a delirium. And then with a renewed determination in his eyes, he kicked his horse and sprinted out of there.

Joshua knew where he was going. And he let him go.

Othniel almost shouted with desperation to Joshua, "Commander, permission to join my brother."

"Granted."

Othniel leapt onto his horse and followed Caleb's exit.

Joshua prayed after his galloping comrade, "May Yahweh have mercy on you, Caleb ben Jephunneh."

He then sent a division of one thousand men after them to Gilgal, to protect the camp. He would never let something like this happen again.

He looked back down on Hoham and the others on the ground, and commanded his men, "Hang them on five trees until the evening. Then put them back in their cave of cowardice and seal it with the stone. Tomorrow, we devote Makkedah to destruction, and then the entire Shephelah lowlands."

CHAPTER 50

The brothers Arba and their squad of five surviving Anakim saboteurs had arrived at Kiriath-arba with their hostages several days earlier.

When they received the news that their king Hoham was dead, they could not be more joyous at the news. They did not need to lead a coup or secret assassination after all. Ahiman would simply step into the royal vacancy provided by the tragic murder at the hands of the Habiru. The brothers would turn it into a propaganda campaign of revenge that would fuel their people and strengthen their grip on the reins of power.

It could not have been a better gift to them. But for the next few days, they would have to put on a façade of mournful faces. They would not want the populace to be aware of their celebration or their political schemes.

The brothers presided over funerary ceremonies for their dead missing king at the megalithic circle of stones, called a gilgal, at the top of their ridge. Since they did not have the body, they used a carved statue of him in effigy and placed it beside the body of his wife, whom they killed to accompany him into the afterlife, as was the custom. Her body was left to the vultures in excarnation. The bones would be buried in a royal ossuary in the catacombs below the gilgal.

Next was the coronation of Ahiman as king. It was an elaborate affair that was shortened to the ceremony alone, without the seven-day celebration, because of the urgent nature of the war that was upon them.

A long procession strode through the main thoroughfare of Kiriath-arba.

Ahiman was at the front of the parade standing in his royal iron war chariot, a huge golden-plated ceremonial vehicle drawn by a dozen horses because of Ahiman's gargantuan size and weight.

Talmai, the new general of the army, flanked him on his left, Sheshai, his Right Hand. In truth, Sheshai was Ahiman's puppet master, ruling by proxy through his brother who did not have the intellectual ability for statesmanship. The brothers Arba would bring in a new era for the Anakim, a new reign of terror that would forever shake off the chains of Egyptian vassalage and would grind these Habiru into dust and scatter their seed to the four winds.

Behind them were the musicians, beating heavy military percussion and blowing a hundred trumpets and horns of grandeur.

Next came the dancers, men and women who jerked and spasmed in chaotic movements and cut themselves in expression of the dissonant religious philosophy of the Anakim.

They left a trail of their blood drippings to be tread upon by the next section of the parade: the new administration, consisting of some carryovers from the old administration and replacements for those killed for lack of trust by the new administration.

A long train of marching soldiers came next, in rigid lockstep, with the Anakim salute of power. Their straight right arms held in a fist, with the other arm bent at a perpendicular angle; fist thrust into the elbow joint. This was an affirmation of the new focus on militaristic rule that the brothers would bring.

At the end of this long parade was a caged cart that carried Rahab, her brothers and sisters, and Achsah. They were included in the ceremony for propaganda purposes to incite more support for Ahiman's preparations for war.

It made the masses rabid.

After the cheering of the new king and his administration and forces, the crowds then turned to hatred, pelting the prisoners at the tail with dead rats and excrement, chanting with hatred, "Habiru, Habiru, Habiru!"

Inside the cart, Rahab tried to protect her pregnant belly from the putrid splattering. She felt as if their vileness and hatred could be transferred from the fecal matter to her precious unborn child.

Rahab's sisters wept, and her brothers sought to shield them from the thrown feces.

The youngest, Yasha, noticed Achsah's lack of concern. She stood stoically looking forward, with a determined and slightly satisfied look on her face.

Yasha said to her sister, "Rahab, why is Achsah without fear? She looks—happy."

Rahab looked at Achsah herself with a satisfied knowing look.

She said to Yasha, "Because she knows her father is coming to get us."

· · · · ·

Ahiman and his brothers ended up at the temple of Ba'al to offer sacrifices to their god of power.

They entered the courtyard with their sacrifice of bull, goat, and lamb. But the coronation and obeisance to the Most High would not be complete without the necessary human sacrifice on the tophet in the inner sanctuary.

It would be neither customary nor expedient to sacrifice the captured women and children, because that would deprive them of their more calculated usefulness as hostages.

What *was* customary during dire times of suffering or war was to sacrifice the offspring of significant figures in the city in order to appease the gods and stave off disaster. They would be the children of elders, political officials, or rich merchants. In this case, it would be the five children of the newly deceased King Hoham. They ranged in ages from twelve to twenty-years old. It was both standard practice and convenient opportunity to eliminate any rival to the throne of past monarchs.

But after the flesh of Hoham's children was burning like incense to Ba'al's nostrils, Sheshai asked the high priest, "Where is Lord Ba'al?"

The high priest gave a shady look at his assistants and muttered, "He has left Kiriath-arba."

"What? When did he leave?" asked Sheshai, perturbed.

"The morning you brought the hostage Habiru into the city."

Talmai butted in, "What kind of coward is he? He runs because he knows the Habiru are coming?"

"Silence," said Sheshai. He turned back to the priest, "Did he say he was returning?"

The high priest paused uncomfortably.

"No."

Talmai stepped forward and picked up the high priest with a roar and threw him against the wall with all his strength, killing the poor fool.

Talmai then bellowed another roar of anger.

The other priests scattered to escape the temple with their lives. Sheshai shouted, "CONTROL YOURSELF!"

Talmai heaved with angry breaths. "He was a traitor to keep that from us. To keep it from the king. Without the god's presence we will be weakened. You know that, brother."

"Yes, I do," said Sheshai. "Nevertheless, your rage will be your undoing, if you do not control it! Fear is not the only passion that blinds a warrior against his *own* weakness. Rage is its equal."

They were both interrupted by the voice of the unheard Ahiman, with his deep base resonance. "We need no gods."

They turned to look up at their towering sibling, now king, now more confident than ever.

"There is only one god: Power."

• • • • •

Rahab was brought before the king and his brothers at the throne room. Ahiman sat majestically on the throne of bones. Sheshai to his right, Talmai to his left.

The fact that Rahab was guarded by two Anakim was ridiculous looking as her small frail pregnant figure was dwarfed by the nine foot tall colossal monsters. It was like ordering two grizzly bears to guard a kitten.

Sheshai spoke sarcastically, "So, you, a common harlot, are the chosen vessel of this god, Yahweh? How would he know if the child is his or one of a hundred others?"

Talmai sniggered.

Rahab was not intimidated. She stood her ground proudly.

"I am not a harlot. I have been redeemed, made clean by Yahweh's atonement, and adopted into Israel as a royal child."

Sheshai said, "What a strange deity, this Yahweh. To use such lowly dregs, such—outcasts. So is this child inside you his?"

"The child in my womb is the son of Caleb ben Jephunneh, the Right Hand of Joshua ben Nun, the leader of Israel. But if he is Yahweh's chosen seed, you can do nothing to thwart his plans."

Sheshai chuckled, "You are a courageous little one."

Rahab said, "Why does the king not speak? Is he your stooge?"

Ahiman burst out with a roar that almost knocked Rahab down, "DO NOT MOCK ME, WHORE!"

Rahab swallowed in fear. But she knew her evaluation was correct. These fearsome monsters were just as ego-driven as every male of every species. They were giants, but they were men, with men's weaknesses. So she also knew them better than they knew themselves.

Talmai asked, "Can I eat one of her sisters in front of her?"

"Not yet," said Sheshai.

Sheshai was calm with Rahab, like a king cobra. "I can see you are cunning enough to know you are safe at the moment, harlot. But I assure you, as soon as you outlive your political usefulness, you will wish you could die. You and all your family."

Rahab shivered. She knew Sheshai was calculated and he meant what he said. The hothead was unruly and could cause incalculable damage with his outbursts. She had to be careful with him. The big one was frighteningly huge, and enigmatic. God only knew what he was capable of.

Ahiman said to Rahab, "You will tell us what you know of your leader Joshua ben Nun."

Sheshai changed the subject, which clearly angered Ahiman, "This mate of yours, Caleb ben Jephunneh, rumor has it he was the one who killed Og of Bashan. Is that true?"

Rahab said, "Yes."

"Og was an impressive Rephaim. How did he do it? Does he have a special talisman or talent?"

There was no way she was going to tell him about Caleb's whip-sword or Karabu skills.

One talent she had developed in her past that became useful now was her ability to lie convincingly. It had saved her life, and now she needed it to protect her husband.

"He does not tell me about the details of war, for this very reason, should I be captured by his enemies."

Sheshai stared at her, trying to read her. Was she lying? His instincts told him no.

He said to his brothers, "I believe this Caleb is more critical to Yahweh's plan than Joshua. His is the seed for this "chosen womb" after all. He has been given the identity of a guardian."

Talmai interjected, "He has not fulfilled his calling too well if it is to guard this wench."

Rahab said proudly, "He will be here soon enough and you can argue with him over that."

CHAPTER 51

Caleb and Othniel arrived at Gilgal galloping at top speed. The horses of his team were near exhaustion. They had ridden them hard.

They arrived at the tents of Judah. Caleb's tents were among those that had been burnt down by fire.

He got off his horse, and stumbled over to the empty charred remains that had been his dwelling.

He fell to his knees and prayed to the Lord God through burning eyes. The pain was too great to bear.

His men stood back respectfully, allowing him to mourn.

Othniel went desperately in search of Achsah amidst the remains.

Caleb looked over and saw a pile of some items that had been rescued from the fire. They were charred and blackened by soot. There was a brass pot, some clay pottery, and even some garments. One of them, Caleb noticed was a tunic of Rahab's. He grabbed the light under cloak and pressed it to his nose and mouth. He breathed in the scent and his eyes filled with tears.

He reached down and pulled up Rahab's dagger she had carried with her through her life. The blade that had saved her more than once was not able to save her this time.

His sadness turned to anger as he placed the dagger into this belt for safekeeping.

Othniel approached him, looking like a dead man, holding Achsah's bow broken in half. He was trembling.

They both shared a pain that could not find words. All of Othniel's regrets flooded his soul and nearly broke him. He should have revealed his love. He should have overcome his fears. He should have married Achsah.

One of the few surviving Israelite males approached Caleb. He was wounded. He had a bandaged arm and leg and limped up to Caleb.

"Sir."

Caleb said, "Tell me what happened."

"We were ambushed at night. There were eight of them. Giant Anakim. They split into two squads coordinated to strike at the same moment. One hit the northern camps of Benjamin and Ephraim and the other one—here."

Caleb trembled with anger. "Diversion."

"They were gibborim. They wiped us out. Only one of theirs was killed, decapitated."

Caleb knew the Anakim killed their wounded rather than be bogged down by them.

Caleb could barely say it, "Where are the bodies?"

"They only killed Rahab's parents. The rest of them, they kidnapped."

Caleb looked up at him stunned.

"They bound them up and carried them in sacks. Some of us tried to chase them down, but they were fast. They lost us in the forests."

Caleb got on his feet. He could not believe it. His family was alive. His Rahab was alive.

Othniel demanded, "Was Achsah with them?"

"Yes. They took everyone."

Caleb said, "Where is this dead Anakite?"

The wounded survivor brought Caleb to the monster. They had kept it in a tent for the dead outside the camp. Dead bodies were unclean and should anyone touch one, they would be unclean and would have to wait outside the camp for seven days.

The head was laid on top of the chest of the nine-foot tall warrior. It had red hair and beard.

When Caleb saw it, hatred welled up within him. He saw the tattoo markings on the face and chest. They were the same as those of the Anakim who had captured him and Joshua over forty years ago. He had never forgotten them. They were Canaanite and occultic. Black astrological symbols and spells for power over their enemies.

"We found this on his person." The survivor handed Caleb a piece of leather with a map drawn on it. And the only city marked as an origin was Kiriath-arba.

Caleb and Othniel would have to get back to Joshua and the armies of Yahweh as quickly as possible.

But first, Caleb wanted to pay his respects to Rahab's parents.

He found their graves outside the camp and spent a quick moment in silence before them with Othniel by his side. They had not been the best of parents. In fact, Rahab had been far more gracious to them than they had deserved. But that grace had transformed them, and over the years they became the parents they should have been in thankfulness for the forgiveness they received.

But now, they lay in their undeserving graves, Caleb staring at the dirt to which they had returned, and he mumbled another prayer to Yahweh that he would avenge their murder with justice.

• • • • •

After Makkedah, Joshua had conquered Libnah, and was preparing to attack the cities of the Amorite coalition they had just defeated, when Caleb and Othniel returned from Gilgal.

Caleb told Joshua that the Arba brothers had kidnapped Achsah, Rahab, and her family. Joshua felt like he was hit by one of the hailstones of Aijalon.

"You are sure of this?" asked Joshua.

"Yes. The markings on the dead Anakim confirmed it. And he carried a map indicating Kiriath-arba as their origin."

Joshua said, "I need to secure the lowlands region before we can take Kiriath-arba."

Caleb said, "My Commander, I beg of you, let me lead the forces against Kiriath-arba. They have taken my family to the land that you promised me."

Othniel jumped in, "Allow me to join my brother, I plead,"

After a few moments of silence, Joshua got up and said, "Caleb, you will lead the siege on Kiriath-arba with three thousand of our soldiers. Let Othniel be your Right Hand."

Caleb brightened with hope.

"I will take the other three thousand with me and finish conquering Lachish, Eglon, and Jarmuth, and then join you."

Caleb protested, "But Commander, Kiriath-arba will be the most difficult battle we will face. They are the mightiest in all of Canaan and they have walls that reach up to heaven."

"You mean, like Jericho?" said Joshua with a smirk.

Caleb was caught off guard.

"Be strong and courageous, Caleb. It should only be a matter of days for me to finish my campaign, because those cities no longer have their kings or their full armed forces." These were the cities whose kings were now buried in the caves of Makkedah.

"I will devote them to destruction and meet up with you at Kiriath-arba. We will deal with Adonizedek's Jerusalem later."

Caleb thought it through. It just might work.

Othniel was thinking of Achsah and revenge.

"Well, get moving, man," said Joshua. "We have no time to delay."

CHAPTER 52

Caleb led his coalition of three thousand Israelite and Gibeonite forces to the city of Kiriath-arba. They surrounded the valley side of the walled fortress. The backside was a cliff several hundred feet steep and impossible for any military attack. It was both a blessing and a bane for the Anakim. A blessing because it cut off half of the opportunities of hostile forces, and a bane because it meant a higher concentration of those forces on the open fields before the city gates.

The Anakim had prepared for the impending conflagration. They had sealed up their threefold gates at the approach of the Israelites. Both sides placed watchmen on lookout as the siege began. Caleb's army was camped a thousand feet away under the cover of the nearby cedar forest.

Caleb entered his war tent with Othniel as his new Right Hand and his commanders of thousands and hundreds. Six spies had returned with intelligence and were waiting for him.

"What news do you bring?"

"Commander," said the captain of the spies, "we have canvassed local villages in the area, and we have a possible number of warriors in the city."

"How many?"

"Three thousand."

Caleb swallowed. Three thousand human warriors would be an equal contest with their three thousand. Three thousand Anakim giants, however was a different matter altogether. Those numbers gave the Anakim a three to one advantage.

Caleb could see the fear in the spies' faces.

Othniel spoke up, "We should consult our two Hittite commanders on siege warfare. We can begin building siege engines and mining under the walls."

The Hittite commanders were from their new vassal city of Gibeon. Their expertise with siege warfare might just be a providential blessing that came from Joshua's otherwise mistaken treaty with the Gibeonite deceivers.

Another commander protested, "But that will take too much time."

Caleb knew he had to have faith, and to build that faith in his men with strength and courage.

Caleb said, "I will wait for Joshua to join us with his three thousand within the week. By then we could have mines dug and siege engines built and ready. We will devote them all to destruction as Yahweh commanded."

The encouragement did not apparently work well for the spies, or the other commanders as the darkness never left their somber faces.

The sound of a trumpet drew their attention to the walls of Kiriath-arba. The commanders left quickly for the city front, barking orders to their captains of fifty to assemble for battle. Unlike Caleb, the Anakim were not going to wait for Joshua to arrive.

The Israelites arrayed in formation three thousand strong, slingers in front, then the Gibeonite infantry, and behind them Israelite archers.

Caleb strode to the front on his horse, followed by Othniel and his three commanders of thousands.

Another horn blew from above the city gates and the Israelites grew tense.

Caleb shouted, "Be strong and courageous, Israel! For our god Yahweh is a warrior!"

The soldiers responded with a shout through the ranks.

They were ready for anything.

And then, the front gate creaked open. Caleb could barely see it from his distance of a few hundred feet.

But it was opening. Just enough for a person to walk through.

Enough for nine persons to walk through.

It slammed shut behind them.

The archers nocked their bows.

Caleb yelled, "Hold your fire!"

They were not Anakim. They were not even warriors. It looked like four cloaked priests were leading five young people away from the gates that now slammed shut and locked.

Caleb said to Othniel and his commanders, "Follow me!"

They galloped out to meet the nine refugees.

When Caleb got closer, he recognized who the young ones were. They were his daughter Achsah and Rahab's four siblings!

The "priests" pulled off their hoods to reveal Mikael, Gabriel, Raphael, and Uriel.

Caleb leapt off his horse and ran to embrace Achsah.

She jumped into his arms and he hugged her with all his might.

She was crying.

"My Achsah! My precious Achsah!"

He released her to hug the others, who had gathered around him.

Achsah looked up at Othniel on his horse. He could not break his military posture. He could not jump off his horse and embrace her and tell her he had been a fool and that he had loved her all these years and that he wanted to marry her.

He had a responsibility as the Right Hand of Caleb to be sharp of senses and ready for war.

But she saw his broad smile and the pools in his eyes that he briskly wiped away.

Caleb looked at the archangels.

"What did you do? How did you acquire their release?"

They were all solemn-faced. Mikael said with urgency, "Not here. Get us back to the camp behind your lines."

Caleb and the other commanders quickly helped everyone up on the horses to ride tandem back to the Israelite forces.

Achsah got up on Caleb's horse with her father, but her eyes were on Othniel the whole time.

They arrived back at the front line guarded by battle formations.

• • • • •

"I do not understand," said Caleb, "You came from Joshua's campaign out west in order to secure the release of the hostages?"

"Yes," said Mikael.

The archangels were alone with Caleb in his war tent. The family members were safely guarded in the middle of the army camp.

"But why did they give them to you?" said Caleb.

"Because Joshua turned himself in to Ahiman in exchange for their release."

Caleb's face went white.

"Joshua exchanged himself for my family?"

"Yes."

"Did you try to stop him?"

Uriel said, "Of course we did. We are not a bunch of morons."

Gabriel explained, "It is the nature of moral freedom. We cannot make you obey."

"But he is Yahweh's chosen one to lead the army of Israel," said Caleb.

"That is what we told him," complained Uriel. "But he would not listen."

Mikael said, "He left the leadership of his forces in the hands of his generals. And he told us that you would do just fine leading the siege of Kiriath-arba."

Caleb was still incredulous. "I cannot believe he would do such a foolish thing."

Mikael now became more sympathetic, "To the mortal mind, it may seem a foolish thing for a man to give his life in exchange for another. But in Yahweh's kingdom, it is the essence of redemption. Substitution."

"But he could have been double-crossed," said Caleb.

"That is why he made us the negotiators," said Mikael.

"Why did you not double-cross those evil Anakim?" said Caleb.

Mikael said, "Joshua told us not to. He feared there would be more terrible consequences if we were not completely successful. He did not want to risk the lives of any of your family."

Caleb said, "And now they have Joshua and my wife Rahab."

Mikael said, "The children were mere collateral. Their goal has always been the Chosen Seed and the leader of Israel."

"Will you help me liberate them?" said Caleb.

"Actually, we cannot," said Mikael. "We have been commissioned by Yahweh on our own course that will lead us far up north."

"You are leaving me here without your protection against the mightiest of giants in the land, who have the Chosen Seed as their hostage."

"Believe me," said Uriel. "I wish we could change places."

The others gave him an annoyed look.

Mikael said, "Caleb ben Jephunneh, be strong and courageous. Be vigilant. Trust in Yahweh, and you shall have victory."

"That is easy for you to say," said Caleb. "You are archangels."

Uriel said, "You do not think *we* have to have faith? What do you think it takes to face a Watcher, my witty sense of humor?"

"Leave him be," said Mikael. "Caleb's responsibility is no less than our own."

Caleb knew he was right. He knew it was all leading to this. Yahweh would test his faith in the fires of adversity to burn out the dross like purified gold.

That night, Caleb prayed for the salvation of Rahab and Joshua from the hands of their enemies.

That night, the archangels left but did not tell Caleb that they were hunting down Ba'al.

There had been a change of plans. The angels had originally doubled as guardians to protect the hostage exchange, in order to find out where Ba'al was hiding in the city so that they might catch him and bind him into the earth. But when they entered the gates, they soon discovered that Ba'al had long gone.

But they knew their adversary better than Ba'al's own priests. They knew he was not running from cowardice. Ba'al was no coward. He was the mightiest of all the fallen Watcher gods. No,

Ba'al was calculating. He was fleeing to draw his pursuers into his own web of power. He had fled to the far reaches of the north, where he had finished building his palace on Mount Sapan.

The gods were strongest on mountains, and the archangels would face their most deadly battle on Ba'al's own turf, at the mercy of his cunning devices. Uriel was not joking when he had said he would prefer to switch places with Caleb. Fighting the giants of Kiriath-arba would be child's play compared to the maelstrom of unleashed fury that they were walking into.

But rather than take the long over-land route of two hundred miles to Sapan, they decided to ride twenty five miles west to the shoreline city of Ashkelon and take a ship up the coast. It would be quicker.

They could only wonder what diabolical plans Ba'al had in store for them.

CHAPTER 53

"You what?!" shouted Talmai.

He was in the war room of the king with Ahiman and Sheshai. He was staring at his brother Sheshai with unbelief.

"Those hostages were valuable bargaining shekels for our scheme!"

Sheshai responded, "Calm down, brother. I exchanged them for a more priceless bargaining shekel."

"But they are the Seed line. If we do not destroy them…"

"They are not the Seed line. The harlot is. They were mere collateral. Besides, after we win this battle, we will kill them all anyway. So I simply hit two birds with one slingshot. Now we have both the Seed and the Destroyer of Canaan."

Ahiman grinned maliciously, "We have Yahweh in our grip."

• • • • •

The dungeon was cut into the rock about fifty feet beneath King Hoham's palace. It was a large holding cell behind bars where the Anakim could hold as many as a hundred prisoners. But the only prisoners who resided in it now were Joshua and Rahab.

Joshua was laid out on his back with a bloody nose, a black eye, and a body full of bruises from his captors. They were not allowed to kill him, but they swatted him around just to vent some of their contempt upon him.

"I am going to have to move it back into place," said Rahab. She was referring to Joshua's nose, crooked from being broken.

He nodded silently.

His head was resting in her lap. He had just come back to consciousness.

She swallowed and placed a hand on each side of his nose, like a potter sculpting clay. She could feel where it was off, and she made one quick movement to jerk it back into place.

Joshua groaned in pain.

But it was not quite in place.

"I am so sorry, Joshua. One more time."

She made another quick jerk and she heard the cartilage crunch and felt it finally snap into place.

Joshua blacked out for a moment.

Rahab cringed.

He became conscious again and sat up. He felt disoriented, but his vision quickly came back into focus as he looked at her. At her dirty, but angelic face. Even in this moment of grave danger it struck him how bewitching and stunning her features were to him.

He shook his head to clear it from the intrusive thoughts.

"Why did you do it, Joshua?" she said. "Why did you endanger the Wars of Yahweh by exchanging yourself for mere hostages?"

Joshua sighed and looked away. He could not look into her eyes. He was disgusted with himself. He had experienced a personal moment of revelation and repentance from his covetous desire. He had realized he was a failure at living up to Yahweh's holiness, and had felt a renewed lease on his life. And yet, here he was again, finding himself irresistibly enticed by her alluring beauty like some kind of teenage juvenile. What was wrong with him?

He sighed. "Rahab, God will not be thwarted if I am dead. He will raise up another to take my place. I am not the indispensable one. You are."

She covered her pregnant belly and looked away with anger. "Do not say that, my lord Commander."

He looked down at her belly. "The child you carry in you is the promised seedline of our deliverance. Do you despise the word of Yahweh through his prophets?"

Rahab would not answer him. She was disgusted with herself. After all she had learned about atonement, and after experiencing such grace through the freeing love of Caleb, she still could not believe that Yahweh would choose her for such a royal honor.

Joshua said, "We were both there, Rahab. There comes a point where you have to trust what Yahweh says of you, and not what you feel or what you see all about you."

"Even still," she said, "They did not return me to Israel, they returned my family."

"I owed that to Caleb as well," he said. "And so I am here to protect you."

She smiled. "You look like you need protection more than I."

He shared her smile. "Now, there you speak the truth."

He paused a moment to decide how he would say what he would say next.

"Rahab, I was a fool to reject you at first."

"You have already apologized and more than made up for such mistakes, my lord."

"But there is more to it than that," he said. "I have sought to be a holy and righteous man. I have followed the law of Yahweh with rigorous devotion. I thought that my obedience was my assurance and security. Until I met you."

"What do you mean?"

"Yahweh has shown me through you that he accepts *goyim* from any nation who repent and turn to him."

Her eyes began to tear up. "Goyim" was the word used of those who were not Israelites and were under the judgment of Yahweh; such as she had been.

Now he was looking at her, looking right into her penetrating eyes.

"He has also shown me through you that I am not the holy man I thought I was." He hesitated. It was very difficult for him to get it out. "I am as much a man of flesh and weak desire as I am of spirit and faith."

Suddenly, in her heart, Rahab knew what he was saying—what he was trying not to say. She wanted to hold him. To share the forgiveness that she had felt. But she dare not.

For she knew that she too felt the flesh and weak desire he was speaking of.

For that moment, Joshua felt the urge to reach out and grab her, draw her to himself and embrace her as a lover. But he turned instead and moved to the iron bars of the cell. "I am as much deserving of judgment as any other alien to the covenant."

She said, "Do we not all labor under the conflict of flesh and spirit? Is this not what makes us human?"

Was she offering him an excuse? Was she trying to tell him something?

"It is what makes us human," he said. "But what makes us holy and separated unto Yahweh, when we have such blackened hearts?"

"Faith," she said. "It is all I have."

They were interrupted by the arrival of a contingent of Anakim guards.

One of them said, "The king wants to see you two."

Joshua and Rahab were taken into the king's throne room by the giant guards.

Ahiman was seated on his throne of bones, Sheshai stood to his right as usual, and Talmai to his left.

Joshua saw Sheshai whispering to Ahiman when they stepped near the throne.

Sheshai then spoke to them, "Joshua ben Nun, you stand before the mighty King Ahiman of Kiriath-arba. I am his Right Hand, Sheshai of Arba, and this is the general of his forces, Talmai of Arba."

Joshua did not want to let Sheshai know that he had met him and Talmai forty years ago when they had been captured spying out the land. Any secret he could keep may become an advantage later—if there was a later.

Instead Joshua stood firm and announced, "King Ahiman, I beg of you to release this simple pregnant woman."

Rahab gave Joshua a dirty look. Simple?

"She is of no value to you. I am the Commander of the forces of Israel. With me, you hold the advantage in this battle."

Ahiman spoke in his booming voice, "If she is of no value, then why did you seek to trade yourself, the "strong and courageous commander of Israel" in exchange for this "simple harlot."

Joshua said, "She is not a harlot."

Though they were facing certain death in the hands of the enemy, Rahab's soul rose with hope at the words of Joshua. To hear that pronouncement from the very leader of Israel's lips made her believe her identity had been transformed. She was a daughter of Israel, an adopted child of Yahweh, the living god. Her past was dead and gone.

But now her future did not look much different.

Sheshai butted in. He was overly eager to be the spokesman and it was obvious. "Many generations ago, your ancestor Abraham and his family infested this land like a plague. He invaded this very city of King Arba, and butchered every one of our ancestors with impunity—save one. Abraham did not know that our queen Naqiya would give birth in her death to the child within her womb. That child was Anak, the father of my people. For over four hundred years we have waited for the opportunity to exact revenge upon our enemies, the Seed of Abraham."

Joshua responded with equal confidence, "The War of the Seed goes back farther in time. In the Garden of Eden Yahweh pronounced a curse upon the Seed of the Serpent at war with the Seed of Eve. He prophesied that Eve would crush the head of the Serpent. King Ahiman, the creator Yahweh has claimed your land and he will possess it for his people."

Sheshai and Talmai laughed. Ahiman did not. He remained rock faced. He stood and walked down to Joshua and Rahab, still staring at Joshua with hardened eyes.

Joshua looked up at his fifteen-foot tall frame. Massive. Twelve hundred pounds of muscle. Joshua stood in front of Rahab, as if he could protect her from this titan of maleficence.

Ahiman reached down and grabbed Joshua by the neck, lifting him up in the air to be eye level with Ahiman.

Joshua choked and sputtered. He held onto Ahiman's six-fingered hands so he would not break his neck as if dangling from a noose.

Sheshai spoke behind Ahiman, "There is only one problem with your zealous bravado, Joshua. We have the Seed of Eve in our hands at this moment. We will crush it, and we will eat it in the face of Yahweh."

Rahab trembled with horror at her fate.

"King," said Sheshai, "I have a question for the Commander."

Ahiman dropped Joshua to the floor and returned to his throne. Joshua and Rahab could see who was the real ruler here in this kingdom.

Joshua rubbed his throat as Rahab helped him back up.

Sheshai said, "This Caleb, who leads in your absence, does he have full authority over your forces?"

Joshua said, "Yes. And he does not need me to grind your army into dust. He is my mightiest gibbor and Yahweh is with him."

Rahab spit out, "He will destroy all of you! He is a Karabu warrior!"

The moment after she said it, she regretted it. She had let her emotions get the better of her. She had stupidly given away a secret that she knew would endanger her beloved. She felt sick to her stomach.

Sheshai grinned and said, "Thank you for the intelligence, wench. It will help secure our advantage."

"I have an idea," said Ahiman. The brothers looked at him. He rarely had ideas of his own. This should be interesting.

"I will propose a face off of singular champions. I am the mightiest of the Anakim, Caleb, of the Israelites. I will challenge this Caleb to a duel."

Joshua gulped. Rahab went white.

"If Caleb wins, we will return you two worms. If I win, we will flay and gut you both, and eat you on the walls before your armies."

Ahiman looked at Rahab, "And your child shall be my dessert."

Rahab's entire body trembled at the thought. She wanted to vomit. But she would not give them the satisfaction.

Sheshai and Talmai were pleasantly surprised at the political wisdom of their otherwise nonpolitical sibling. There could be nothing more demoralizing than losing their two leaders and their seed of hope.

Caleb would not stand a chance.

CHAPTER 54

"Caleb, you cannot do this. It is madness!" said Othniel. He had always felt in the shadow of his older brother's reputation, and had therefore constantly sought to prove himself worthy of the family name, sometimes by taking dangerous risks. But this time he was the reasonable one.

The commanders of thousands and hundreds surrounded Caleb in his war tent. He had just received the challenge by Ahiman to a fight of champions at the base of the city walls.

Another commander added, "This Ahiman is the most feared Anakim in the land. He is eighteen feet of pure sinew and muscle."

"That is an exaggeration," said Caleb. "He is only fifteen feet tall."

"Oh, you are right, brother," interrupted Othniel with sarcastic anger. "That should be an easy kill, then, only fifteen feet tall. Do you know Ahiman is rumored to have killed an entire platoon of fifty men with his bare hands? He has been reported to have ripped a bear's body in half."

"He will not touch me," said Caleb. "His size makes him slow. And I am trained in the way of the Karabu."

Othniel said, "Angelic warfare. All fine and good, except this titan is an Anakim, a hybrid of angel and human. He comes from the

Nephilim. They are not mere humans, like you. They have the advantage of both earthly and heavenly realms."

"But I have Yahweh on my side."

Yet another commander complained, "Caleb, if we lose Joshua *and* you, we will surely never see the possession of this Promised Land."

Caleb answered him, "You could lose me in any of our battles. I am not indispensable."

"We would rather you face twenty average soldiers on the field than this giant monstrosity."

Caleb sighed, "Men of Israel, be strong and courageous. We do not win our battles by our own strength, but by the strength and might of our god, Yahweh. You should not be trusting in me anyway."

"We are not discrediting Yahweh," said Othniel. "We are trying to be discerning and wise, to use the minds Yahweh gave us for strategy."

Caleb said, "This is not a time for safety and caution. You forget whom you are talking to, brother. That is my Commander and friend in there. That is my wife and child and the hope of Israel in there. I am fighting Ahiman in the morning."

Another commander offered, "What if it is a trap? What if they lure you in and capture you?"

"That would be no better than killing me. You would still have to trust Yahweh."

"You think you are being faithful, Caleb," said Othniel. "But you are being foolish and stubborn. Is that your faith, or is it pride that guides you?"

"Enough" shouted Caleb. "Counsel is adjourned. Good night, my commanders. I will fight in the morning, and Othniel will lead the armies in my place."

Caleb went back to his tent, where Achsah and Rahab's siblings were staying until they could be brought safely home.

He entered the tent and hugged and kissed each of Rahab's siblings. They looked at him strangely. He was an affectionate brother-in-law, but he had never been this demonstrative. It worried them.

Then he said, "Achsah, let us go for a walk." He held up a bow and some arrows in his hand. "I brought a gift for you."

The two of them went for a walk in the cedar forest where they were encamped. They always had several guards follow them just out of earshot.

The moonlight broke its way through the thin foliage above to shed some light on their path. They followed a well-worn trail.

Caleb smiled. "Your mother and I used to go for walks in the evening. It was the only way we could get some peace and quiet sometimes."

Achsah smiled. "Was I a problem baby?"

"You were never a problem for us. You were always a joy. This was just our way of maintaining our communication. Time alone. To refresh our souls with adult conversation."

He paused. She could see him tearing up.

"But now you have become a fine adult woman. And you will one day marry a man and have a family of your own. I just want to get a little of your time now before you have so much less of it."

"What is wrong, father?"

"Nothing is wrong. Can I take a walk in the woods with my daughter?"

She said, "It has been a long time since we did target practice together."

"See? That is my fault, and I am trying to rectify a bad habit. Besides, you need to get used to your new weapon. Practice sighting."

She sidled up to him and put her arm around him, hugging him.

"You have been busy with the war. I do not hold it against you."

He held her as they walked.

He asked, "Do you like Rahab?"

"Yes. She is the most sensitive yet strong woman I have ever seen."

"What about as a mother?"

"You are speaking as if she is here with us. She is a hostage in the Anakim camp and we do now know if she…" She choked up. She could not finish the sentence.

"She will return. Have faith."

"How do you know? Is there something you are not telling me?"

Caleb would not answer her. He kept walking, kept holding her tight.

She started to cry.

"Father, I am scared."

"Do not be scared, my Achsah. Yahweh will deliver us."

He could not do it. He could not tell her what he was about to do. But he had to. It would be the most horrible betrayal not to let her face his last possible moments on earth without the opportunity to face them together, truly together.

"Tomorrow I am going to fight their champion warrior alone on the battlefield."

"No! No! No!"

She clung to him like she was not going to let him leave the forest.

"Shhh," he whispered to her. "Yahweh will deliver me."

"Then why are you talking like I will never see you again?"

"Because we do not know the will of Yahweh. And our faith must never become presumption. We must always prepare ourselves for the worst but hope for the best."

"I cannot lose, you, Abba, I cannot." Abba was an adult term of endearment for a father.

"I need you to be the mature woman of the household and watch over everyone for me until I return with your mother."

"Why are you doing this? Why can it not be someone else?"

"It must be me, my sweet child. Only I can fight for the freedom of Rahab and Joshua. If I win, they will be freed. So you see, this is much bigger than me, than you, than our entire family. This is for our nation and its existence."

She could not argue with that. She could only let it sink in to her soul.

He knew he could not stop there. "And if I do not return with your step-mother Rahab, I expect you to carry on the family name. To marry and have children. That would make me happy. Can you promise me that?"

She could only cry harder into his chest.

"Achsah, I need you to promise me. Or I will not have the strength to face my own challenge tomorrow."

She looked up into his face, and whimpered out, "I promise."

He kissed her forehead gently.

"My little turtle dove. I love you."

She said, "I love you."

But her countenance suddenly strengthened and she added, "Father, Rahab has brought new love and life to this family. Bring her back."

"I will."

There would be no target practice tonight as father and daughter held each other in the forest and would not let go.

CHAPTER 55

The morning sun rose over the hills around Kiriath-arba. Its rays spilled out onto the clearing before the city gates, lighting what would be the field of battle for a contest of champions.

Anakim giants lined up for a good view high upon the city walls.

The army of Israel lined up outside the field with archers in ready position in case there was any betrayal on the part of the Anakim. But they were also there to cheer on their champion Caleb who stood before them.

Othniel stood by his horse as field commander in Caleb's absence.

The large city gate opened.

The giants on the wall howled wildly, accompanied by the percussion of war drums.

It was a loud affair intended to strike terror into the hearts of their enemies. And it worked. Caleb had been stretching his legs, back, and arms in preparation for combat when he saw the titanic colossus step out into the sunlight.

The Israelites were silent with awe of the nemesis that stood in the morning light like a god of war.

Caleb swallowed and took a deep breath. He felt Othniel's hand on his shoulder. He turned to him and they grasped wrists with knowing eyes and solemn silence. No words were needed.

Caleb dropped to one knee to pray.

Othniel joined him.

And then the Israelite's secret weapon was brought to the fore of the lines: The Ark of the Covenant.

The gold plated box glittered in the sun. It was carried on its poles by priests and accompanied by the high priest Eleazer.

Caleb rose and Eleazer pronounced a benediction on him.

"Caleb ben Jephunneh, Yahweh is with you! Yahweh is with Israel! Trust in him with all your heart and lean not on your own strength, but upon the Spirit of Yahweh Elohim! He will fight for you! Be strong and courageous! Do not fear this Seed of the Serpent!"

Caleb turned to address the soldiers with Othniel proudly by his side. "Let all of Israel stand in awe and wonder, for our god will deliver us!"

The men cheered. They believed him for the moment, as all good soldiers do.

"Shout to the Lord and praise his name before the shadow of thine enemies!"

The army of Yahweh responded with a shout that rang throughout the valley in such thunderous unison that it was now the Anakim's turn to have their confidence shaken. It was a predetermined praise of Yahweh that they had been taught. And it almost sounded like the indomitable voices of the Seraphim before the throne of Yahweh, the sound of many voices as one.

The Anakim had heard of this golden box that was paraded before the front lines. They heard it was a talisman that brought devastation upon Jericho. The gossip was that it released powerful lightning bolts that struck the walls and collapsed them into dust. It was a container that their god Yahweh was trapped inside to be let out like a Jinn or "hidden daemon." Legends claimed that Abraham had brought this god with him from the Arabian desert into Canaan.

It did not matter that their legends and lore were lies, twisted half-truths, and misunderstandings. It still struck fear into their hearts, such that many of them jumped off the walls back into the city, thinking they would be smashed in the same way as Jericho.

But Ahiman was unmoved.

He had only one adversary with whom he had to concern himself: the puny human now approaching him on the field with javelin and shield.

Ahiman was dressed in his traditional Anakim berserker outfit that he used in the Pit of Death: A simple loincloth and leather belt, with the addition of shin greaves and leather foot toppings. Because of his vast height, it was easier for small opponents to wound his lower legs and feet, so leather wraps with some metal attached made it near impossible for them to hurt that sole vulnerable location.

He was covered in occultic tattoos. He was shaven bald and his face covered with war paint. Normally, he would have the lightning bolt of Ba'al across his face, but since that coward divinity's desertion, he simply painted his skin gold so that he would appear to shine like a god himself, like a Shining One.

His extra-long neck made Caleb think of a serpent. It swayed back and forth with ritual movement. It was the tradition of the Anakim as they faced battle to strike fear in the hearts of their enemies, but all it did was make Caleb think of striking off his head as he would a snake.

Ahiman's armaments were frightening. He carried no shield because he did not need it for protection. He was one hundred percent on the offensive without concern for defense. This aggressive confidence was another element of the Anakim that struck fear into their foes.

He carried a large mace in his left hand, and a strange new weapon in his right called a "flail." It was a handle with a chain and a spiked ball attached to the end of it. Caleb had never seen it before, but he could instantly see its advantage. Such flexible weapons could strike with an additional pulverizing force not attainable with straight solid weapons. The lack of a sword meant that he was not interested in cutting Caleb; he wanted to pulverize him into a bloody pulp.

Caleb carried Rahab in his belt, but he would wait for the right moment to use it. He too had lighter weighted armor on, leather breastplate, a fighting kilt and flexible sandals. Israelites tended to have lighter armor in general, but in this case, it was even less helpful as a single hit from this beast would crush him to a pulp or cut him in half no matter what armor he wore. Minimal armor was an advantage for the way of the Karabu.

He grasped his javelin in his hand and his round shield in his other as he stepped up to meet the giant on the field half way between the armies.

The Anakim drums died down as the combatants circled one another.

Ahiman's neck continued to sway, cobra-like, ready to pounce. He jeered Caleb, "You have one shot with your toothpick, Habiru. Make it count. Your shield will not protect you from my blows."

Because Rahab was curled up in its peculiar sheath, Ahiman assumed it was some kind of hammer or dagger, which seemed more foolish to him. It was exactly the misunderstanding that Caleb had hoped he would have.

They continued to circle at a distance from one another.

Ahiman continued his swaggering and taunting, "I do not know what magic you used to defeat Jericho and the Canaanite coalition, but magic is of no impact on me."

"It was not magic. It was the might of Yahweh against your perverted Seed of the Serpent."

Ahiman replied, "Your god will shudder before my plans for your wife. And when I gut her of *your* child, I will swallow it whole. And I will excrete your chosen Seed into the dirt as fertilizer!"

Caleb said simply, "You have blasphemed my beloved and my god for the last time. As Yahweh lives, you will not leave this field today alive!"

They stopped in their pacing. Ahiman's back was to the walls. He snorted contemptuously and said, "Take your last look at your beloved on the walls of the gate. I have many more blasphemies for them to watch."

Behind Ahiman, Caleb could now see the forms of Rahab and Joshua, tied to poles that rose above the city walls for them to see the spectacle of death that was about to occur.

A shiver went down Caleb's spine.

But it did not have the effect that Ahiman intended. Instead of disheartening Caleb, it energized him. It filled his body with a burning blast of determination, knowing he had their audience.

Which was a good thing, because Ahiman had done it all as a ruse to distract Caleb. He swung his ball and chain over his head. The six-foot long chain whistled through the air and the iron-spiked ball slammed into the ground where Caleb had been standing.

But he was no longer there, having jumped out of the way.

Caleb then ducked and rolled as the mace came swinging around from the other hand.

Up on the wall, Rahab and Joshua watched the battle from their imprisonment on the poles. Their arms were tied tightly to the cross pole of a T-shaped post. They could not move, and the rope caused bloody burns on their flesh from the rubbing pressure. But they felt no pain. Their hearts were too caught up in praying for Yahweh to fill Caleb with strength, speed, and favor.

Down on the field, Caleb's shield was a bit clumsy and slowed him down dodging from the attacks. It was a little strange for him to be carrying such a useless piece of metal against the enormous titan that attacked him.

But it was not intended by Caleb to protect him. Rather, it was intended as a strategic distraction.

Ahiman began to deride Caleb again.

But the act of verbally attacking your enemy meant you were off your guard ever so slightly to focus your attention on your words instead of your actions.

That was when Caleb made his move.

The moment Ahiman began to blurt out another insult, Caleb immediately dropped his javelin and pulled off his shield, spinning in a circle to build momentum for a throw into the face of the gargantuan.

The shield flew through the air at the face of Ahiman. It hit his face and bounced off, falling to the ground. Of course it did not hurt him, it only surprised him for just a moment. It threw his attention. And as he shook his head back into attention, it was already too late.

Caleb had picked up his javelin, aimed, and thrust the "toothpick" at his opponent's head.

Ahiman had not been prepared to protect himself against such trickery.

The javelin lodged into Ahiman's ear and pierced his eardrum. He screamed in painful anger and reached up to pull the spear from his bloody ear and snapped it in two. He discarded the pieces and reacted immediately with more pummeling of his flail and mace at Caleb.

But what he did not anticipate was the result of the injury. Caleb had aimed for the ear with specific intent, and it was not merely to make him partially deaf. It was to throw him off balance. The inner ear is part of the stabilizing mechanism for the body. By puncturing it, Ahiman had lost his strong sense of balance. His twelve-toed feet may have had good grip on the ground, but that grip was not of much use with an unstable sense of balance.

Ahiman backed up to catch himself from falling. But as soon as he realized what had happened, he responded with a counter move. He knew he could not target Caleb directly now, so instead he unleashed a fury of blows, one after the other in rapid succession in the general direction of Caleb with the intent to overwhelm him with a tempest of blows—like a storm god.

One after another, the mace, followed by the flail, slammed into the ground where Caleb was. They were crushing blows that shook the ground with their force. And they would have submerged any other warrior in a rumbling deluge of destruction.

But Caleb was not any other warrior. He was a Karabu warrior. And he was unencumbered with weapons, so he danced, and dodged, and flipped and flew around the crushing blows.

It frustrated Ahiman, but he kept his attack until Caleb noticed he was slowing down. He was tiring.

Caleb jumped through Ahiman's legs and rolled to a stand behind him.

Ahiman's long neck turned to keep his eye on Caleb. But it caused him to stumble a bit from the dizzying motion. He brought his weapons around to continue the pummeling.

But Caleb had already drawn Rahab and unfurled it in preparation.

As Ahiman's mace hit the ground near Caleb, Caleb snapped his blade at Ahiman's face and it took off a chunk of his cheek in a bloody splash. He had been aiming for his eye.

Another mad swing of the flail and Caleb ducked and whipped. The deadly sting of Rahab connected with Ahiman's neck and ripped another mass of flesh off him. But it also cut through his carotid artery.

Ahiman screamed in pain. Blood gushed out of his neck. He dropped his mace and put pressure on his neck with his hand to stop the bleeding.

Now he was only one handed. The spiked ball and chain however were the most dangerous.

Ahiman extended his arm for a swing, and Caleb whipped Rahab around the giant's forearm.

If he got lucky, he could yank it and hopefully slice it down to the bone, making it completely ineffective.

Unfortunately for Caleb, he had underestimated the mass of the Anakite's flesh. It was much stronger than he had anticipated.

Ahiman dropped his flail and jerked his arm back.

Caleb went flying twenty feet in the air away from Ahiman and tumbled to a heap.

Ahiman removed the flexible angelic blade from his bleeding forearm and tossed it twenty feet in the other direction.

He stumbled toward Caleb, still off balance, bleeding profusely from his Rahab-inflicted gashes, with one hand holding his neck wound. He knew he was done for as a warrior. The damage this insect did to him was significant. He would no longer be the leader of his people. They might even execute him out of mercy for his weakness.

He had no weapon, no balance, and only one useless arm ripped to shreds by the whip sword. But he still had his twelve hundred pounds and that was enough to extinguish the life of this dirty little Habiru.

Caleb was beat up by his landing on the ground. He turned in time to see Ahiman approaching him. But he had no javelin, no sword, and no protection. He was flat on his back and disoriented. He barely had enough sense left in him to realize that this roaring giant was lunging at him in the air.

He could not think straight enough to move. But his warrior instinct did.

Caleb rolled out of the way and was missed by inches as the ground quaked with the weight of the gigantic hulk landing in the dust.

After Caleb rolled, he pulled out the dagger he had stashed in his belt. It was his wife Rahab's secret dagger he had retrieved from the smoldering ruins of his camp back in Gilgal.

He leapt onto the back of the humongous monster, sliced the other carotid artery on the other side of his neck and jammed the dagger into the base of his skull up into his brain.

A loud screeching cry of death escaped Ahiman and the entire Anakim army knew that their champion was dead.

Caleb was huffing with the exhaustion of the fight. He leaned into the ear of his nemesis and whispered, "Compliments of my wife, you filthy serpent seed."

He had been holding onto the dagger for just this very purpose since the kidnapping.

He pulled the blade out and raised it high to his forces.

They cheered with victory and ran to meet their champion commander.

Up on the poles, Rahab was crying with joy, and Joshua gave thanks to Yahweh for his victory.

But immediately, they were returned to their dungeon by Sheshai.

Sheshai and Talmai were dumbfounded with shock. They could not believe a rodent Habiru had just defeated their mightiest of gibborim. It was humiliating. They watched as warriors surrounded Caleb and gave him a sword with which to cut off the head of Ahiman.

Caleb then walked with weary legs closer to the wall to present the head to Sheshai and Talmai. He yelled, "I have triumphed over your champion! Now release the captives!"

But the Anakim did nothing.

"Fulfill your covenantal obligation in the name of Yahweh of Israel!"

But Talmai yelled back in response, "Go sodomize yourself, vermin! We have no obligation to keep our word with bloodsucking Habiru!"

Caleb stood in rage as his men surrounded him.

"Sheshai and Talmai of Arba, I will cut you in pieces and send them to the four corners of this land as a testimony of your judgment!"

Talmai responded, "I will see you on the battlefield, grasshopper!"

Caleb spun around like a discus thrower and hurled the king's head at Talmai, who had to duck to avoid the bloody mess from hitting him.

Caleb led his men back to camp.

At a short distance he saw that the three commanders who were with Joshua had arrived with their three thousand men, fresh from their victories in the Shephelah lowlands.

They now had six thousand warriors ready for battle.

Caleb grinned and said to those with him, "Prepare the siege ladders. We attack tomorrow."

CHAPTER 56

Sheshai entered Ahiman's personal chambers to gather the crown and royal robe used for ceremonial occasions. He had told his brother to ready the elders of the city for an emergency coronation of him as the new king of Kiriath-arba. Sheshai had taken a personal guard with him of ten soldiers. He was the next in line for the throne, but he wanted to intimidate the elders to move quickly without questioning.

There would be no time to even perform the ceremonial march through the city as Ahiman had done when he was crowned. He would simply go before the elders and they would give their unanimous approval and he would ascend to his rightful place.

He could not believe it. What luck. He had spent so much energy trying to rule by proxy through Ahiman. It had been so bothersome and tricky. But now, thanks to the unexpected blessing of Ahiman's surprise defeat at the hand of a despicable Habiru, he had his dream. He would be the direct ruler of his people, something he had coveted for so many years.

He was trembling with excitement as he rushed over to the palace to meet the elders of the city in hurried assembly for crisis.

The gathering was in the throne room. The eight elders arrived out of breath. They knew they had to deliberate quickly, something governments were not accustomed to doing.

They stood along the walkway up to the throne. They would have to unanimously agree to Sheshai's ascension, and then he would walk up to the throne, have the crown and robe placed on him. Then the royal scepter and a large mace would be given to him by the head elder who would cite the ceremonial words of approval of the elders, and Sheshai would be king.

Sheshai pushed open the doors and marched up to the front of the room with his ten guards following him. They took their places surrounding him protectively as he placed the crown and garment on the throne of bones.

He was rushing. Everyone was rushing. They had to move quickly. They were at war.

Sheshai looked around and said impatiently, "Where is my brother? He should be here by now! Elder Adab, do you have the royal scepter?"

"Yes, my lord," said Adab.

"We will have to move ahead without Talmai."

Sheshai was interrupted by the big oak doors opening to Talmai. He was dressed in his general's garb of armor and cape with metal necklace covering his long neck.

"Brother Sheshai!"

Everyone turned to see Talmai strutting forward to the throne, followed by a company of fifty armed soldiers.

"What in Sheol are you doing?" complained Sheshai as the soldiers split apart and walked behind the elders, surrounding them ominously.

Talmai stood in the midst of the walkway staring up at Sheshai with a maleficent look on his face.

"My dear brother, what I am doing is engaging in what is commonly known as a coup d'état."

Talmai clapped his hands twice and the soldiers all grabbed the elders from behind and drew daggers across their throats, dropping them all to the floor.

Sheshai was so surprised by his brother's actions; he stood there with frozen face in shock. He had not seen it coming.

Sheshai quickly gathered his wits and barked to his ten guards, "Arrest the general immediately!"

But his guards did not move.

"I said, arrest him!"

But the guards slowly stepped away from Sheshai and turned to face him, displaying their loyalty to Talmai.

"You see, brother," said Talmai, "there are advantages to being the general of the army. A certain access to necessary power."

Talmai nodded to the guards and they grabbed Sheshai. They bound his hands behind him with chains.

"Talmai, why are you doing this? We would be coregents. It was our plan."

"It was *your* plan. It has always been *your* plan, and *your* schemes, and *your* ambition to the throne. I am fed up with your insatiable lust for control. I will not be your puppet or your dog."

Sheshai was uneasy with alarm. "You have neither the temperament nor the political maturity to rule our people."

"I have the power. That is all I need to rule our people. For that is all we respect."

Sheshai said, "At least let me help you strategize for this battle. I do not think you realize just who you are facing."

"I am facing greasy little Habiru who do not know who they are facing."

Talmai turned to the guards, "Throw him in the prison with the others. And keep him bound."

One of the guards said, "Shall we bring the hostages to you?"

"Keep them there for now. I will kill them and eat them at our victory feast after the war."

· · · · ·

Achsah was alone in a small clearing facing the northeast, where the tabernacle in Gilgal was. She had been praying to Yahweh on behalf of her father and had not heard the news.

But she heard the sound of someone approaching her from behind.

She jerked around to see Caleb standing at the clearing edge.

She yelped, "Father!" and ran to his arms.

He caught her and embraced her so tightly, she told him she could not breathe. So he released her.

He noticed a figure standing just inside the shadows of the forest like a sentry watching over her.

It was Othniel. Caleb had asked him to set a guard over her. He had not anticipated it would be Othniel himself. But he should have. Othniel had been watching over her for most of her life.

Achsah interrupted his thoughts, "I knew Yahweh would deliver you! I knew it. I was praying for you."

"I know you were. Thank you, my little turtle dove."

"Where is mother?" she asked. "And Joshua?"

Caleb's countenance dropped. "I am sorry, child, but we were betrayed. They did not release them to us."

Achsah's face went dark. "They are going to die?" she said.

"No. They are still alive, and we will still have time to save them."

Even he did not believe his own words.

CHAPTER 57

Sheshai's hands were chained to the rock wall of the prison area. Rahab stood a safe distance away, as the long-necked giant commented on Caleb's victory.

"I am impressed with your Karabu gibbor," said Sheshai. "My people respect power and fighting skill. I cannot but admire Caleb ben Jephunneh."

Joshua said, "Yet you said we were to be returned with his victory."

"Yes," said Sheshai. "And I would have released you as soon as I ascended the throne. I seek to be a ruler of my word, regardless of the loss it may bring upon me. But my brother is not so honorable."

Rahab remembered that one, the one she knew whose unbridled temper was dangerous.

Sheshai continued, "And unfortunately, my brother was also general of our army. So when he pulled a coup on me, I had little choice but to submit to his superior power."

"What will he do to you?"

"There is only one fate for a deposed claimant to the throne: execution. And the manner in which it is done is excruciatingly painful and humiliating."

Rahab could not believe how nonchalant the giant was about his blood betrayal and impending doom. But then again, warrior cults were so hardened by their violence that they left little room for sentimental emotions.

They were interrupted by the arrival of a company of four guards.

The lead guard took out some keys and placed them in the door to unlock it. He said, "Time for dinner, Habiru. Only, for this meal, you are the main course." The others with him chuckled.

Before he could turn the key, the four guards were suddenly overtaken by another group of four Anakim. These were not reinforcements, but rather saboteurs. They chopped down one guard before they could realize what was happening. The guard pulled the key back out of the lock and turned to fight the attacking Anakim.

These giants were fierce, and close quarters only seemed to amplify their brutality. Swords clanged with fury, and body slammed against rock with rumbling as Joshua turned to Sheshai for an explanation.

Sheshai said, "They are part of a contingent loyal to me."

Joshua thought that was not particularly of any advantage to him and Rahab, since both brothers wanted them dead.

What should I do? He thought. *What could I do?*

Rahab clung to him in fear and Joshua had to suppress his instinct to respond to her.

The fight waged on. Two were dead on both sides. Two were left.

Their swords clanged with rapidity and ferocity.

And then it was down to one on one. And swords were on the ground.

The last two Anakim were wrestling against the prison bars that kept the hostages. Sheshai's soldier was on top and pummeling the other guard bloody.

But he did not notice the other guard grab hold of his dagger in his belt.

The other guard plunged it underneath his opponent's sternum.

That guard then made his last dying move, snapping his enemy's neck with a twisting jerk of his hands.

The other guard went dead limp.

But Sheshai's guard stumbled back, glanced at his commander Sheshai with an apologetic look and fell back dead to the ground.

They were all dead. The guards had fought to the death. But because of that death battle, now no one would be releasing them.

"I have it!" said Joshua. "I have the key!"

He had reached through the bars and had retrieved it from the dead guard lying against those bars.

Seshai said, "I can help you escape."

Joshua and Rahab gave Sheshai skeptical looks.

"You will never find your way out of here without being discovered. But I can take you to a secret tunnel that leads you out of the city down the back cliff."

It suddenly struck Joshua that this whole thing could have been a ruse to gain their confidence. But that was impossible. As Sheshai could do whatever he wanted to hostages anyway.

Joshua said, "And why would we trust you when we are the prize of both your pursuits?"

"I have nothing left. I will be executed. If helping you keeps me alive to overcome my traitor brother, then I will gladly trade one priority for another. Revenge is far more important to me than your deaths."

Joshua looked long and hard at Sheshai weighing his options.

Sheshai added. "Do not get me wrong, Habiru. After I release you and regain the throne, I will hunt you both down and kill you. But only after I have returned your favor of help."

It was the frankness of this giant's intent that persuaded Joshua to take the risk. It was strictly a bargain with the enemy of a mutual enemy. Power knows no loyalty, only victory.

And Joshua had no other way out of this city of Serpentine Seed.

Joshua opened the cell door and said to Rahab, "Gather the weapons and put them in the far corner."

Joshua kept the guard captain's dagger for himself. It was almost the size of a sword for him.

Rahab responded obediently as Joshua warily unlocked the chain on one of Sheshai's hands. Then he handed the key to Sheshai and backed down to guard the access to the weapons as Sheshai finished unlocking his other hand.

Sheshai said, "I will walk in front of you, so you can keep your eye on me."

He finished unlocking the other hand.

Joshua tightened his grip on the dagger sword.

Rahab stepped back placing a protective hand on her belly.

Sheshai said, "We are going to the catacombs beneath the gilgal of death on the top of the ridge. Follow me."

They did—with great caution.

CHAPTER 58

Philistines were master ship builders. They were part of the Sea Peoples who had settled the coastlands of Canaan. They had come from the distant Aegean islands of Caphtor, across the Great Sea of the Mediterranean. Their Mycenaean culture was overrun and they fled to Canaan to rebuild their civilization. Over the years, they had grown from their original settlement in Gerar to control a pentapolis of five coastal cities: Gaza, Ashdod, Gath, Ekron, and Ashkelon.

The principal god of the Philistines was Dagon. He was half-fish, half-humanoid, and was a god of storm. His cult center was near the shoreline of Ashkelon where the boats were docked for their journeys of trade, diplomacy, and battle.

The four archangels, Mikael, Gabriel, Raphael, and Uriel had disguised themselves as monk priests on a pilgrimage to Mount Sapan. They had boarded a ship to follow the coast up north. They wore long billowy cloaks that hid their armament and weapons beneath.

When they settled on board, they noticed several other unusual ships at port that were loading unusual cargo and sailors. The ships were larger and heavier, built for long distance voyage, and the sailors were giants. Several ships of Anakim and several of Rephaim. The angels overheard some of their sailing companions explain that the ships were going to sail to the end of the western horizon where the sea meets the mountains that held up the firmament above them. They were exploring for distant islands, but the local feelings were that they were also fleeing from the destruction of the evil Habiru that had invaded their land.

The Philistine ship that the angels were on was a shorter distance sailing vessel, sleek and parabolic in shape. And they were fast. They had traveled the couple hundred miles of shoreline in a mere two days.

The angels could see Mount Sapan on the Syrian coastline.

"Thank Yahweh, for this strong headwind," said Uriel to his companions. "I do not think I could stand the stench of these Philistines and their rotting fish for much longer."

"Hush," said Gabriel. "Do you have to complain about every petty inconvenience?"

"Gabriel," said Uriel, "Please do not tell me you delight in the repugnant odor of these Dagon worshippers."

Mikael was not listening to their spat, because his attention was concentrated on the two priests of Dagon at the back of the ship trying not to be noticed.

They were bald, shaven of all hair including eyebrows, and were tattooed to look like their skin was scales. They looked like human fish hybrids. Of course they were not, but it was their way of identifying with their deity.

But they also carried burlap sacks that looked like they were full of vegetables or something.

Mikael had noticed them earlier making surreptitious glances at his fellow band of travelers that warranted Mikael's suspicion.

Mikael had gestured to Raphael who joined him in observation while the other two bickered.

"You know, Uriel," said Gabriel, "You have not bathed in quite some time, so you are quite sour-smelling if I may say so."

"Oh, I am sorry," said Uriel, "I did not notice my own odor because yours was so overwhelmingly noxious and rancid."

When the Dagon priests opened their sacks and poured their contents overboard it could have been like any other passengers dumping refuse into the water. But after a few moments the priests then ran and jumped off the ship into the water to swim away from them.

Mikael and Raphael had figured out what was happening.

Mikael, said, "Hold your tongues, scrappers, we have company."

"Very large and ferocious company," added Raphael.

The two of them had figured out that their true identities were not successfully concealed from the Philistines in Ashkelon. Dagon must have sensed their presence and sent spies to follow them. And he had evidently also given them magic elements to cast in the waters. Elements that would draw something to the ship, something the spies did not want to be around to experience with the angels.

Mikael and Raphael ran to the edge of the ship and looked in the water. There was only one thing they could think of that was terrifying enough to warrant such fear.

Then Raphael saw it. "Leviathan!" he shouted.

But it was too late. The shadowy form that had been speeding toward them from the depths was already upon them.

It broke out of the water and landed on the hundred-foot long sea vessel, smashing it to smithereens. Leviathan was over four hundred feet long and hundreds of tons of pure sea dragon.

The angels and other passengers catapulted into the air a hundred feet away and landed in the water.

One simple collision with the beast and the ship was reduced to splinters and floating debris in the water.

And now, the sea dragon of chaos was circling back for a second pass.

CHAPTER 59

Sheshai had made good on his promise to Joshua. He had led them to the surface of the palace, killing a couple of guards on the way, and still did not pick up any weapons to fight Joshua.

He had led them through the palace and upper city streets, which were virtually empty because all available hands were at the walls preparing to fight the Israelites.

They made their way up to the gilgal of megaliths at the top of the hill. The gilgal consisted of concentric rings of huge stones that aligned with star constellations in astronomical precision to create a microcosm of the universe. Rahab was very familiar with this astral worship from her days with the serpent clan of Gilgal Rephaim. It was all too familiar to her and made her nauseous at the sight. But she pressed on.

A large tumulus mound was at the center of the circle. This was an altar for excarnation of the dead, but also an entrance to the catacombs of tombs below. After the bones of the deceased were picked clean by vultures, they were placed in ossuaries in the catacombs.

Sheshai had explained that the catacombs included a secret tunnel pathway that led down the cliff edge at the back of the city. If discovered by the enemy, it would provide stealth access to the city at an otherwise unscalable cliff wall. Soldiers could only pass through the tunnel one at a time, but it would still be a secret passage for a small strike force of assassins.

The tumulus entrance was guarded by ten human servants and one Anakite warrior because all the Anakim were needed for the battle royal that was unfolding in the valley below. The likelihood of Israelites discovering the secret tunnel at the bottom of the cliff was virtually impossible, but this squad would serve as an early warning in case the impossible did happen. What they did not anticipate was that Israelites would be entering the tunnel from their city side guided by the rightful king of Kiriath-arba.

When the Anakite saw Sheshai approach, he stood to attention with the human servants. Sheshai counted on the fact that word of the coup and Sheshai's imprisonment would certainly not have been transmitted to this incidental outpost, so he had the element of surprise.

Joshua and Rahab had circled around the long way by tracing the edge of the cliff to the back of the tumulus. Rahab looked down hundreds of feet below and got dizzy. She backed away from the edge and walked closer to Joshua as they approached the backside of the tumulus.

On the front side, Sheshai had arrived and was greeted by the Anakite. "My king, what need have you to visit this humble gilgal?"

"I have intelligence that the Israelites may have found the tunnel entrance below."

"Shall I alert general Talmai to bring back-up forces?"

I was right, thought Sheshai, *he is not aware of the coup.*

Sheshai relaxed and tried to figure out a way to disarm the soldier and kill him as he peered into the tumulus.

But unfortunately, that lowering of Sheshai's guard was all the soldier needed to draw his dagger and plunge it into the back of Sheshai.

The soldier had deceived him. He *had* been briefed on the coup and was loyal to Talmai. He knew he needed to trick Sheshai or he would not have had a chance against the mighty warrior king.

Sheshai yelled and turned to face the soldier who now drew his sword.

The servants backed off in fear.

But they were not prepared for Joshua who got the jump on them and hacked down three of them before they even fought back.

The Anakite swung wildly at Sheshai, striking stone as Sheshai dodged and darted from the deadly blade. His back was searing in pain and leaking precious lifeblood from his kidney, but his senses and strength had been jolted by the instinct for survival. He finally found his opening to grab the sword hand of the soldier and struggle for control of the blade.

Seven armed servants against Joshua was really not a fair fight. Joshua dispatched them all within mere moments, fueled by the Spirit of Yahweh and bent on bringing back Rahab to his best and truest friend.

Sheshai could have dispatched his opponent in mere moments under normal circumstances. But his kidney wound had weakened him considerably and he stumbled on a rock, falling to the ground with the soldier on top of him.

He tried to hold the blade back, but the soldier was slowly pushing it toward Sheshai's heart. Sheshai's strength was bleeding out of him onto the ground and the soldier would soon end it all.

But before the blade could pierce Sheshai's chest, another blade swung high, hard, and furious, lopping off the soldier's head.

Sheshai pushed the corpse off of him.

"That makes twice," said Joshua.

But Sheshai said nothing. Instead, he stared past Joshua at a frightening sight.

Joshua turned to see Rahab held at knifepoint by the last human servant. Joshua had lost track and had not killed all seven servants after all. He had only killed six.

After all this, thought Joshua, *thwarted by a lowly servant.*

But then that lowly servant yelled out, "Please do not kill me! I am a loyal servant of the lord, my king, Sheshai!"

Joshua and Sheshai breathed a sigh of relief. They had come so close to failure.

The servant let Rahab go.

She ran to Joshua and embraced him.

Sheshai said, "Well done, my faithful servant. But I need your help for one more thing."

He waved him over and the servant ran and bowed to one knee.

Sheshai grunted with pain grasping his back. He could not bend down. "Please, stand up," he said.

The servant stood.

Sheshai cupped his hands affectionately on the servant's face to give him a better look. The servant was trembling.

"What is your name?" said Sheshai.

"Kirum."

"Kirum, I thank you for your service and for your salvation of this woman. Please accept my warmest gratitude at your courage."

Kirum smiled. He had pleased his king.

And then that king broke Kirum's neck.

Rahab screamed and clutched onto Joshua. She yelped, "Why did you do that? He helped us!"

"He saw me help you. That knowledge would become a weapon of blackmail for my enemies during the rest of my reign. It was necessary."

"You are ruthless!" she cried. "A savage barbarian!"

"Ruthless, I am," said Sheshai. "But barbarism is in the eye of the interpreter. Quickly. We have not much time."

He led Joshua and Rahab through the catacombs until he found the tunnel that would lead them back down to the valley floor.

"Follow this to the bottom."

"Thank you," said Joshua.

"Spare me your niceties, Habiru. Remember what I said. When next we meet again, I will kill you."

They split apart, Joshua and Rahab going down and Sheshai finding his way back to the city where he would gather his loyal soldiers to recapture the throne.

When Joshua and Rahab found the tunnel exit at the bottom of the rock bluff, Joshua stopped and pulled her aside.

"You are safe now. Find your way around to the front where the Israelite forces are aligned. You should encounter no Anakim. They are all inside the city."

"What about you?" she asked.

"Tell Caleb I am going to kill the king within as he attacks without."

"Joshua, no. You must not. You are needed by Israel."

"Your husband is a worthy leader. He will do fine."

"But he needs you. Caleb will never forgive himself if you die."

"Then you must make sure that he does. Tell him to be strong and courageous." He looked into her eyes. He wanted to tell her, but he knew he never could. "Tell him to cherish his wife and children.

That he is the most blessed man on the face of the earth to have such an invaluable treasure of infinite worth and beauty."

She knew by the look in his eyes what he could not say. And she respected him for not saying it.

She grabbed him and hugged him. She gave him a kiss on each cheek, the last, lingering with sadness.

Then she was off and on her way back to the Israelite camp.

Joshua returned to the tunnel for his ascent back up into the hornet's nest of evil.

CHAPTER 60

Leviathan was the seven-headed sea dragon of chaos. It was king over all the sons of pride. Its scales were impenetrable armor to javelins and fishhooks. Even its underbelly was like sharp potsherds that seemed indestructible. It had a main head that guided the monstrous bulk through the waters, with massive jagged teeth the size of a man. But its six lesser heads were no less fearsome as they sought prey with equal ferocity. Some of them could even breathe fire.

Its massive double tail provided the power for accelerated speed that could overcome any sea creature or human vessel. So when it circled back to the Philistine ship it had just demolished, there was no hope for any of the human survivors to escape its jaws.

But not all the survivors were human. The four angels swam with all their might toward the shore a thousand feet away. They held off drawing their weapons until the last moment. They were at a double disadvantage because underwater they could not swing their weapons with enough force to cause damage. They would only be able to thrust into the skin of the beast upon contact. This made their situation perilous upon hazardous.

Leviathan passed through the sinking wreckage, snatching up a few bodies here and there, but instead of feasting on the human cargo, it kept moving, zeroed in on the swimming angels.

It became clear to them all what was happening. Centuries ago, when Ba'al was incarnate as Marduk, god of Babylon, he had killed Rahab the sea dragon, also known as Tiamat. His defeat of the dragon of chaos was the establishment of his mighty kingdom and therefore gave him alpha superiority over Rahab's offspring, Leviathan. Now that they were at the shores of Mount Sapan, Ba'al's priestly minions had called up the monster from the depths to attack his enemies.

Uriel was slower than the others. He was smaller and without the power of Mikael or the speed of Gabriel. He would be the first to be eaten.

They were still five hundred feet from shore when Leviathan caught up with them. It was moving so fast, they felt a strong water current push them forward before it struck.

Uriel turned and saw one of the heads target him and open its mouth wide. It happened so fast. He did not have time to even draw his weapon. The monstrous head swallowed him whole.

Gabriel was underwater and saw it happen. He screamed "URIEL!" but all that came out was bubbles and a distorted gurgle. That noise had drawn the attention of another head that swung around and chomped at Gabriel. He barely dodged it, pushing himself away from the rugged scaly head. He drew his sword, but turned to see another head snap down on him.

The suction created by the monstrous head opening its gaping jaws pulled Gabriel in before clamping shut. But Gabriel had held his sword upward, creating a wedge. The sword cut right into the roof of its mouth before it realized what had happened. It instinctively opened its mouth in painful retraction. But it was too late. The sword was embedded deep. And Gabriel left it there. He swam his way out and grabbed hold of the back of the confused head to ride it like a bucking stallion.

Mikael and Raphael dove deep to avoid the passing bulk of the wriggling twisting serpent. It had moved too fast in the water to catch them all in its jaws.

They jammed their swords into the mighty tail and held on for dear life. Raphael's sword had to find the flesh between the scales, but Mikael's steel sword was strong enough to crack through the otherwise impenetrable armor.

The monster felt the sting of the swords and instinctively rose from the depths. It broke the surface and curled back under like a snake, but writhing up and down instead of sideways. This created a momentum so that when its tail broke the surface, it snapped out of the water with a force so strong, it cast off the angels, their swords pulled from the flesh.

And that is exactly what they had hoped for.

They catapulted through the air several hundred feet before landing in shallow waters—mere yards from the shore. In trying to get rid of the annoying parasites, the monster had flung them closer to their intended destination.

They hurried their way to shore. But they did not anticipate Leviathan's relentlessness.

It kept coming at them.

It broke the waters and wriggled up onto the shoreline, its heads snapping at the angels, who responded with powerful swipes of their swords, creating cuts and gashes that were mostly inconsequential on the serpentine colossus.

But just as one head was cut, another head would bite. They would be overwhelmed in seconds.

Mikael noticed that Gabriel was still riding one of the heads and yelling with gusto, "YAHAAAAA!"

Because of the distraction, Mikael slipped and fell in the sand.

One of the heads saw its moment to strike.

But Gabriel had seen the misstep and launched himself at the head just as it was pulling back to strike.

He hit the eye and caused it to bellow a stream of fire from its mouth in agonizing self-protection.

The flames reached Mikael and scorched him. He was wet and had his armor, but it still scorched him.

But at the same moment that Gabriel had jumped, another one of the heads had targeted Gabriel and had lunged.

It was not swift enough. Gabriel was already in the air, so the teeth clamped down on the neck of the other head. The scales of this monstrosity may have been impervious to human devices, but not to its own razor sharp fangs. The wounded head screeched. But the others fangs were stuck between the plates and could not shake loose.

Raphael had moved to the rescue of Mikael and pulled him back out of the way as Gabriel engaged in a Karabu dance of evasion. He did not have his weapon, but he had his training. And even though he was sopping wet, he dove, flipped and spun, drawing the snapping jaws away from his comrades.

And then Mikael and Raphael noticed one of the heads was not chasing Gabriel. Rather, it was jerking around violently as if choking on something.

That something was Uriel.

A sword blade suddenly burst out from its gullet and ripped an incision large enough for Uriel to burst out and fall to the ground with a groan. He had drawn a sword after being swallowed whole and had used it to stick in the monster's throat until he could cut his way out.

He coughed, "It's softer inside than out!"

But his sword was yards from his grasp, and he was stunned by the fall.

"Uriel!" yelled Gabriel, and in a moment, Gabriel was by his side to help him, with the fallen sword in hand.

Another head lunged at them.

They rolled to each side as the jaws hit the ground in an explosion of sand. It swallowed a mouthful of beach, not angel.

Uriel had drawn his other sword. Gabriel had his ready.

And they simultaneously plunged their blades into the soft gums of each side of the creature's mouth. It yanked back with a belch of fire and the angels fell back to the sand.

But then, without warning, Leviathan wriggled its way back into the waters to escape these heavenly sand flies and their troublesome bites.

The angels had done some real damage to the sea dragon of chaos. None of the heads went without significant wounds, from the slashed throat of Uriel's nemesis to the head with Gabriel's sword permanently stuck in the roof of its mouth. But its lacerations and lesions would eventually heal. It would take much more to kill this occultic monster of the Abyss than what these archangels could dish out.

"HAHA!" yelled Uriel. "Did we deliver or did we deliver?"

Gabriel handed Uriel his other sword that he had used to pierce the dragon. "You might want this. Thanks for letting me borrow it to save you."

"Save me?" said Uriel. "I do believe it was my blade that entered its gums, causing it to skulk away back into the depths."

They were back at it again.

"Seconds after mine entered its gums on the other side," responded Gabriel.

Uriel had not realized what had happened in the fray. He sat back. Then he concluded with a grin, "I guess we saved each other this time, brother."

Gabriel smiled and offered his hand to help him up.

"Gabriel, Uriel!" yelled Raphael, "I need your help!"

They turned to see Raphael tending to Mikael's burns by the rocks on the beach.

They ran to their comrades.

Mikael had third degree burns over the left side of his body. He had tried to turn out of the field of fire and had been scorched over the side of his body left vulnerable.

He was moaning through gritted teeth, bearing the pain as silently as he could.

This was bad. Mikael was their leader. He was the mightiest of all four, but now he was impaired. Without him, their chances of overcoming Ba'al were slim. He would heal with preternatural speed, but it would still take days.

"I need something to wrap his wounds," said Raphael.

They had nothing but the armor on their bodies. They had left their cloaks behind them in the sea when the dragon first hit them.

They looked fruitlessly around, but there was nothing.

Gabriel said, "Archons, we have company."

Raphael and the others looked up on the rocks rising above shore that became Mount Sapan above them.

There were one hundred hair-shaven tattooed priests standing in the rocks staring at them.

Uriel said, "You are wrong, Gabriel. We have *bad* company. Those are priests of Ba'al."

"You are dead wrong," said Gabriel. "Those are *armed* priests of Ba'al."

Uriel looked closer.

"We are all dead wrong," countered Uriel. "Those are armed priests of Ba'al *possessed by demons*."

CHAPTER 61

It was early sunrise when the gates of Kiriath-arba opened and a sortie of five hundred Anakim warriors flooded out onto the field before the city. They ran full force at the Israelite alliance.

By the time the Israelite watch guards alerted their soldiers, and prepared for battle, the Anakim were already upon them.

The giants swung battle-axes, chopping three and four men in half with each swing. Maces crunched bones and skulls, and iron swords cut through shields.

Before the Israelites and their Gibeonite allies got back on their feet and pushed back, several hundred of their men were already dead.

It took mere minutes.

But Caleb remembered the tactic against the Rephaim at Edrei. Their size was a disadvantage for one thing, easy sighting for archers. Normally, in such close quarter battle, archers were useless because they would just as equally kill their own men as the enemy. But because the Anakim were eight to ten feet tall, they towered above the five-foot Israelites, which made them easy targets for archers without fear of collateral damage to their own.

Caleb lined up a squad of archers who began filling their opponents with arrows.

The giants blew a horn of retreat and they immediately withdrew back to the city walls.

The Israelites chased them back to the city. But in such situations the defenders used a special tactic. Gates could not be opened to allow the returning soldiers entry, because their chasing adversaries would too closely follow them.

So walled cities had developed a technique used in these rapid strike raids that allowed them quick return to safety behind the walls.

The returning several hundred Anakim reached the walls, where hundreds of ropes dangled to the ground. The soldiers would grab hold of the ropes and would be hauled up with speed back over the walls by a line of fellow soldiers inside who pulled the ropes up with all their might.

It looked like an army of spiders returning to their webs, out of the reach of their pursuers.

They then responded with raining down a storm of arrows and javelins upon the attacking Israelites, who retreated to the edge of the forest.

Talmai smiled with victory. He had been watching the stratagem from the height of the city gates. Although he had his own significant losses, he had struck far more damage on his enemy. The morale of Israel had been shaken, and he had been successful with his first act of war as the new king of Kiriath-arba.

He returned to his control post, a confiscated tavern, with his bodyguard of five gibborim warriors.

As he entered the tavern the sight of Sheshai waiting for him accosted him.

Before he could respond, twenty loyal followers of Sheshai jumped the five bodyguards and overwhelmed them, slaughtering them all.

Talmai killed three attackers before a battery of five gibborim held him down.

Sheshai walked up to Talmai, who pulled fruitlessly at his captors' hold.

"Talmai, my brother, has it come to this? We are now reduced to fighting for petty control over one another? Whatever happened to our family legacy? Our dreams of dominion?"

Talmai looked back with burning eyes. "You betrayed our people long before you handed over those hostages. You have always been interested in your *own* legacy, your *own* "dreams of dominion." Ahiman was your proxy and I have been the fly in your ointment." Talmai stopped and smiled. "Or should I say, your wife's ointment?"

Sheshai went flush. He suddenly realized that Talmai had betrayed him with his wife. That he had been a fool not to see the signs. It only angered him more. He had been stabbed in the kidney at the tumulus, but now he had been stabbed in the heart by his own brother.

"Get him out of my sight. I will deal with him after we wipe these Habiru off the face of the earth."

The guards shackled Talmai and pulled him away.

"And bring me my wife."

Outside the tavern, Joshua pulled back out of sight as the guards carried Talmai away to the dungeon. Joshua was disguised in the clothes of the dead servants from the sacred gilgal. He had found his way through the city pretending to be a lowly servant with a mission from his master.

He now knew that Sheshai was in control of the city again. He wondered how he would be able to get into that control post and kill the commander in chief. Of course, it might enable the rise of Talmai back into power, but he had to risk it because Sheshai was a brilliant tactician who had the experience to outmaneuver Caleb.

Joshua had to assassinate Sheshai.

CHAPTER 62

The four archangels formed a perimeter around Mikael, whose burns had incapacitated him in pain. Sand had rubbed into the burns and increased his agony.

The priests of Ba'al were coming down from the rocks to attack them.

Raphael drew his sword. Uriel drew both of his and tossed one to Gabriel.

"Thanks," said Gabriel.

"I want it back."

"You'll get it back."

The angels noticed something about the priests. They jerked and twitched as if they were human puppets. And they did not move with coordination. They were erratic.

The eyes of the priests were turned up inward into their heads, showing only the white of their corneas. They growled with inhuman presence.

"They are infested with demons of the Nephilim!" shouted Gabriel. They had noticed this happening before, and it was becoming increasingly evident that the spirits of the dead Nephilim, those hybrid beings of human and Watcher killed in the flood and other judgments, were possessors. They were restless wandering mists that sought human bodies to inhabit. The worshippers of idols were prime targets. Once a human opened himself up to dark forces, the demons were allowed to enter and take control.

One of the advantages of having a Nephilim spirit in the body was the increased strength it gave. A possessed human could have the strength of three or four men and an uncontrollable wildness.

And they were harder to kill. A severely wounded human possessed by a demon could continue its villainy by the power of the evil spirit animating its body.

Those superhuman monsters now descended upon the three angels.

The uncoordinated frenzy of the demonic horde was countered by the trained Karabu discipline and synchronization of the archangels.

Uriel sliced and cut like a windmill with his one blade. Raphael hacked with angry protective moves over Mikael.

Uriel and Gabriel were belting out their kills with competitive zeal.

Uriel yelled, "Five demons sent to Sheol!"

Gabriel yelled, "Six!"

"Good for you. Can I have my sword back?"

"Have some patience."

Uriel yelled, "Seven and eight! Beat that!"

Gabriel ducked and dodged a priest who swung a strange blade at the end of a pole. It was curved and sharp and very large. Within moments Gabriel had stolen the weapon from the minion and cut its head off.

Gabriel shouted, "Uriel!"

He threw the sword into the air at Uriel, who had already turned to catch it and continued in his windmill fury without losing a beat.

Now he had two blades of fury.

Gabriel proceeded to spin his new weapon like a scythe and cut down attacker after attacker.

But these creatures were strong. They could take a lot of hits before they succumbed to their wounds.

Uriel had cut off two arms on one priest, but it kept coming at him with chomping teeth. It too two more heavy strikes before it finally dropped dead.

But the next one was already upon him.

Four demon priests surrounded Raphael at once. They pressed in with their swords and he kept them at bay. But when he killed one, another one replaced it before he could gain an advantage. He was starting to wear down.

He kept hearing numbers yelled out, but had lost track of who was saying what.

"Eleven!"

"Twelve!"

"Thirteen!"

"Thirteen!"

Gabriel barked out, "Will you two keep it down? You are distracting me with your rivalry!"

The next words were softer, but just as annoying if not more so because now they were like whisperings.

"Fourteen."

"Sixteen."

"Eighteen."

They had killed over half the priests, but they kept coming. Evil was relentless.

And then Raphael was surrounded by six demon priests and could not see the one behind him lift its battle-axe.

A painful war cry resounded from behind Raphael and a limping Mikael with gritting teeth chopped off the demon priest's head. He had only half his body available to help, but it was his right half and he was right-handed. It was as if he had a surge of power that came over him.

Every movement, every swing, every contact, caused intense pain in Mikael's burnt flesh. But he had to keep going. He was not going to sit back in misery as his comrades fought this demonic horde on his behalf.

Suddenly, the air was filled with the sound of a deep long horn from on top of the mountain.

The demon priests responded by melting away and running back up the mountain.

It was over as quickly as it had begun.

The angels stood with heaving breaths over the bodies of over sixty Ba'al priests dead on the ground.

"Well?" said Uriel looking at Gabriel. "Total?"

"You first," said Gabriel.

"I asked you first," said Uriel.

"No exaggerating," said Gabriel.

"No exaggerating."

"Okay." Gabriel paused. Then he said it like a confession, "Twenty two."

Uriel gave him a surprised look. He had been one-upped.

"Truly?" he said.

"Yes, truly," said Gabriel with a twinge of anger. "I do not lie, Uriel."

"Twenty two?" he asked again.

Gabriel started to grin, and said with devious triumph, "And what is your total, little angel?"

Uriel sighed.

Then he whispered, "Twenty five."

Gabriel's smile turned to stupor, as Uriel's frown turned to a smirk.

"You trickster," complained Gabriel. "I ought to…"

They were interrupted by Raphael, "Stop your quibbling, you two, and help me!"

The both of them saw Mikael on the ground again, but passed out. Raphael wrapped Mikael's wounds now with cloth from the garments of the dead priests.

Gabriel helped Raphael, but Uriel stood looking down on them as if he had just figured out the secret to the universe.

"Wait a minute, archons."

They looked up at him.

"With all the surprise that has taken us off guard, has it even entered into any one of our thick skulls to pray for healing from Yahweh?"

The angels looked at one another dumbfounded.

Gabriel said, "I guess we were so busy fighting one devilish fiend after the next, that we must have taken our eyes off Yahweh."

"Indeed, we have," said Raphael humiliated. Then he just fell to his face in the sand and prayed, "Yahweh forgive us for our neglect."

They prayed over Mikael as only archangels can pray. If a human were there, he would have said it sounded like heavenly tones of music. There was nothing quite so elevating of the soul as the beauty of archangel sonic harmony.

They sang praise to their god and maker.

They prayed for the healing of their leader.

And when they were done, they looked at Mikael. He was awake. But he was still softly groaning from his pain.

He had not been healed.

Uriel looked up into the heavens to make sure Yahweh had been listening.

But they knew he heard them wherever they were on earth, in the heavens, or even in Sheol. They knew that when the righteous cry out, Yahweh hears them.

But Mikael was not healed.

"Well," said Raphael, "I guess Yahweh has other plans for our brother Mikael that he has not revealed."

"He is inscrutable," said Gabriel.

Uriel added, "And humans think they have it difficult. We are archons of Yahweh's heavenly host and even we do not get things our way sometimes."

"Stop your grumbling and complaining," Mikael butted in. "You are starting to sound like Israelites. Now help me up, and let us find the temple of this bully deity, Ba'al."

Gabriel and Uriel grabbed Mikael and they started toward the top of Mount Sapan looming before them.

Uriel looked up. "This is one high mountain."

"Yahweh's footstool," said Mikael.

He groaned in pain and stumbled. It was going to be a very high footstool for this severely wounded angel to climb.

CHAPTER 63

Caleb oversaw the retrieval and burial of his four hundred and fifty dead warriors. More than half of them were their Gibeonite allies. But he also made sure to use psychological warfare against the Anakim that he had learned from the Rephaim. Because of Caleb's archery tactic, they had thrown off the giants and were able to kill close to one hundred attackers. Of these, Caleb impaled fifty bodies on poles before the city walls and burned the others in a bonfire of giants on the field in full sight of the Anakim inhabitants.

Since the Israelites were in the midst of war and were too far from home camp, they would have to bury their dead in the wilderness area near their war camp. But this would be entirely appropriate because this land would be theirs so they were simply the seed of death that would bring forth the fruit of conquest of this very land.

It was a mass grave, but the bodies were laid side by side rather than in a heap, which would have been degrading. They were dressed in their war garments as a symbol of their sacrifice for the people of Israel. It marked their communal unity in the pursuit of Yahweh's war. For a soldier in such a holy endeavor, it was a more important connection than even family burial, since they were a brotherhood of shed blood, as opposed to born blood. And faithful sacrifice was deeper than blood.

Caleb looked over each and every one of the dead warriors. Some of them he recognized and had fought beside. But all of them were just as important to him because he knew that each one was a special child of Yahweh. Each had a family just like him. Each had a story, a history, just like him. Each had an entire life of human connections and bonds to dozens of beloved family and friends, who would suffer the emotional pain of tragic loss—just like him.

The true spiritual reality of war swept over his soul like never before. These were not statistics or numbers of men, these were hundreds of precious human lives interconnected to others who were ripped from their hope and cut short of their promise for the sake of others.

The true cost of this war of Yahweh pierced his entire being and he broke. He had tried to pray and devote the warriors to Yahweh, but he could only weep for their misfortune.

Othniel finished the prayer for Caleb.

The men were covered with the dirt of the Land of Promise, their inheritance.

Caleb stayed on his knees with his face in the dirt.

Until he felt a hand touch his shoulder.

But it was not Othniel's hand.

He knew that touch, that lightness, that very presence. It could not be.

He stopped and looked up—into the face of Rahab, eyes wet with pain for him.

"My beloved?" he said. He thought it was a vision.

She smiled. It was not a vision; it was her flesh and blood.

He jumped up and grasped her tightly in his arms.

"How did you escape? Where is Joshua?"

"There is a civil war within the city. Two brothers are fighting for the throne."

This was good news to Caleb. Great news.

She told him of their escape and how Sheshai helped them to the catacombs in exchange for his freedom to overthrow his brother's regime. She told him how it was only a temporary truce for a mutual enemy.

Then she swallowed with difficulty, and said, "Joshua went back into the city to assassinate Sheshai after his coup."

At first, Caleb was horrified that Joshua would attempt such a suicidal mission.

But then he knew Joshua and his spirit of tenacity. He would not let anything go, especially in a situation like this. He was so close to the heart of iniquity he would not pass up an opportunity to pierce that monstrous heart with a stake of death.

Caleb could see Joshua's strategy as if it were his own: Killing the top three brothers in chief of their clan would devastate their morale, and tremendously weaken their military organization. Joshua's plan could well be the Israelite's victory call—and the Anakim's death knell.

Caleb turned to Othniel and said, "Have the commanders muster the forces for attack. We have little time."

Othniel said, "Yes, commander," and left the gravesite.

Caleb turned to the gravediggers, "Finish the burial and report immediately to your sections for orders."

He wondered if he would be ready in time to coordinate with Joshua's mission behind the enemy walls. If they could breach those walls at the right moment, they might be able to save Joshua before he was caught and swallowed up by Anakim retaliation. If they were too late, Joshua would not have a chance to survive his deed.

It seemed impossible to Caleb.

But he remembered that he served the god of the impossible, so he bowed his knee and prayed to Yahweh.

Then he looked up to Rahab. "Can you show a strike force where that tunnel is?"

"Yes," she said. "But it is very small. You will not be able to use it for anything like a major breach."

"I do not want it for a breach. I want it for an extraction team. We are going to rescue Joshua."

CHAPTER 64

The four archangels made their way up Mount Sapan's lofty heights. Raphael helped to carry Mikael on his shoulder as they pushed through the wooded forest at the base. When they broke out from the tree line, they saw the summit was veiled in cloud, and the sky above was turbulent. Thunder was already rumbling in what was sure to be a storm of large magnitude.

"Well," said Uriel, "I can see the storm god is preparing for us. They do not call him 'Cloud Rider' for nothing."

Cloud rider was a term in Canaanite religion that symbolized control over the weather as a tool of judgment. The phrase "coming on the clouds" or "riding the clouds" was a symbolic statement of the storm deity arriving to punish his adversaries.

Uriel chided, "Yeah, well, Yahweh is coming on a swift cloud to Mount Sapan."

Somewhere in the midst of those clouds, they knew they would find the palace of their enemy storm god, Ba'al.

But the final leg of their journey was a four hundred foot steep rocky ridge with difficult overhangs to traverse. Beyond that towering edifice of rock was their target.

Uriel whistled. "Whew, *that is* steep."

"We can hoist you up using rope," said Gabriel to Mikael.

"Our rope went down with the ship," said Mikael through clenched teeth of pain. His body would heal, but not quickly enough.

Raphael said, "You can hang on my back and I will carry you."

Gabriel said, "That should not be too difficult. Even Uriel was able to carry Noah on his back out of the pit of Tartarus in ancient days."

Uriel was offended. "What do you mean, 'even Uriel'? Do you realize how deep that pit was?"

Gabriel raised his hands in mock surrender.

Mikael said, "You three will be facing the king of the gods at the seat of his throne on his sacred mountain of power. You will need all your strength focused on binding him, not protecting me in my weakness."

They were silent. They knew he was right.

Uriel said, "It still vexes me that Yahweh would not answer our prayer for healing when we need it the most, *on the person* who needs it the most."

Mikael said, "Apparently, Yahweh wants you to rely on his strength and not mine."

Uriel said, "You always see the clay pot half full."

Gabriel said, "And you never *see* the clay pot."

Uriel said, "Gabriel, the next clay pot I see, I promise to break it over your head."

"Enough, you two," said Mikael. "I think we have all missed the point. This is more than a simple lesson of faith. My incapacity is Yahweh's intent for a strategic offense: prayer. I will plead to the Lord of Hosts as you are fighting his nemesis."

"Of course," said Gabriel. "How could we be so thick of head twice in a row?"

"Speak for yourself," said Uriel.

Raphael said, "What if those surviving minions discover you here alone? You have not the strength to defend yourself against their numbers."

"I will be all right. Raphael. Now get going. The more you delay, the more ready Ba'al becomes."

The angels began their climb. Mikael grunted and got up on his knees. Sharp jolts of pain burst through his burned knee like lightning bolts. He felt faint, but continued through until he was on his face prostrate in prayer, and began to seek Yahweh's face.

It was not the four hundred foot climb that was difficult; it was the massive overhangs where the angels had to hang by their fingertips with feet dangling over a death drop of six hundred feet down. As angels, they could not die. But the fall would place any one of them in a worse condition than Mikael and guarantee failure on their mission.

As they were breaking the ridge past the overhang, Gabriel was in the lead. He was moving too quickly out of an impatient desire to attack their enemy.

His foot slipped.

But when he grabbed a rock to catch himself, it gave way and he plummeted past Raphael.

Uriel was at the tail end and saw him coming. He fastened his foot firmly and reached out to grab Gabriel.

He caught his wrist with his right hand and gripped the rock for all his life with his left.

The jolt almost ripped him from the ledge. But he held it.

Gabriel hung over the ledge, the death drop below him.

He looked up at Uriel with gratitude.

"Thank you, Uriel," he gasped.

Uriel managed a jab through gritted teeth, "I guess I saw that clay pot coming."

"Very funny."

Then Uriel crowed, "Would you like me to carry you the rest of the way? You know, like I did Noah. Since you do not seem strong enough to make it."

Gabriel was not going to apologize just because he was dangling over a precipice. "Why do you not just let me go? Unless you think you need me."

Uriel smirked and pulled Gabriel up so he could get his footing again.

Gabriel said, "I do believe I got you on that one, brother. You have to admit it."

Uriel would not.

"Come on, Uriel. I got you and you know it."

They cleared the ridge and all bickering went silent.

They stood before the entrance of the palace of Ba'al.

It was magnificent. It towered over them like an imposing giant. Huge pillared columns surrounded the massive entrance.

Uriel noticed it first. "Hey, this is a counterfeit of Yahweh's heavenly temple above the waters."

It was true. Ba'al's past as one of the *Bene ha Elohim*, meant that he was intimately acquainted with the architecture of Yahweh's temple. But whereas the heavenly temple was marble with gold trimmings, it appeared that Ba'al's palace was megalithic stone blocks and gigantic cedar trees gilded over with silver and gold.

Ba'al had sought to set his throne on high in a new mount of assembly of the gods.

Uriel mumbled to himself a paraphrase of a well-known Canaanite myth from the city of Ugarit, just south of their location.

"I will ascend above the heights of the clouds. I will make myself like Elyon, the Most High."

After a pause, he finished the verse with his own words of biting contempt, "But you will be brought down to Sheol. To the far reaches of the Pit."

Gabriel stepped up next to Uriel and said, "Let us go bind this son of Belial and be done with him."

Belial was a derogatory name given to the Accuser Mastema for his heinous crimes against Israel. It carried the meaning of malevolent lawlessness.

Raphael found a golden plaque at the entrance that said "House of Ba'al. Built by Kothar-wa-Hasis."

Uriel said, "Whoever this Kothar-wa-Hasis is, he will be one disappointed deity when we are through."

They drew their weapons and stormed into the palace ready for a fight.

But the storm god was not awaiting them inside.

The palace was empty.

They walked cautiously into its hallways and rooms. One led to another and to another. And no one was present anywhere. It was not long before they realized that the entire edifice was like a giant maze meant to reduce one to madness. Once you were inside, you could not find your way out.

They stuck close to each other in order to avoid the dilemma they had in Mount Hermon when they were separated and hunted down by Ashtart. They were not going to let that happen again.

Unfortunately, they were now lost in the labyrinth.

CHAPTER 65

His commanders on the wall called Sheshai from his war room to the gate of the city. He had his kidney wound wrapped and hidden, for fear of being discovered and considered weakened by his commanders. That would surely lead to a coup against him.

Every step brought a stab of pain, but Sheshai made sure no one saw it in his face or his walk. He was not going to lose control again.

When he arrived he saw the Israelite army ready and a small contingent of soldiers wheeling a vehicle toward the city gates. It was a battering ram. It was made of cedar, and it looked like a tower on wheels.

Sheshai knew immediately from his experience that it was Hittite in construction. He figured that Israel must have Hittite advisors, probably taken from Gibeon, because these Habiru were largely ignorant of such practices having come from desert wandering for so many years.

The Hittite ram had a swinging pole inside the enclosure that was operated by a battery of some twenty men. It contained a long cedar tree with a metal tip on the outside that hung from the pole inside like a pendulum. When placed against a wall, they would swing the ram back and forth, and it would eventually pound the normal brickwork into rubble. The men inside were protected from arrows by the enclosure.

Only the men wheeling it up to the walls were vulnerable.

Sheshai cursed Yahweh and ordered his men to prepare for their Sodom defense.

But then he saw that the ram was not being wheeled up to the wall but up to the front gate.

The fools, thought Sheshai. *I will have them for lunch.*

The reason for Sheshai's confidence was the construction of the city gate. Rather than being a straight gate that opened out onto the field for easy access, instead, it was a casemate enclosure that jutted out from the wall and opened to the left side of the wall. The approach to the gate was up an incline, making it harder to wheel the ram, and making the attackers vulnerable to assault from the walls above to their right.

Had the attackers approached the wall straight on, the defenders could only attack when the Israelites reached the wall. But by attacking the gate, the Israelites were subjected to abuse from above all along their approach to the gate along the wall.

It would be devastating—had Caleb not simultaneously launched a scaling attack on the far side of the city with a division of a thousand men with ladders.

Sheshai was forced to split his army in half to address both issues at once, thus dividing his attention.

The third prong of attack was the strike force, led by Othniel through the catacomb tunnels from the backside of the city cliffs. He led fifty of the mightiest gibborim warriors on their way up to the city. They were to find Joshua and extract him, while also seeking opportunity for assassination of the king if Joshua had failed.

Projectiles of rocks and arrows assaulted the soldiers pushing the battering ram. They wore their shields strapped to their backs to protect them, but it was not enough. Too many were killed and had to be replaced.

But then Israelite slingers and archers strafed the walls above the battering ram to force the Anakim back behind the parapet.

The ram made it to the gate and began to swing and hit with powerful percussive force. It shook the walls with each hit.

Flaming arrows launched at the vehicle were useless because it had been covered with a resin coating of deciduous tree sap that acted as a fire retardant.

On the other side of the city, ladders were thrown up against the walls for Israelite and Gibeonite soldiers to scale.

There was an art to using ladders in a siege. If they were placed too close to the wall, they could be easily pushed over by the defenders with poles. So they were laid out at a lower angle to make that impossible.

But the problem with a low angle was that the ladders could not bear the weight of too many soldiers and would often break under the strain of the weight. So the Hittites supervised the proper angle and height that could achieve maximum offensive capability with minimum risk of collapse.

The first wave of attackers was not immediately successful and suffered high losses trying to gain a foothold against the wall. But they kept coming with the faith and ferocity of Yahweh.

Rahab was left in Caleb's tent under protective custody of a platoon of gibborim. Caleb was not going to allow any other possible danger to assault her while he was still alive, especially since she was due to deliver any day now.

But he also could not allow himself the luxury of being around her for it would distract him from the most serious battle of his life. This was more consequential than facing the mighty Ahiman in hand to hand combat, for now the sands of time were running out on Joshua's life, and if they did not break through in time, all would be lost.

CHAPTER 66

Uriel left markings with one of his swords on the walls to mark their direction in the maze of palace rooms through which they traversed. Upon entry of each room, they prepared for surprise attack, but there was none. It was as if they were being drawn deeper and deeper into a spider's web of peril.

Raphael stopped with sudden awareness. The others gripped their swords.

"What is it, Raphael?" asked Gabriel.

And then they all felt it. But it was not what they had expected. It was not the preternatural tingle of danger, but of faith and hope.

Raphael said, "I can feel the effect of Mikael's prayer."

Gabriel said, "I also sense it."

Uriel said, "It is a good thing we finally listened to Yahweh, or we might be a trio of morons wandering aimlessly without supernatural guidance. Not that I feel entirely comfortable with our current situation."

It was at that moment that they entered the final room, a large wide-open area with a huge twenty-foot golden statue of Ba'al. He was posed in a walking stance, wearing a Canaanite conical horned hat of deity, and brandishing a war mace in one hand held high, and a lightning bolt in the other, ready to strike.

They approached the statue and glared up at it with contempt.

"Phew," exclaimed Uriel. "These gods sure are a self-aggrandizing lot."

"Obviously fictional," quipped Gabriel.

Uriel said, "At least we now know one of his weaknesses. He has an inflated view of himself."

Gabriel said, "And he is probably impotent."

Suddenly, the ground opened up below their feet.

They fell through a trap door and slid countless yards down a shaft that was so smooth; they could not grip it to stop themselves. It was like glass. It must have been made through intense heat melting the rock surface.

When they finally landed, it was into a cavern that reminded them of the seat of assembly inside Mount Hermon. But in this assembly hall, there were no stalactites or stalagmites, but glorious silver pillars that filled the room with regal splendor. And there was no throne of simple stone but an elevated throne of gold with a canopy and footstool.

Uriel said, "Well, is he not just a pompous little divinity, trying to outdo both Yahweh and his own pantheon with vaingloriousness."

"Welcome to my throne room, archons," said a booming voice. It came from nowhere but echoed throughout the cavern.

They looked around, and then Ba'al appeared out of the shadows and sat down upon his throne.

The angels saw that between them and the throne was a six-foot tall bronze barrier that blocked their immediate access to him. It looked like a huge round pillar lying horizontally. Uriel figured it was an occultic barricade since Ba'al seemed too at ease on his throne in the face of their impending attack.

Ba'al was dressed as his statue was, up above in the palace: Bare-chested with conical horned hat and mace. But he wore a battle kilt tied to his waist.

Uriel retorted, "We were just debating your impotency, King Kumquat."

Ba'al bellowed with fearsome volume, "SILENCE, GODLICKER!"

And then as quickly as he exploded, he returned to calm—an ominous calm. "I am the Most High, king of the gods. Yet, you dare invade my palace with such audacity, and speak with such brazen incivility?"

It was just a thought to Uriel to insult Ba'al by reducing the god's realm of authority over vegetation and storm into sarcastic jabs. But he did not realize it would have such effect. What he did not know was that it reminded Ba'al of the insolent sarcasm of Ashtart when she would insult him in a similar way through the ages. He was a deity of calculated coolness, but for some reason, those verbal digs really got under his skin.

Too bad for Ba'al, Uriel's wit was sharper than Ashtart's.

Uriel muttered to the others, "Another weakness."

Raphael said, "Good for us it is *your* strength."

Gabriel added, "For once."

Uriel shot Gabriel an angry look.

Ba'al stood from his throne and removed his horned hat and grabbed a chalice full of blood on a stand before him. He took a drink and then poured the rest over his head in a baptism of gore. The crimson red glistened over his shining body that now flashed like burning bronze. This Watcher god's intensity was brimming over like a volcano ready to erupt.

He said, "You think this is a replay of your battle with Ashtart? You have no idea. Ashtart was my slave."

Uriel muttered to Gabriel under his breath, "I have to hand it to you, Gabriel. He *is* impotent."

"You said it first, brother," returned Gabriel.

It was like their rivalry could turn on a shekel into loyalty—if either of them could just stop competing so much.

Ba'al said, "Where is your lead archon? How dare he send his lackeys to do his work."

At that very moment, Mikael was outside where the others had left him, praying to Yahweh with all his might. His archangelic voice could not be heard above the whirlwind of fury that was above him tearing the heavens in half. Bright flashes of lightning struck the rocks near Mikael, thunder pounded his eardrums, and sheets of rain attacked his skin like pine needles.

But Yahweh could hear him.

The angels moved slowly but determinedly toward Ba'al. Uriel said, "Well, god of temper tantrums, we apologize for being so unimpressive to your royal windbag. But Yahweh has a way of using the weak things of this world to confound the muscle bound."

Ba'al was shaking with fury. He was shining with such brilliance from his anger that it would have blinded a human.

But these were not humans. They were archangels.

Ba'al gave a fangy grin and raised his hands in the air as if summoning his powers.

He proclaimed, "NEHUSHTAN, ARISE!"

Suddenly, the large, round, bronze barricade began to move.

To slither.

It was not a fallen column.
It was alive.

CHAPTER 67

The fighting at the city walls of Kiriath-arba was intense. The battering ram was beginning to break down the iron-gilded gates with its pounding force. The Anakim were breaking down the besiegers' ram engine below with large rocks. Israelite archers and slingers kept picking off Anakim defenders on the walls with their projectiles.

On the far side of the city walls, units of climbing Israelite and Gibeonite warriors were barely kept at bay by Anakim using long poles to push back the increasing number of siege ladders.

Sheshai had chosen to use the high roof of the tavern inn as his command tower from which he could see the field and forces for battle strategy.

Several military captains accompanied him, his trumpeter for sounding orders, and messengers to carry more specific commands to the field.

He felt the loss of his brothers weigh upon him. He had thrown Talmai in prison and would later prosecute him for treason and mutiny. Not to mention the torture he had in mind for Talmai's betrayal with his wife. But Talmai had been a mighty warlord. He had not only inspired his soldiers when he was their general, but he had engaged in death defying feats of valor. Ahiman had been the largest most fearsome Anakite in all the land and had garnered allegiance and devotion through his gibborim exploits of terror. But now he was dead by the hand of that Habiru grasshopper, Caleb of Israel.

Together, the three of them had been an unstoppable united force that even garnered respect from the Most High Ba'al. But now Sheshai was on his own. He had always been the smarter of the brothers, and therefore the brains behind their strategic climb of power. And he had certainly achieved his ultimate plan of becoming king of Kiriath-arba. But he now understood how much he had relied upon his brothers' support and unique talents to compliment his own.

And his strength was ebbing away because of the wound in his back. If they discovered Sheshai's vitality was fading, they would kill him and replace him. Weakness was not tolerated.

He was light headed. He took a long drink of ale and pushed aside the past and all thoughts of weakness to set his mind like iron toward the task at hand: Repelling and exterminating the godforsaken Habiru termites at his door.

The three generals stood nervously silent around Sheshai. They had counseled him to engage their stratagem without further delay. But he had shut them up and was waiting patiently for just the right moment to spring his trap.

He wanted to lure the enemy in, give them the false hope of apparent victory, like flies drawn to poisoned honey. When he struck, it would be a hammering blow of such high losses and crushed morale; he would turn the tables and make the besiegers the besieged.

One of the generals noticed Sheshai was pale and sweating. He asked him, "My commander, are you well?"

Sheshai looked at him with offended eyes.

Then he drew his sword and cut the general down.

He summoned every ounce of strength within himself to do it. The thrill of the kill brought new energy to his weakened disposition. He turned to the others. "Are there any others who question my power?"

The two surviving generals stepped back slightly and almost in unison said with frightful eyes, "No, my lord."

Sheshai looked out onto the field from his vantage point. His eyes focused like a falcon's sighting on its prey. His mind observed every soldier's movement with godlike calculation.

A slight grin spread across his lips.

Joshua had found his way to the back of the tavern when he realized that the security inside the headquarters was far too heavy for him to penetrate. Dozens of Anakim gibborim. He would not make it past the entrance to the bar. But he had seen that Sheshai was using the roof as an observation post.

His first order of business was to dispatch a stray giant and grab his dagger after dragging him into the alleyway and hiding the body with garbage.

In the hands of the human Joshua, an Anakim dagger was almost the size of a sword. But that was perfect for his purposes. He did not want a sword fight; he just wanted to slit the king's throat.

He slipped the dagger into the sash of his servant's outfit and began his climb of the tavern wall.

The building was built from a stone lower foundation with hardened mud bricks higher up. It made for relatively easy grip; at least until he got to the final wooden overhang eighty feet above. He had no idea how he was going to scale that perilous structure. But he did not have the luxury of an easy approach. He left that up to Yahweh when the time came.

The climb had been harsh on his hands. The rocks were roughly hewn and the bricks were old and jagged through years of weathered abuse. It made for a good grip, but it was tearing up his hands. His fingertips were bloody and starting to quiver from the strain.

He had to stop a moment to rest, shaking out the cramp in one of his hands while he held on with the other. But then the other one cramped up and he had to switch holds to shake out that one.

He was now about seventy feet up and nearing the impossible overhang. This would be the moment he needed his strength the most, but he had barely any left in him. And now he could see that the overhang was tightly constructed wood with no places to grip.

He figured his only chance would be to use the dagger to dig out handholds.

He took a moment to pray to Yahweh for help.

When he started to move upward, he lost his grip momentarily and almost fell. His body scraped against the wall. His sash came undone.

And then the one chance he had left slipped out of his sash and fell clanging to the ground below.

It was his dagger.

Now he did not know what to do. He had come so far and was now quite literally up against a wall, with no way out.

But it was worse than he realized.

For Joshua did not see that below him where his dagger had fallen, was the companion Anakite looking for his fellow missing guard. He had just noticed an awkward looking pile of garbage in the alleyway, when the sound of the dagger hitting the pavement had caused him to glance above where he had not thought to look.

Just as Joshua prepared to start crossing the side of the building to find another way up, a large rock the size of a watermelon hit the wall near him, startling him, and making him freeze in confusion.

It could not be rock loosening from the wall above. It had come from below. Rocks do not fall upward.

As he realized what was happening, another rock the size of a human head hit him in the back and knocked the wind out of him. It was not big enough or hard enough to break any bones. It was just enough to jar him loose from the wall.

And he plunged to his death seventy feet below.

But today was not the day of Joshua's death.

The large ten foot Anakite was directly below him on the ground and caught his plummeting body like a pet in a master's arms.

The Anakite did not want to get in trouble for failing to secure this obvious assassin for questioning by the king. Death was too good for such seditious villainy.

Torture was more fitting.

Up above on the roof, completely oblivious of the assassination that had just been thwarted, Sheshai saw the moment he had been waiting for. His Nephilim senses came alive and he shouted to his trumpeter, "Sound the call!"

The trumpeter was startled. Even though he had been waiting for his command, Sheshai's voice was so intense and sharp, it jarred him. He lifted the war horn to his lips and sounded a prearranged bellow that would announce to the captains on the wall their next move.

Because of Kiriath-arba's close proximity to the southernmost Valley of Siddim, the Anakim had explored the valley for its natural resources. This was the location that had survived the destruction of Sodom and Gomorrah centuries ago, and was just outside the shores of the result of that destruction, the newly expanded Dead Sea.

It was also the location of one of Sodom and Gomorrah's most precious resources: The bitumen pits of the Siddim Valley.

The black pitch substance had been a profitable source of water sealant as well as other various economic uses.

One of those various uses was a flammable device. The pitch could coat a torch and burn half the night as a light source.

Or it could be set aflame and poured upon enemies at city gates with a fire that could not be quenched with water.

The Israelites were making great headway with the battering ram and scaling ladders. The gate's iron gilding had been pierced and the wood beneath was splintering.

The scaling ladders had become too numerous to hold back at the other side of the city. The Israelites and Gibeonites were about to breach the wall and enter when the sounds of Sheshai's war horn reverberated across the walls.

The Israelite allies paused with surprise.

The Anakim along the walls and at the gates moved cauldrons full of boiling pitch forward to the parapet.

They then poured the pitch down upon the battering ram and upon the scaling ladders.

The blistering heat burned alive dozens of men in its river of pain. But the real damage came from the fiery tipped arrows that lit the pitch and set afire the wheeled battering ram, scaling ladders, and the ground all around the attacking forces.

It was a wall of fire burning everything in its path with unquenchable flames.

Israelites and their allies screamed in agony.

Anakim laughed in derision above them.

The battering ram became an oven of wood that cooked the men within.

Caleb looked upon the chaos with horror. He sounded the retreat, but it was too late. Hundreds of men were trapped in an inferno of torment.

But that was not the only subversion to occur in this stratagem of Anakim terror.

The team of fifty gibborim led by Othniel through the secret Anakim catacomb tombs were now at the top near the tumulus.

Caleb had made the mistake of not considering the fact that once Sheshai had led Joshua to the tombs, he would know that Caleb would now have the knowledge of that entry point.

And Sheshai had set a small army of several hundred Anakim to guard it.

Othniel's band had cautiously exited the tumulus entrance to the gilgal of astral worship. But the Anakim lay in wait and caught them off guard.

Othniel's' warriors put up a mighty defense, but it was not enough for their small number and they were overwhelmed.

They were butchered.

Joshua looked up at the towering form of Sheshai marching in front of him, as he was escorted toward the prison cell by a dozen guards. He wondered why the king would bother to waste precious time accompanying a prisoner to his incarceration while there was a crucial battle going on above.

But Joshua was unaware of the stinging loss that Caleb had just experienced.

And he was not prepared for the sight before him in the cell.

In the corner of the chamber were not one but two prisoners chained to the wall. The giant Talmai was beaten and bruised against one wall, staring into oblivion. Joshua thought he would be dead by now, but evidently, Sheshai had more nefarious punishment in mind for his seditious brother.

Part of that punishment was chained to the wall crosswise from Talmai.

It was another Anakite. A dead female Anakite with her eyes and tongue gouged out.

Sheshai could see Joshua's confusion. He said, "That was my brother's lover. My wife."

Sheshai was torturing his brother mentally before he would torture him physically. He stuffed Talmai's double betrayal into his face and forced him to choke on it.

These Anakim monsters were a vicious and brutal lot.

"Brother," said Sheshai, "I have company for you."

Talmai looked up from his delirious stare. When he saw Joshua, his eyes focused and he came out of his delirium. His eyes filled with seething hatred.

Sheshai said with a wry bite, "Have you had sufficient time to contemplate the betrayal of your blood?"

Then Talmai's broken look hardened with a smirk spread across his lips.

He said, "You have lived a life of betraying blood. You used our brother Ahiman and you used me as pawns in your ambitious quest for power."

Sheshai said, "It is the way of our people, Talmai. As Ahiman once said so poignantly not too long ago, there is but one god: Power."

Talmai said, "And you could not achieve it through strength or might, but through deception and cunning. Like a woman."

Joshua could see that stung Sheshai. Their worship of power led the Anakim to despise the nature of the female gender. They dismissed nurture, compassion, and empathy as weakness. Women were reduced to property. They were tools of male gratification and breeding vessels for the growth of the clan. To accuse another male Anakite of female qualities was the highest of machismo insults. And it was enough to justify a demand for satisfaction through a duel in the Pit of Death.

But Talmai's insult was not shallow macho bravado. Sheshai's treatment of his wife illustrated a deeper truth. He would not have reacted with such emotional vengeance on his wife if he had seen her as merely property. He would not have lashed out at her or his brother if he did not have affection for her that was deeper than mere property.

Sheshai had loved his wife.

Despite the evil that seemed to reign throughout the land, all human creatures, even half human creatures like the Anakim, displayed a trace of the image of Yahweh suppressed in their soul that leaked through the cracks of their hardened violent exterior. Even evil monsters were capable of love, of kindness, of affection—of weakness.

Talmai broke Sheshai's silence, "I shall go to Sheol with the pleasure of knowing that I exposed your frailty: your humanity."

He said 'humanity' with such disdain because these Seed of the Serpent detested their human side and desired to be fully gods, like their divine progenitors, the Watchers.

Finally Sheshai spoke. "Talmai, your entire life you have been nothing but a lawless juvenile. I have rescued you from your own inability to control your passions so many times I have lost count. You have always lacked the character and discipline to achieve the notoriety you sought but could not grasp. You will not be remembered as the most feared son of Anak, as you had desired. Rather, you will be forgotten as just another criminal with delusions of grandeur."

Talmai responded through gritted teeth, "Brother, if you fancy yourself such a noble example of Anakim justice and kingship, then I demand that you fulfill our law of blood vengeance and allow me a duel in the Pit of Death."

Sheshai burst out with a laugh. "Do you really think my honor is sullied by your childish invectives against me?"

"I am not referring to you," said Talmai. "I am referring to him."

Talmai glanced at Joshua, whose blood ran cold.

"That Habiru is the commander of the forces, whose surrogate leader killed our brother Ahiman. Anakim justice demands blood for blood. Do with me what you will, but first allow me to satisfy our family's vengeance."

Sheshai knew Talmai was correct. He may have been a wild and unruly savage, but he knew enough of the law to use it to his own benefit when necessary.

Anakim laws of retribution stipulated the right for any citizen to wreak vengeance upon a killer of family members in any way they so desired, including a duel in the Pit of Death. Because Talmai had no access to the offender, Caleb ben Jephunneh, his superior officer was judicially guilty as his superior representative. Should Caleb be captured after blood vengeance was taken, he would still face judgment, since substitutionary atonement was never accepted as full satisfaction like it was in Israelite justice.

Talmai knew Sheshai's other weakness, a tendency to respect the law.

He had gambled on his appeal to Sheshai's sense of justice and played it as his last peg on the game board.

And he was right.

Sheshai thought about it. Then he looked down at Joshua and said to Talmai, "To the Pit of Death you shall go."

CHAPTER 68

When the large bronze colored barrier between Ba'al and the archangels began to move, the angels knew they were in trouble. It had been stretched over a crevice that encircled Ba'al's throne. That crevice led to a river of molten lava a hundred feet below. The gargantuan Nehushtan had been warming itself over the heat fumes of the volcanic magma.

But now as it slid into position its head came into view, a flat-headed cobra with piercing blue lapis lazuli eyes. And behind its head were a series of four reptilian wings that began to unfold. It was a winged serpent, the size of which the angels had never before seen. Its head alone was twice that of the bulky Ba'al, and its body must have been one hundred feet long when uncoiled.

It rose to a height of twenty feet over them with its hood and wings spread in a frightening hissing display ready to strike.

The three archangels took combat stances with weapons ready to return blade for fang.

Uriel could not help but blurt out, "Not another snake. What is it with all these snakes in this land?"

Raphael said, "I for one plan on having snake steaks this evening."

Gabriel added, "And a pot of cobra stew. So stop your belly aching and get your dicing blades on, Uriel."

The huge reptile brought to mind the divine uraeus cobras of Egypt that guarded the Pharaoh's throne and tombs. But this one's size was fitting for its divine liege.

Ba'al belted out, "Archons, you have trespassed in my palace! Now face the wrath of Ba'al Most High!" He pointed his iron mace in their direction and shouted, "Nehushtan, smite them!"

The copper gargantuan hissed and struck at the closest foe, the small figure of Uriel, who rolled out of its way with nimble dexterity.

Raphael and Gabriel synchronized slashes on either side of the flared hood and drew blood.

But it would take much more than the tiny claws of these rodents to faze Nehushtan.

It followed its original strike with a series of snapping fangs at each of the angels who had to dodge and dance out of the way with Karabu flair.

Unfortunately, it was not three angels against one gigantic serpent; it was three angels against one gigantic serpent and the mighty storm god of Canaan, who now leapt forward to engage the angels with his smiting mace and piercing lightning bolts.

Within his palace, Ba'al apparently had the ability to call forth balls of lightning out of the air above them. A charge would gather around his hand. He would then throw it at his opponent like a catapult of fury.

The first one hit Raphael and sent him flying backward ten feet to the ground shaking with a seizure until the lightning charge dissipated.

At the same moment, Nehushtan's tail came around behind Uriel and wrapped around him in a cocoon of scales.

It was about to be all over for the angels.

CHAPTER 69

Caleb had just withdrawn his forces and was still reeling from his losses at the gates and walls of the city. The Anakim filled the parapets swaggering their necks and jeering the Israelites.

Caleb strategized in his war tent surrounded by his commanders when Othniel arrived from his failed raid. He was bloodied and beaten and he delivered the news that would push the dagger deeper into Caleb's guts.

"We were ambushed by a platoon of giants. We never made it out of the gilgal tumulus. I alone survived."

It was a devastating setback for Caleb. All three of his attacking forces had been crippled and repelled. He had lost close to three hundred men. And now he was unable to rescue Joshua from the jaws of that hellish titan, Sheshai.

It was a dark day for Israel.

Just like those who died in the failed siege attacks, every one of those men was a valuable human being who had a family with wife and children. They each had goals and dreams of a life that impacted countless other people. They were stories cut short, narratives unwritten, painful losses to a multitude of other people.

But he was the commander of the forces of Yahweh. He had to keep his mind on his objective, on his duty to Yahweh.

Caleb placed his hand on the weary Othniel's shoulder and said, "My brother, I am grateful for your service to Yahweh."

He turned away to consider the implications of this failure. Joshua would not be coming back to the congregation of Israel.

All the commanders knew it too.

But their dread silence was broken by the arrival of another messenger.

"General, the sappers are successful! They await your command!"

Caleb turned to his commanders and said, "Ready your forces. This is our last chance."

When the Israelites had first arrived at their siege of Kiriath-arba, Caleb had set about in preparation for several plans of attack. The battering ram and siege ladders had failed. But the third stratagem was to use the mining knowledge of the Hittite war counselors from Gibeon to dig tunnels into the Anakim city.

They had started behind the Israelite lines out of sight of their enemies. They had been patiently digging all the past week underneath the skirmishes and battles that had led to this very moment.

And Caleb had directed the mining sappers to tunnel to the one location that the Anakim would never suspect: the gates of the city. He had correctly surmised that if their battering ram tactic had failed, the Anakim would assume Israel too demoralized to attempt another attack on the gates. That they would seek another approach.

Caleb had even left the burning remains of the battering ram blocking their entrance up the rampart of the gates. This was surely interpreted as a sign of resignation on Caleb's part.

It was not anything of the sort. It was a ruse.

A significant force of several hundred warriors traveled through the tunnels to the end point just inside the city gates.

The sappers prepared to make their breakthrough. They had used a rigging to hold the ceiling of the tunnels in place as they dug to within inches of the surface.

Outside the city, Caleb led three divisions of men in what looked like another ladder attack, away from the city gates.

The Anakim focused their attention on the foolish Israelite attempt to repeat their previous failure.

But underneath the city gates, the sappers used ropes held by the hundreds of waiting soldiers to pull the rigging down and with it, the ground surface beside the gates.

A huge sinkhole opened up, the size of ten men wide. By the time nearby Anakim had figured out what was happening, a flood of Israelite warriors was already pouring in like a bursting dam.

They cut their way up into the gate towers and opened the threefold doors like a gaping wound.

The Israelites outside the walls then abandoned their ladders and ran along the walls toward the gates. Their enemies above killed some, the removal of the battering ram slowed others down, but the ruse had worked. Thousands of Israelites poured through the city gates like a bleeding artery.

They held their bridgehead with fierce determination fueled by the memory of their fallen brothers.

The Anakim regrouped and came from every corner of the city to meet their Habiru enemy with every giant in arms.

But it was too late. The Israelite allied forces pushed inward like their long lost battering ram.

Giant met human. Metal clashed with metal. The Anakim were spread out, the Israelites were concentrated and overwhelmed their enemies. If these forces met on the open battlefield, giants had the superior numbers because of their size and strength. But within the city, size encumbered agility and speed moving within and around the obstacles of buildings and alleyways.

The Anakim were under the ban of *herem*, so the Israelites slaughtered every living thing—man, woman and child. They set homes on fire and left in their wake a frightening destruction.

Yahweh had turned the tables.

CHAPTER 70

Joshua stepped out into the large arena surrounding him with empty seats. It was the Pit of Death. There would be no audience for today's contest, except for six guards at the perimeter, for everyone else in the city was along the walls in battle against Israel.

Normally, in a blood vengeance duel, the offended Anakite would have the right to handicap his opponent with a wound of some kind to ensure victory for the justified.

But not today. Talmai was avenging his brother Ahiman's death at the hands of Caleb, but he wanted his justification to be entirely of his own power. So he did not wound Joshua, but left him unscathed with full capability.

Talmai wanted it to be an equal match so that his victory would be that much more glorious—his revenge that much more satisfying. This half-pint human would not stand a chance against his skill or force.

But no matter the outcome, the victor would be brought back to the dungeon by the watching guards for a later execution. So this fight was for personal satisfaction not justification.

As Talmai entered the Pit, Joshua turned to face him.

Talmai towered four feet over Joshua's near six-foot height. And Talmai was frightening in his special Anakite fighting attire: He was naked, except for his short loin covering, leather belt, and war necklace of gold showcasing his long warrior neck. His head was completely shaven of his blond locks, and he carried nothing in his huge six-fingered hands.

It was going to be a hand-to-hand fight to the death. Talmai was going to rip off Joshua's limbs one at a time and feast on his brains with relish.

Talmai's occultic tattoos appeared to move on his skin as he approached Joshua.

Though his opponent was a puny human, Joshua was no mere warrior. He was a gibborim of the Habiru who had terrified the Canaanites and colluded with Talmai's treacherous brother.

For his part, Joshua knew that once they began to physically grapple, he would not last long in the giant's grip. He was out-muscled by his opponent. He had to stay out of his reach if he wanted to live.

So how would he be able to kill him if he could not touch him? This was not going to be easy.

This was going to be impossible.

They circled each other, feeling out their adversary, planning their strategies.

What Joshua would not give now for just a scrap of Caleb's Karabu training.

He saw now, too late, that all his discipline, all his strength of will that he had spent his life cultivating, was no match for the will to power of a creature of this size and capacity.

What good would Joshua's brute force be against a monstrous brute twice his size and probably three times his brute strength? He felt like a hyena facing down a lion. He did not have a chance.

This would not end well for Joshua.

He did the only thing he could do when facing his certain death; he uttered a prayer. A simple prayer.

"Yahweh, help me."

CHAPTER 71

On the other side of the city, Caleb's forces were decimating the enemy. Yahweh had struck fear into the hearts of the Anakim. They were massacred by the hundreds. The streets ran red with blood. It would all be over shortly.

Othniel captured Sheshai from the tavern and dragged him out to the street. He was thrown down before Caleb's feet.

Caleb put his foot on Sheshai's neck.

But then he realized Sheshai was pale, barely conscious, and mumbling with delirious eyes.

Caleb noticed a blood soaked wound on Sheshai's back and knew he did not have much time left. It looked like his kidney had been pierced.

He took his foot off Sheshai's neck, grabbed him by his collar, and slapped him back into consciousness.

"Where is Joshua? What have you done with him?"

Sheshai could only mumble. He was slipping.

"What have you done with Joshua, you Anakite dog?"

Sheshai looked up at Caleb and as his life ebbed out of him, he managed to smirk and mumble, "You are too late, Habiru. He is receiving his judgment in the Pit."

Sheshai's face went still and he died in Caleb's hands.

Caleb screamed in agony.

He shook the Anakite. He tried to slap him awake again. But the giant would not awaken from his death slumber.

Caleb punched him.

And he kept punching him with furious fists as if trying to resurrect the monster by bludgeoning his life back into his broken body.

The grief that overwhelmed Caleb's soul at this moment was inconsolable.

How dare this worthless Seed of the Serpent murder the mighty general of Israel and claim that Yahweh was judging him in the pit of Sheol.

But Othniel yelled, "Caleb!"

Caleb looked up at his brother with burning red eyes.

Othniel said, "He is not talking about the Pit of Sheol, he is talking about their arena, "the Pit of Death."

Caleb's eyes suddenly popped wide open. "Of course," he said. He yelled to his surrounding men, "To the arena! Now!"

• • • • •

Inside the Pit of Death, Joshua and Talmai could hear the tsunami of battle that was now washing through the city.

It fueled Talmai's wrath. He bellowed with venomous rage at Joshua, "Your ancestor Abraham tried to wipe out my people. But out of the ashes mighty Anak was birthed, and with him, our revenge. Now you seek to finish what you began. But this day will not be your victory, Habiru."

Joshua said nothing. He was watching Talmai's extra-long neck swaying like a cobra.

· · · · ·

Caleb, Othniel, and their two platoons of soldiers about one hundred strong ran at full force toward the arena they could see towering next to the royal palace. One of the platoons was pikesmen with long spears and the other was archers.

They arrived at the gates of the arena.

They were gargantuan doors thirty feet high made of cedar wood and gilded with iron.

They were about as strong as the gates of the city.

And they were locked.

There was no way they were going to walk through those doors.

Caleb shouted a command, "Twenty five of you go this way and twenty five of you the other! Find a way in!"

Then Caleb could hear a voice thundering in the arena inside. It was the voice of a giant. It was Talmai.

"We will exterminate every last one of you! We will enslave your women and children! And after we are through eating your flesh, I will dance on the holocaust of your burning bones!"

Caleb said to Othniel, "Joshua is still alive! We have time."

But none of the soldiers could find another way in. The arena was sealed tight, prohibiting escape or entry.

Their time was running out.

CHAPTER 72

The gigantic Nehushtan had Uriel wrapped in its coils, Raphael was on the ground stunned and disoriented by Ba'al's lightning bolt, and Gabriel was starting to buckle under Ba'al's powerful hammering.

What Gabriel did not see was that Nehushtan had reared its head behind him and was preparing to strike at the same moment that Ba'al had conducted a more powerful surge of lightning into his hands.

He threw the lightning bolt at the angel.

As soon as it hit him, he would be incapacitated, just as Nehushtan's fangs struck.

But it never made contact with Gabriel because a sword swung in front of Gabriel and diverted the electrical jolt upon itself.

It was a steel sword.

It was Mikael's sword.

In Mikael's hands.

Steel was a conductor of electrical current, so the sword effectively absorbed the surge and Mikael leapt behind Gabriel in time to strike at Nehushtan's open jaws with his newly electrified blade.

He pierced the giant serpent's upper palate. The electrical current flowed into the creature's head and it spasmed with paralyzing force.

Its coils loosened and dropped Uriel to the ground coughing and catching his wind.

Raphael was already up in full force and moving in unspoken synchronicity with Gabriel who had now traded places with Mikael as he faced down the mighty Ba'al.

Raphael and Gabriel took the moment of the serpent's paralysis to jump on either side of its huge trembling head, and plunge their swords into the beast's eyes, blinding it.

It hissed with fury as its muscles came back under its control. It snapped blindly at the smell of the archangels. But it was all for naught as Uriel joined them in a trio of dancing Karabu warriors slicing and stabbing the giant reptile over and over.

Since they did not have the size to deal significant cuts, they were using their small advantage to bleed it out through a multitude of insignificant cuts.

Uriel was the most efficient with his two swords and whirlwind spinning that cut a swathe of open wounds and gushing blood.

Nehushtan was like a big lumbering cow being attacked by a school of piranhas. It would only be a short matter of time before the thing would be consumed by a thousand small bites.

Uriel noticed that Mikael had been completely healed of his burns. He blurted out to Gabriel, "A delayed answer to prayer!"

"But it was an answer," said a huffing Gabriel.

"In Yahweh's time," said the usually silent Raphael.

They were actually having a bit of fun now with their handicapped opponent.

Mikael however, was not having fun. He may have been miraculously healed, and he may have been the strongest of the band of archangels, but he was still no match for the mighty storm god who was pummeling him relentlessly with his battle mace in one hand and a newly drawn battle-axe in the other.

Mikael's steel sword was about the only blade that could withstand Ba'al's thunderous force, but he was tiring under the relentless storm of blows. Ba'al handled battle-axe and mace with unrelenting synchronized blows.

Uriel shouted, "It is time to finish off this over-bloated worm, and help our brother!"

Nehushtan was now swaying around deliriously with loss of blood and stinging pains all over its body. Its heart was pumping feverishly as its lifeblood leaked from a multitude of cuts.

Raphael had seen that desperate pulsating just a few yards down the gullet from the monster's reared head.

He shouted, "Gabriel, on your knees!"

Gabriel responded immediately with obedience. Over the millennia they had learned to respond with fluidity to each other's commands in such hectic moments. Because there was no time to explain strategy in the heat of battle, they trusted one another, even if they did not know the other's intent. The result was that they acted in union like a single warring organism divided into four separate parts.

Gabriel was right under the serpent's head. He went down on his knees.

Raphael took a running leap.

He used the back of his comrade as a ramp and launched into the air with sword grasped in two hands above his head.

He hit the belly of the beast at the spot where he had surmised the beating heart was.

His blade pierced the monster's scales and plunged deep into its life muscle, all the way up to the handle.

Raphael's weight ripped the sword downward, slicing the heart in half.

The creature had a momentary jolt from the shock to its system.

And then its head fell to the ground, dead.

Raphael was trapped underneath the reptilian corpse, so the other two cut through the scaly flesh until they found him and pulled him out, covered in the blood of his nemesis.

When they turned to join Mikael, they saw that he was barely holding his own against Ba'al.

In fact, Mikael had been backed up against the crevice that surrounded the throne. They knew he was moments away from being pushed off the ledge down into the abyss of molten lava below.

They had no time to plan, only to act.

Gabriel called it. "Enki at the War of Gods and Men!"

The three of them bolted for Ba'al without thinking.

The archangels had also developed a shorthand way of communicating strategy in a battle when appropriate. They called out references to other battles they had won, so that they would know what move to make together if needed. In this case, Gabriel was referring to the war on the fields near Erech before the Flood. Gabriel had been struggling with the god Enki by a crevice when the humans Tubal-cain and Jubal simultaneously rammed into Enki, sending them all down into the waters of the Abyss where he was bound until judgment. The humans had died by sacrificing themselves to achieve their victory.

In this case, Uriel had planned on saving Mikael. He yelled, "Under!"

Gabriel and Raphael launched into the air.

Uriel dove to the ground underneath Ba'al's legs in order to grab Mikael's leg's to keep him from falling to his doom.

Mikael was between the god and the chasm. He would be pulled over into the lava below if they did not time it just right.

The two angels hit Ba'al's lower back, throwing the god forward in a tackling motion.

Uriel grabbed Mikael's ankles.

The two angels grabbed for the ledge to stop their own descent.

Mikael's ankles slipped out of Uriel's grasp as the bulky god hit the archangel and the two flew over the ledge.

The plan had failed.

Uriel screamed, "MIKAEL! NO!"

He scrambled to the edge only to see the body of Ba'al hit the flowing lava with an explosion of fiery slag. He sunk beneath the burning crust. They were not able to bind the god's hands and feet, but this would be the next best thing. The river of flowing magma would take Ba'al deeper into the earth and deposit him in an encrusted solidified pool of hardened volcanic lava. There he would await his judgment, unable to escape his imprisonment in the earth.

And then Uriel saw Mikael, dangling over the precipice just a few yards down. But his hands were slipping. The rock was slick from the massive heat, and there was no grip above him.

So Uriel called out, "Raphael, hang on to me!"

Raphael grabbed Uriel's hands and dropped him over the edge until his ankles were within Mikael's reach.

The rocks in Mikael's hands crumbled and gave way.

But he reached up just in time to grab Uriel's ankle with one hand without plummeting to his own volcanic imprisonment.

Raphael and Gabriel pulled the two of them to safety.

Gabriel said to Uriel, "You lost your grip on Mikael."

Uriel said, "If you would not have hit Ba'al so hard, I would have been fine."

"Would you have preferred a love tap?"

Uriel turned professorial. "Successful strategy requires sufficient intelligence to appropriate the correct amount of force in order to achieve one's objective. I apologize, Gabriel. I forgot you had a smaller brain."

Gabriel retorted, "And I forgot you had smaller hands."

Mikael broke in, "Archangels, I hate to interrupt your underestimation of each other's abilities, but we have a job to do. Let us burn this diabolical palace to the ground."

"With pleasure," said Uriel looking up at the structure above them. "Cloud Rider, my rear end. Yahweh rides the clouds."

CHAPTER 73

Inside the arena, Joshua continued to stare at Talmai's swaying cobra-like neck. He remembered something Caleb had taught him long ago: *Knowing your enemy's weakness is better than facing his strength.*

Joshua could never best Talmai on strength. He had already calculated the giant's height and weight as dwarfing his own. His six-fingered hands could squash Joshua in their grip. Talmai was a bonfire of fury.

Joshua had already concluded that he did not have a chance.

All he had was a prayer.

And a simple lesson from Caleb he had learned several years ago.

It was that single Karabu lesson he needed.

Without warning, Joshua ran directly at Talmai and jumped up into his arms.

The giant could not believe this puny little wart would do such a stupid thing. He welcomed Joshua into his bear-crushing hug and squeezed the life out of him.

As Joshua was passing out, he could barely hear the sound of a distant shouting voice from outside the Pit.

It was Caleb. He shouted, "Joshua! Joshua, we are here!"

• • • • •

Outside the walls, Caleb could hear that Talmai stopped taunting Joshua. He was most likely fighting him now.

He knew Joshua was no match for the titan.

He knew he would not stand fifteen seconds in the ring with the crazy son of Arba.

Fifteen seconds passed in silence.

Then he heard a crack echo through the empty stadium.

He cinched his eyes in pain. It sounded like the cracking of a human skull.

Caleb started to pound uselessly on the door.

NO, NO, NO, NO! JOSHUA!"

Caleb sunk to his knees in defeat.

Othniel filled with rage. He knew there was nothing he could do to help Caleb.

The other soldiers arrived back at the gates with sorrowful eyes and no intelligence of a way in.

Caleb knelt there wondering why would Yahweh allow such a thing? Why allow him to get so close to helping his commander and friend, only to snatch the opportunity from his hands? Was Yahweh a cruel god after all?

Suddenly, the clinking of chains followed the sound of oxen grunting behind the gates.

The arena gates opened. It was an ox-driven gate mechanism.

Caleb shouted, "Prepare to back me up, soldiers! I want this Anakite for myself!"

The soldiers lifted shields and prepared weapons. They lined up phalanx style behind Caleb, all one hundred of them, long spears in front, archers behind.

Othniel stood beside his brother and commander with drawn sword.

Caleb unfurled Rahab as the gate opened wide.

But they were not aware that there were six Anakim warriors guarding the duel inside. And those six were lined up shoulder to shoulder blocking the entrance to Joshua's body.

The six of them gave a unified war cry.

Only to have their bodies punctured like pin cushions by a dozen arrows each, launched by the elite archers.

The Anakim were stunned. But not dead. It took more than a few needles to take down these giants.

It took the long spears to take them down, piercing their hearts, lungs, and vital organs. The phalanx had moved in synchronized precision with the archers. The bodies of the Anakim guards fell and Caleb could now see the inner arena.

In the center of that arena lay a corpse.

A lone figure walked toward Caleb.

It was stooped over and stumbling.

But it was not a giant.

Caleb yelled, "Joshua!"

He ran to him.

Othniel stayed protectively close behind.

Caleb tried to embrace Joshua, but Joshua groaned. Caleb pulled back.

"Sorry, Caleb. I am a little crunched."

"My Commander, you are alive."

"My loyal friend," said Joshua, "it was you who saved me."

"What?"

Joshua replied, "It was you who told me a small amount of faith can move a mountain. So a small amount of pressure can topple the mightiest gibborim."

"How did you do it?"

Joshua recalled the technique that Caleb had taught him years ago.

After he had foolishly jumped into the muscle-bound arms of Talmai, and just before he passed out from being crushed, he thrust his thumbs into each side of the long neck of his adversary, hitting the pressure point near the carotid artery.

Before Talmai could do anything with his massive strength, his eyes turned upward, his knees buckled, and he fell to the ground like a sack of dead meat.

But he was not dead, he was unconscious.

Joshua then pulled himself out of the lifeless arms. He grabbed the giant's head and jerked it with a hard twist, snapping the spine and paralyzing Talmai instantly.

That was the crack that Caleb and his men had heard resounding through the arena.

The fight was over before it had begun.

Talmai's massive bulk of muscle and power was incapacitated by a small little thrust of two thumbs. How the mighty are fallen.

Talmai had come back to consciousness just in time to look up at the victor as his lungs and heart ceased to function from his spinal cord injury.

He suffocated to death.

Caleb smiled and repeated the proverb, "A small amount of pressure and a small amount of faith."

So this was the irony of faith. This was the revelation that victory could not be won against their mighty enemies by might or by strength, but by Yahweh's Spirit and deliverance.

Joshua said, "I want you to teach me some more of that Karabu training. I think I am warming to it."

Caleb smiled.

But then he turned serious.

He said, "The battle is over. But the killing will go on into the evening. This city is under the ban of *herem*."

"And your family," said Joshua, "are they well?"

"They are safely guarded in my war tent behind the lines. Rahab will be happy to see you."

But Caleb was wrong. Rahab was not safe. The entire platoon of gibborim warriors that had been ordered to protect her were circumvented by one mysterious spy.

CHAPTER 74

When the final thrust of Caleb's operation launched on the city, there were only a few hundred soldiers left guarding the camp.

The fifty dutiful guards watching Rahab were all itching to be out in the battlefield killing giants. Half of them had gone to the edge of the camp to watch the fighting. Most of the other soldiers kept watch on the perimeter for any Anakim spies or saboteurs leaving the city.

But no Anakim spies made it out alive that night.

The spy that had slipped into the camp undiscovered was not a giant, it was something else—something from Rahab's past.

And it took the most inopportune time to strike.

Rahab had several midwives with her in her tent prepared for delivery. She had felt the birth pangs coming earlier but had made sure that the guards would not know about it. She did not want Caleb's attention distracted from his military mission. It could cost him his life.

Rahab and Achsah had grown close to each other through these difficult times, and Rahab considered Achsah her best friend. Though she was technically her stepmother, their closeness of age allowed a closeness of relationship Achsah could not have had with her birth mother.

She had told the guards that she wanted them to keep their distance this evening as she and Achsah were going to have a long bath in her tent, and she wanted privacy.

Two wooden tubs hand crafted by Philistine artisans were the one luxury Caleb had allowed Rahab in this otherwise rough existence. The guards obliged them by pulling away to eat some dinner a couple tents away.

But Rahab had not been entirely untruthful. They were indeed going to have a bath this evening, but for a different purpose. Rahab had learned one interesting technique from the Snake Clan of Gilgal Rephaim: water birth. They would deliver their children into the water pool as a transition between the womb and the real world.

Rahab forced Achsah to join her by bathing in the second tub. She wanted Achsah to relax since there was not much she could do.

Achsah was a bit uncomfortable with it, but she obeyed, in order to please her stepmother.

By the time the birth pangs had climaxed and the midwives were delivering, Rahab had managed to gag herself on a towel so as not to draw attention.

Achsah's silent eyes teared with delight when a midwife pulled up a baby boy out of the water and cut the umbilical cord.

Rahab whispered with delight, "Welcome, little Boaz."

It was the most quiet celebration of ecstatic joy that any of the women had ever experienced. They were crying without sound and moving their arms around without making noise. They almost blew their cover by laughing at themselves.

Rahab handed the baby to Achsah to wash in her own bath.

It was an honor that made her heart full. She gently washed the afterbirth that was still clinging to the baby's skin.

A midwife took the boy and wrapped him in swaddling clothes. The women prepared to get out of their baths.

That was when the spy completely smashed their celebration.

He was virtually invisible to the surrounding soldiers. He blended into the night and the forest as if he was a part of nature itself.

He was in fact a master of nature.

He slipped into the tent, and snuck up behind the two women in the wooden tubs.

Everyone's focus was on the man-child in one of the midwives' arms.

By the time the spy showed himself, he was already upon Achsah with a dagger at her throat.

"Do not scream or I will kill you."

Rahab saw the hair and the horns. She recognized his face from many years ago.

He was a satyr.

"Xizmat."

"Arisha. Or should I call you Rahab? It has been quite a task tracking you around all of Canaan with your different identities."

She gestured to the two midwives not to move.

"Release Achsah. We will not scream."

She gestured to the midwives be quiet. They obeyed.

He pulled back his blade.

"Rahab. The name of the sea dragon. I like it. A feisty name for a feisty woman. Get up and put on your clothes."

"I just gave birth, Xizmat."

"I do not care, quim. Get up. Not you," he said to Achsah.

Rahab got out of the water, dried off and put on her clothes. She moved slowly from her labor.

"How did you find me?"

"I do not know how you disposed of Izbaxl's body back in Panias, but you left behind the evidence that condemned you of the crime of murdering my brother."

"What evidence? That was over twenty years ago."

"Do you not remember what you shamefully cut off of my brother in your hospital room?"

Achsah was not following, but realization flooded over Rahab like the Deluge. She had castrated Izbaxl.

"I could find no other evidence of your whereabouts so I told no one. The whole incident would have dissolved into an unsolved mystery. But then many years later, your family was redeemed from Panias by a mysterious benefactor in Jericho. I never forgot they were your family, so I had spies follow them."

He stood up. Achsah could now see his lower body with goat legs and hooves. And his eyes were wet with rage.

"My Izbaxl was so loving and giving. He saved my life. You murdered him."

"He was eaten by dire wolves, and he deserved it."

Xismat held back his fury. "He was my brother, you bitch. And rest assured, I have elaborate plans for retribution."

Rahab backed up.

"Oh, I am not going to kill you. That would be anti-climactic. I am going to bring you back to Panias, and you will return to what you always were and always will be, a worthless harlot of Azazel."

Achsah gasped.

Xizmat pointed his finger at her to shut up. His face was full of fury.

"I will go with you quietly on one condition," said Rahab. "You kill no one in this tent, and you leave my child with Achsah."

Achsah's eyes went wide. She had been so intent upon understanding what was going on in front of her that she did not stop to consider what this goat demon beside her would do to her or baby Boaz. A chill went down her spine.

"Granted," said Xizmat.

Achsah knew that Rahab had just saved their lives from this despicable smelly chimera. Now it was her turn. She got up from the tub to dry herself.

Xizmat watched her with interest.

"No," countered Rahab. "Only me."

Xizmat looked around. "I need some rope and a gag. I do not want you alerting anyone until we are far away."

He bent down to pick up a sash from a pile of clothes. It would be good enough.

"As for the child…"

But when he turned back toward Achsah, he saw her standing and aiming a notched bow and arrow at him.

"You little rodent," he said.

She was shaking.

He was about eight feet away from her. Close enough for one leap with his strong goat legs.

He smirked. And took one step closer.

"You have never killed anyone before, have you?"

She did not answer.

Rahab breathed out, "Achsah." She was not sure if Achsah had it in her. And if she did not, she would surely be dead in seconds. And maybe even her son as well.

Xizmat looked deep into Achsah's eyes and said, "You cannot do it, little girl. Killing someone is a gruesome thing. And you are too young and innocent. And beautiful."

He had a hypnotic effect on her. He was manipulating her. She did not notice he had taken one more step closer.

She continued to tremble. Her aim faltered.

Xizmat's legs imperceptibly lowered, preparing to spring.

Then Achsah said, "I tried to kill a monster before, but I could not." She was referring to the Anakite who kidnapped her from the camp at Gilgal.

Xizmat said, "Well, then…" and he jumped. He attacked her in the middle of his sentence in order to take her completely by surprise.

But the moment before he did, she had already released the arrow, which found its target and entered his left eye, penetrating into his brain.

He jerked backward and fell to the floor in a seizure.

The last thought that was in the dirty old goat's mind was what supple breasts Achsah had.

And then he died.

Rahab gasped.

Achsah said, "I promised my father I would never let it happen again."

CHAPTER 75

The army of Israel stood in the field before Kiriath-arba. The city was secured, all life was devoted to destruction. The Anakim received no mercy as the Seed of the Serpent. The bodies of the brothers Arba—Ahiman, Sheshai, and Talmai—were impaled upon poles on the city walls.

Joshua stood proudly with Caleb as he offered him the ownership of the city and its area for his inheritance. Caleb renamed the city Hebron for future generations. Of course, he would not be able to settle in until they had completed their conquest of the land. But Rahab, Achsah, and Rahab's family were more proud of him than anyone could be of a man who obeyed Yahweh and followed him faithfully.

Joshua proclaimed, "Warriors of Yahweh, you have been strong and courageous! We have achieved mighty feats of faith in overthrowing the Transjordan! King Sihon of Heshbon and King Og of Bashan!"

The men cheered.

"By faith, Yahweh toppled the walls of Jericho! And by faith, we defeated the Anakim of Kiriath-arba, our most difficult enemy in the land of our forefather, Abraham. And we have captured the hill country!"

The men cheered again.

"But our conquest is not yet complete! I am old and very advanced in years. But there is still much land to possess. Before we can apportion out the territories to the tribes of Israel, we must strike down the Anakim city of Kiriath-sepher just south of here! I need a leader to take a force and capture the city!"

There was a hesitation in the crowd. They had just been through so much, and now they were being asked to jump into the fire again?

Caleb saw his precious Achsah in the crowd watching with pride. Then he glanced over and saw Othniel standing like a miserable lonely rock. Caleb knew he desired Achsah but was so emotionally incompetent, that he could not declare his love these past five years of war. So Caleb decided to give him one last chance or lose it all. He yelled out to the soldiers, "He who attacks Kiriath-sepher and captures it, I will give as an inheritance."

He paused, then added, "As well as my daughter Achsah in marriage!"

Before anyone else could even consider the offer, Othniel stepped up and shouted, "I will take Kiriath-sepher! I will grind it to dust!"

Othniel's men cheered.

And Othniel could not believe he did it. He finally did it. After all these years of fear, he finally did what it took to get Achsah's hand in marriage.

Othniel looked over to see Achsah beaming with an ear to ear grin. She had known he was in love with her for so long, but he had never had the liver to say so. He would face death against a thousand giants in battle, but he did not have the courage to proclaim his love for her. It had taken years of patient waiting for him, years of lonely unfulfilled desire. Oh well, if it took a battle of giants to get him to win her hand instead of just asking for it, then so be it. She knew he was a good man. More than that, he was the best man she had ever known, after her father.

She burst out into tears of joy.

Caleb smiled with his own satisfaction.

Finally, thought Caleb, *My daughter will find happiness. And finally my high strung young brother will find happiness and release from his pent up humility.*

Othniel was already busying his mind with how he might take Kiriath-sepher as quickly as possible, so as to marry Achsah as quickly as possible.

Rahab and Achsah stepped up to Caleb. Rahab was carrying baby Boaz in her arms. The three of them embraced and kissed.

Little Boaz looked up into their faces.

Othniel stood next to them staring at Achsah, who smiled back at him. She reached her hand out to him. Timidly, he reached and grabbed it.

Her soft small hand in his felt like a treasure of silk. Caleb's precious turtle dove would soon be his turtle dove.

Rahab glanced over Caleb's shoulder and saw Joshua watching them with a grin. Their eyes locked and they knew they had made the right choices in their hearts; choices to stay their passions, choices to obey their Lord, choices to suffer and sacrifice rather than take and indulge.

Caleb approached his commander. They clasped wrists. They stared into each other's eyes with a friendship deeper than marriage, for they had faced life and death—and resurrection together. Were there any words that could express their commitment to one another? Words that could carry the thankfulness that filled their souls?

"I am old and tired," said Joshua.

"You?" said Caleb. "I am your elder by twenty years and I am ready to finish this. Are you backing out on me after all we have been through?"

Joshua smiled. "No, I just need to find what it is I lost in all this bloodshed and carnage. I want to retire in the hill country of Ephraim, a place without much significance to our enemies."

Caleb said, "Joshua, I have been a fool. Yahweh has kept me alive, just as he promised forty-five years ago when you and I first gave our spying report of the land. Now, behold, I am eighty-five years old and I am as strong today as I was in the day that Moses sent us. But now that I have the land of our forefather Abraham's grave, I must confess I am unsatisfied."

Joshua said, "You strove for an identity you already have."

Caleb said, "All my life, I have felt like an outsider. And no matter how much I proved myself, I was still an adopted child in a family of natural born sons."

"Caleb, was it not you who taught me that faith is what Yahweh desires?"

Caleb listened, but it was difficult as his own words now came back at him.

Joshua continued, "I have always envied you. My quest for a perfect holiness broke me, and only then I saw a glimpse of what you had all along: Beauty and grace."

Caleb chuckled, "And I have always envied you for what you have had: Your chosen status, your holiness and justice."

Joshua said, "We covet in each other what we do not have."

Caleb said, "Then the one thing we both have lacked—is faith."

He paused, then added, "We are both men of flesh."

"And spirit," added Joshua.

He placed his arm on Caleb's shoulder. "Caleb, you have bested me in this life. In trust, in grace, in family, and in battle. I am proud of you. I am proud to be your friend. And proud to have learned the true value of faith as the Seed of Abraham."

"You broke the Seed of the Serpent's backbone," said Caleb. The hill country that traversed the center of Canaan was truly the backbone of control of the land and Israel now owned it.

Joshua suddenly got serious. "This people are not able to serve Yahweh. He is a holy and jealous god. Even after all the deliverance he has brought, after the Red Sea, the water from the rock, and Jericho, and every other miracle, they will still worship foreign gods and will not put away the idols of the land. They will fail to drive out the Canaanites."

"Is this a prophecy?" said Caleb.

"No," replied Joshua. "It is merely my knowledge of their nature—of the nature in all of us. We need a king who can bring final triumph. Until then, the Seed of Eve will never find rest or victory."

Caleb said, "When he comes, he will be like you. Only perfect."

They both chuckled at it.

"Indeed," said Joshua. "Something I could never be."

"Yahweh saves," said Caleb. It was the meaning of Joshua's name.

EPILOGUE

The four archangels arrived at the camp of Joshua outside of the newly named Hebron. Othniel was consulting Joshua and Caleb for his plan of attack on Kiriath-sepher.

When the angels entered, the generals saw a grim look on their faces.

Caleb said, "You are late as usual, archangels. But do not worry, we do not need you for our next campaign. Feel free to take a vacation, get some rest."

"For your information, jester," said Uriel. "We were binding Ba'al the Most High and demolishing his high place in the northern regions of Mount Sapan."

Gabriel jumped in, now defending Uriel with unusual favor, "No rest for the righteous. And you are welcome."

Caleb drew down. He knew that if Ba'al would have been fighting against them, they might have doubled their losses and might not have won at all.

Joshua could see the solemn look on Mikael and Raphael's faces.

"What news do you bring?"

Mikael said, "On our way back we discovered that the nations of the north country have formed a massive coalition of armies from north, east, and west, led by King Jabin of Hazor. The Amorites, the Perizzites, the Jebusites, and even the Hivvites from under Mount Hermon. They are assembling their armies at the waters of Merom to launch a joint attack on you."

Gabriel said, "You have not faced this many before."

Joshua said, "How many?"

Mikael said, "Forty thousand."

That was six times the number of Israel's army. That was like the sand on the seashore to them. But Joshua had learned to have faith in such situations since Yahweh had promised them ultimate victory.

But that victory was given a stab to the kidney when Mikael added, "But they also have something you have never faced before."

Uriel threw in, "You might want to ask us to delay our vacation."

"What is that?" said Joshua. "What do they have?"

"Iron chariots. A multitude of them."

It is here that the Chronicle is broken off and lost to history. One may read more about the incident from the Book of the Wars of Yahweh. If new archaeological discoveries bring to light this small missing segment of manuscript, we will publish it as a novella available for devoted readers of Chronicles of the Nephilim.

Otherwise, the Chronicles continue with the next book, David Ascendant.

Buy *David Ascendant* here.

If you liked this book, then please help me out by writing an honest review of it on Amazon (click here to write review). That is one of the best ways to say thank you to me as an author. It really does help my exposure and status as

an author. It's really easy. In the Customer Reviews section, there is a little box that says "Write a customer review." They guide you easily through the process. Thanks! — *Brian Godawa*

an author. It's really easy. In the Customer Reviews section, there is a little box that says "Write a customer review." They guide you easily through the process. Thanks! — *Brian Godawa*

CHAPTER 76: FREE DIGITAL BOOK

GET THIS FREE DIGITAL BOOK!

For a Limited Time Only

FREE

The Biblical Research of All 8 Chronicles of the Nephilim Together in One Book!

By Brian Godawa

Chapters Include:
- The Book of Enoch
- Sons of God
- The Nephilim
- Leviathan
- Cosmic Geography in the Bible
- Gilgamesh and the Bible
- Mythical Monsters in the Bible
- Goliath was Not Alone
- Jesus and the Cosmic War
- AND MORE!

Click Here to Get Your Free Book!

www.godawa.com/free-giants-book

APPENDIX
CANAANITE BA'AL AND OLD TESTAMENT STORYTELLING POLEMICS

For many Christians, the word *apologetics* conjures a picture of defending the faith with philosophical arguments, archeological evidence, historical inquiry, and other rational and empirical forms of discourse. Apologetics also involves *polemics*, which are aggressive arguments against the opposition. Sometimes a good offense is the best defense. But what is often missed in some apologetic strategies is the Biblical use of imagination. This is illustrative of a distinct imbalance when one considers that the Bible is only about one-third propositional truth and about two-thirds imagination: image, metaphor, poetry, and story.[3]

With the discovery in the nineteenth and twentieth centuries of pagan religious texts from ancient Near Eastern (ANE) cultures such as Babylon, Assyria, and Ugarit, Biblical scholarship has discovered many literary parallels between Scripture and the literature of ancient Israel's enemies. The Hebrews shared many words, images,

---

[3] I discuss this fact and its ramifications in my book *Word Pictures: Knowing God Through Story and Imagination* (Downers Grove, IL: InterVarsity Press, 2009).

concepts, metaphors, and narrative genres in common with their neighbors. And those Hebrew authors of Scripture sometimes incorporated similar literary imagination into their text.

With regard to these Biblical and ancient Near Eastern literary parallels, liberal scholarship tends to stress the similarities, downplay the differences, and construct a theory of the evolution of Israel's religion from polytheism to monotheism.[4] In other words, liberal scholarship is anthropocentric, or human-centered.

Conservative scholarship tends to stress the differences, downplay the similarities, and interpret the evidence as indicative of the radical otherness of Israelite religion.[5] In other words, conservative scholarship is theocentric, or God-centered. Both liberal and conservative hermeneutics err on opposite extremes.

The orthodox doctrine of the inspiration of Scripture states that it is composed of "God-breathed" human-written words (2Tim. 3:16). Men wrote from God, moved by the Holy Spirit (2Pet. 1:20-21). This is a "both/and" reality of humanly and heavenly authorship. While I affirm the heavenly side of God's Word, in this essay I will illustrate how the authors of the Old Testament used the imagination of their enemies as a polemic against those enemies' religion and deities. In my book, *Word Pictures: Knowing God through Story and Imagination*, I describe the nature of this subversive storytelling as the act of entering the opposition's cultural narrative, retelling it through their own paradigm, or worldview, and thereby capturing the cultural narrative. God used literary subversion in the Bible as a means of arguing against the false gods and idols of that time.

---

[4] A significant author of this view is Mark S. Smith, *The Origins of Biblical Monotheism: Israel's Polytheistic Background and the Ugaritic Texts* (Oxford: Oxford University, 2003).
[5] A significant author of this view is Gleason L. Archer, *A Survey of Old Testament Introduction* (Chicago: Moody Press, 2007).

Baal in Canaan

In 1929, an archeological excavation at a mound in northern Syria called Ras Shamra unearthed the remains of a significant port city called Ugarit, whose developed culture reaches back as far as 3000 BC.[6] Among the important finds were literary tablets that opened the door to a deeper understanding of ancient Near Eastern culture and the Bible. Those tablets included Syro-Canaanite religious texts of pagan deities mentioned in the Old Testament. One of those deities was Baal (alternate spelling of Ba'al).

Though the Semitic noun *baal* means "lord" or "master," it was also used as the proper name of the Canaanite storm god.[7] In the Baal narrative cycle from Ugarit, El was the supreme "father of the gods," who lived on a cosmic mountain. A divine council of gods called "Sons of El" surrounded him, vying for position and power. When Sea is coronated by El and given a palace, Baal rises up and kills Sea, taking Sea's place as "Most High" over the other gods (excepting El). A temple is built and a feast celebrated. Death then insults Baal, who goes down to the underworld, only to be defeated by Death. But Anat, Baal's violent sister, seeks Death and cuts him up into pieces and brings Baal's body back up to earth where he is brought back to life, only to fight Death to a stalemate.[8]

The Dictionary of Deities and Demons in the Bible explains of Baal:

"His elevated position shows itself in his power over clouds, storm and lightning, and manifests itself in

---

[6] Avraham Negev, "Ugarit," *The Archaeological Encyclopedia of the Holy Land*, 3rd ed. (New York: Prentice Hall Press, 1996).

[7] Karel van der Toorn, Bob Becking, and Pieter Willem van der Horst, *Dictionary of Deities and Demons in the Bible* (*DDD*), 2nd ext. rev. ed. (Grand Rapids: Eerdmans, 1999), 132.

[8] N. Wyatt, *Religious Texts from Ugarit*, 2nd ed., The Biblical Seminar, vol. 53 (London: Sheffield Academic Press, 2002), 36-39.

his thundering voice. As the god of wind and weather Baal dispenses dew, rain, and snow and the attendant fertility of the soil. Baal's rule guarantees the annual return of the vegetation; as the god disappears in the underworld and returns in the autumn, so the vegetation dies and resuscitates with him."[9]

Baal in the Bible

In the Bible, Baal is used both as the name of a specific deity[10] and as a generic term for multiple idols worshipped by apostate Israel.[11] It was also used in conjunction with city names and locations, such as Baal-Hermon and Baal-Zaphon, indicating manifestations of the one deity worshipped in a variety of different Canaanite situations.[12] Simply speaking, in Canaan, Baal was all over the place. He was the chief god of the land.

On entering Canaan, Yahweh gave specific instructions to the Israelites to destroy all of the places where the Canaanites worshipped, along with their altars and images (Deut. 12:1-7). They were to "destroy the names" of the foreign idols and replace them with Yahweh's name and habitation (vv. 3-4). God warned them, "Take care lest your heart be deceived, and you turn aside and serve other gods and worship them" (Deut. 11:16).

Yet, turning to other gods in worship is exactly what the Israelites did—over and over again. No sooner had the people settled in Canaan than they began to adopt Baal worship into their culture. The book of Judges describes this cycle of idolatry under successive

---

[9] "Baal," *DDD*, 134.
[10] Judges 6; 1 Kings 18; 2 Kings 10.
[11] Judges 2:13; 1 Samuel 12:10; Jeremiah 2:23.
[12] "Baal," *DDD*, 136.

leaders.[13] In the ninth century BC, Elijah fought against rampant Baal worship throughout Israel (1 Kings 18). In the eighth century, Hosea decried the adulterous intimacy that both Judah and Israel had with Baal (Hos. 2:13, 16-17), and in the seventh century, Jeremiah battled with an infestation of it in Judah (Jer. 2:23; 32:35).

Baal worship was so cancerous throughout Israel's history that Yahweh would have to intervene periodically with dramatic displays of authority in order to stem the infection that polluted the congregation of the Lord. Gideon's miraculous deliverances from the Baal-loving Midianites (Judges 6-8) and Elijah's encounter with the prophets of Baal (1 Kings 18) are just a couple examples of Yahweh's real-world polemic against Baal. But physical battles and miraculous signs and wonders are not the only way God waged war against Baal in ancient Canaan. He also used story, image, and metaphor. He used literary imagination.

Yahweh Vs. Baal

Literary subversion was common in the ancient world to affect the overthrow or overshadowing of one deity and worldview with another. For example, the high goddess Inanna, considered Queen of Heaven in ancient Sumeria, was replaced by her Babylonian counterpart, Ishtar. An important Sumerian text, *The Descent of Inanna into the Underworld*, was rewritten by the Babylonians as *the Descent of Ishtar into the Underworld* to accommodate their goddess Ishtar.[14] The Babylonian creation epic, *Enuma Elish* tells

---

[13] Judges 2:11; 3:7; 8:33.

[14] Stephanie Dalley, trans., *Myths from Mesopotamia: Creation, The Flood, Gilgamesh and Others* (New York: Oxford University Press, 1989, 2000, 2008), 154-62. The Sumerian version can be found in Jeremy Black, trans., *The Literature of Ancient Sumer* (New York: Oxford University Press **2004, 2006**), 65-76.

the story of the Babylonian deity Marduk and his ascendancy to power in the Mesopotamian pantheon.[15] And then when King Sennacherib of Assyria conquered Babylon around 689 BC, Assyrian scribes rewrote the *Enuma Elish* and replaced the name of Marduk with Assur, their chief god.[16]

Picture this scenario: The Israelites have left Egypt where Yahweh literally mocked and defeated the gods of Egypt through the ten plagues (Exod. 12:12; Num. 33:4). Pharaoh claimed to be a god, who according to Egyptian texts, was the "possessor of a strong arm" and a "strong hand."[17] So when Yahweh repeatedly hammers home the message that Israel will be delivered by Yahweh's "strong arm" and "strong hand," the polemical irony is not hard to spot. Yahweh used subversive literary imagery, which in effect said, "Pharaoh is not God, I am God." Nothing like an arm wrestling match to show who is stronger.

But now, God is leading Israel into the Promised Land, which is very different from where they came, with very different gods. "For the land that you are entering to take possession of it is not like the land of Egypt, from which you have come, where you sowed your seed and irrigated it, like a garden of vegetables. But the land that you are going over to possess is a land of hills and valleys, which drinks water by the rain from heaven" (Deut. 11:10-11). And the god of rain from heaven in this new land was believed to be the storm god, Baal.[18]

---

[15] Alexander Heidel, trans., *The Babylonian Genesis* (Chicago: University of Chicago, 1942, 1951, 1963), 14.

[16] C. Jouco Bleeker and Geo Widengren, eds., *Historia Religionum I: Religions of the Past* (Leiden, Netherlands: E. J. Brill, 1969), 134.

[17] John D. Currid, *Ancient Egypt and the Old Testament* (Grand Rapids: Baker; 1997), 83.

[18] Fred E. Woods, *Water and Storm Polemics against Baalism in the Deuteronomic History*, American University Studies, Series VII, Theology and Religion (New York: Peter Lange Publishing, 1994), 32-35.

Now the Biblical text begins to reflect that storm god language in its reference to Israel's god, Yahweh. Let's take a look at some Ugaritic texts will give us a literary description of the Baal that Israel faced in Canaan. A side-by-side sampling of those Ugaritic texts with Scripture illustrates a strong reflection of Canaanite echoes in the Biblical storytelling.

UGARITIC TEXTS[19]	OLD TESTAMENT
Baal sits… in the midst of his divine mountain, Saphon, in the midst of the mountain of victory. Seven lightning-flashes, eight bundles of thunder, a tree-of-lightning in his right hand. His head is magnificent, His brow is dew-drenched. his feet are eloquent in wrath. (KTU 1.101:1-6)[20]	Yahweh came from Sinai… At His right hand there was flashing lightning… There is none like the God of Jeshurun, Who rides the heavens to your help, And through the clouds in His majesty… And He drove out the enemy from before you, And said, 'Destroy!'… In a land of grain and new wine; His heavens also drop down dew. (Deut. 33:2, 26-28)
The season of his rains may Baal indeed appoint, the season of his storm-chariot. And the sound of his voice from the clouds, his hurling to the earth of lightning-flashes (KTU 1.4:5.5-9) At his holy voice the earth quaked; at the issue of his lips the mountains were afraid… the hills of the earth tottered. (KTU 1.4:7.30-35)	The voice of the LORD is over the waters; the God of glory thunders, the LORD, over many waters… The voice of the LORD breaks the cedars; the LORD breaks the cedars of Lebanon… The voice of the LORD flashes forth flames of fire [lightning]. The voice of the LORD shakes the wilderness…
now your foe, Baal, now your foe the Sea you must smite; now you must destroy your adversary! Take your everlasting kingdom, your eternal dominion! (KTU 1.2:4.9-10)	And in His temple everything says, "Glory!" Yahweh sits enthroned over the flood; Yahweh is enthroned as King forever. (Ps. 29:3-11)

---

[19] The abbreviation *KTU* stands for "Keilalphabetische Texte aus Ugarit", the standard collection of this material from Ugarit.

[20] All these Ugaritic texts can be found in N. Wyatt, *Religious Texts from Ugarit*, 2nd ed., The Biblical Seminar, vol. 53 (London: Sheffield Academic Press, 2002).

Like the usage of Yahweh's "strong arm" to poetically argue against the so-called "strong arm" of Pharaoh, Yahweh inspires His authors to use water and storm language to reflect God's polemic against the so-called storm god, Baal.

Comparing the texts yields identical words, memes, and metaphors that suggest God is engaging in polemics against Baal through scriptural imagery and storytelling. It is not Baal who rides his cloud chariot from his divine mountain Saphon (Sapan), it is Yahweh who rides the clouds as a chariot from mount Sinai. It is not Baal who hurls lightning flashes in wrath; it is Yahweh whose lightning flashes destroy His enemies. It is not Baal whose dew-drenched brow waters the land of Canaan; it is Yahweh who drops dew from heaven to Canaan. It is not Baal's voice that thunders and conquers the waters resulting in his everlasting temple enthronement; it is Yahweh whose voice thunders and conquers the waters resulting in His everlasting temple enthronement.

Psalm 29 (quoted in part above) is so replete with poetry in common with Canaanite poetry that many ANE scholars have concluded it is a Canaanite hymn to Baal that has been rewritten with the name Baal replaced by the name Yahweh.[21] God was not only *physically* dispossessing Canaan of its inhabitants; He was *literarily* dispossessing the Canaanite gods as well. Old Testament appropriation of Canaanite culture is a case of subversion, not syncretism—overthrowing cultural narratives as opposed to blending with them.

A closer look at comparing just two elements of the Baal cycle with Yahweh's story will yield a clearer picture of the literary

---

[21] Aloysius Fitzgerald, "A Note on Psalm 29," *Bulletin of the American Schools of Oriental Research*, no. 215 (October 1974), 62. A more conservative interpretation claims a common Semitic poetic discourse.

subversion of the Canaanite narrative that God and the human authors were employing. Those two elements are the epithet of "cloud-rider" and God's conflict with the dragon and the sea.

Cloud-Rider

In the Ugaritic text cited above, we are introduced to Baal as one who rides the heavens in his cloud-chariot dispensing judgment from the heights. "Charioteer (or 'Rider') of the Clouds" was a common epithet ascribed to Baal throughout the Ugaritic texts. Here is another side-by-side comparison of Ugaritic and Biblical texts that illustrate that common motif.

UGARITIC TEXTS	OLD TESTAMENT
'Dry him up. O Valiant Baal! Dry him up, O Charioteer [Rider] of the Clouds! For our captive is Prince Yam [Sea], for our captive is Ruler Nahar [River]!' (KTU 1.2:4.8-9)	"[Yahweh] bowed the heavens also, and came down With thick darkness under His feet. And He rode on a cherub and flew; And He appeared on the wings of the wind. He made darkness canopies around Him, A mass of waters, thick clouds of the sky. (2 Sam. 22:7-12)
What manner of enemy has arisen against Baal, of foe against the Charioteer of the Clouds? [then, he judges other deities] Surely I smote…Yam [Sea]? Surely I exterminated Nahar [River], the mighty god? Surely I lifted up the dragon, I overpowered him? I smote the writhing serpent, Encircler-with-seven-heads! (KTU 1.3:3.38-41)	[Yahweh] makes the clouds His chariot; He walks upon the wings of the wind; (Ps. 104:3-4) Behold, the LORD is riding on a swift cloud and is about to come to Egypt; The idols of Egypt will tremble at His presence, (Isa. 19:1)

Yahweh is described here with the same exact moniker as Baal, in the same exact context as Baal—revealed in the storm and riding a cloud in judgment on other deities. Baal is subverted by Yahweh.

This correlation of deity with cloud judgment sheds light on the vision of Daniel's Son of Man that Christians understand as a reference to Jesus Christ.[22] The everlasting dominion received by the divine Baal riding the clouds before the throne of the High God El is apologetically ascribed to the divine Son of Man (Jesus Christ) riding the clouds to the throne of "Elyon," the Ancient of Days.[23]

> Dan. 7:13-14
> "I kept looking in the night visions,
> And behold, with the clouds of heaven
> One like a Son of Man was coming,
> And He came up to the Ancient of Days
> And was presented before Him.
> "And to Him was given dominion,
> Glory and a kingdom…
> His dominion is an everlasting dominion.

Yahweh is God, not the Canaanite El. Jesus is Yahweh's son, as opposed to Baal being El's son. And that "Son of Man" is the one who is given a kingdom of everlasting dominion, not Baal.

The Dragon and the Sea

The second narrative element of the Canaanite Baal cycle that I want to address is God's conflict with the dragon and the sea. In ancient Near Eastern religious mythologies, the sea and the sea

---

[22] This also sheds light on Jesus' prophecy regarding his coming judgment on Israel at the destruction of the Temple: "and they will see the Son of Man coming on the clouds of heaven with power and great glory" (Matt 24:30).

[23] The Hebrew word for "Highest One" used in Daniel 7 is *Elyon*, which is the Hebrew equivalent of *Aliyan* in Ugaritic - another frequently used epithet of Baal! "Aliyan," *DDD*, p 18.

dragon were symbols of chaos that had to be overcome to bring order to the universe, or more exactly, the political world order of the myth's originating culture. Some scholars call this battle *Chaoskampf*—the divine struggle to create order out of chaos.[24] Creation accounts were often veiled polemics for the establishment of a king or kingdom's claim to sovereignty.[25] Richard Clifford quotes, "In Mesopotamia, Ugarit, and Israel the *Chaoskampf* appears not only in cosmological contexts but just as frequently—and this was fundamentally true right from the first—in political contexts. The repulsion and the destruction of the enemy, and thereby the maintenance of political order, always constitute one of the major dimensions of the battle against chaos."[26]

For example, the Sumerians had three stories where the gods Enki, Ninurta, and Inanna all destroy sea monsters in their pursuit of establishing order. The sea monster in two of those versions, according to Sumerian expert Samuel Noah Kramer, is "conceived as a large serpent which lived in the bottom of the 'great below' where the latter came in contact with the primeval waters."[27] In the Babylonian creation myth, *Enuma Elish*, Marduk battles the sea dragon goddess Tiamat, and splits her body into two parts, creating the heavens and the earth, the world order over which Babylon's deity Marduk ruled.

Another side-by-side comparison of those same Ugaritic passages that we considered above with *other* Old Testament passages reveals another common narrative: Yahweh, the charioteer

---

[24] Hermann Gunkel first suggested this theme in *Schöpfung und Chaos in Urzdt und Endzeit* (1895).

[25] Bruce R. Reichenbach, "Genesis 1 as a Theological-Political Narrative of Kingdom Establishment," *Bulletin for Biblical Research* 13, 1 (2003).

[26] Clifford, *Creation Accounts*, 8, n. 13.

[27] Samuel Noah Kramer, *Sumerian Mythology: A Study of Spiritual and Literary Achievement in the Third Millennium B.C.* (Philadelphia: University of Pennsylvania Press, 1944, 1961, 1972), 77-78.

of the clouds, metaphorically battles with Sea (Hebrew: *yam*) and River (Hebrew: *nahar*), just as Baal struggled with Yam and Nahar, which is also linked to victory over a sea dragon/serpent.

UGARTIC TEXTS	OLD TESTAMENT
'Dry him up. O Valiant Baal! Dry him up, O Charioteer of the Clouds! For our captive is Prince Yam [Sea], for our captive is Ruler Nahar [River]!' (KTU 1.2:4.8-9) [28]	Did Yahweh rage against the rivers (*nahar*) Or was Your anger against the rivers (*nahar*), Or was Your wrath against the sea (*yam*), That You rode on Your horses, On Your chariots of salvation? (Hab. 3:8)
What manner of enemy has arisen against Baal, of foe against the Charioteer of the Clouds? Surely I smote the Beloved of El, Yam [Sea]? Surely I exterminated Nahar [River], the mighty god? Surely I lifted up the dragon, I overpowered him? I smote the writhing serpent, Encircler-with-seven-heads! (KTU 1.3:3.38-41)	In that day Yahweh will punish Leviathan the fleeing serpent, With His fierce and great and mighty sword, Even Leviathan the twisted serpent; And He will kill the dragon who lives in the sea. (Isa. 27:1) "You divided the sea by your might; you broke the heads of the sea monsters on the waters. You crushed the heads of Leviathan. (Ps. 74:13-14)

Baal fights Sea and River to establish his sovereignty. He wins by drinking up Sea and River, draining them dry, and thus establishing his supremacy over the pantheon and the Canaanite world order.[29] In the second passage, Baal's battle with Sea and River is retold in other words as a battle with a "dragon," the "writhing serpent" with seven heads.[30] Another Baal text calls this same dragon, "*Lotan*, the wriggling serpent."[31] The Hebrew equivalents of the Ugaritic words *tannin* (dragon) and *lotan* are

---

[28] "Charioteer of the Clouds" also appears in these texts: KTU 1.3:4:4, 6, 26; 1.4:3:10, 18; 1.4:5:7, 60; 1.10:1:7; 1.10:3:21, 36; 1.19:1:43; 1.92:37, 39.

[29] KTU 1.2:4:27-32.

[30] See KTU 1.5:1:1-35.

[31] KTU 1.5:1:1-4.

tanniyn (dragon) and *liwyatan* (Leviathan) respectively.[32] Thus, the Canaanite narrative of Leviathan the sea dragon or serpent is undeniably employed in Old Testament Scriptures.[33] Notice the last Scripture in the chart that refers to Leviathan as having multiple heads *just like the Canaanite Leviathan.*

And notice as well the reference to the Red Sea event also associated with Leviathan in the Biblical text. In Psalm 74 above, God's parting of the waters is connected to the motif of the Mosaic covenant as the creation of a new world order in the same way that Baal's victory over the waters and the dragon are emblematic of his establishment of authority in the Canaanite pantheon. This covenant motif is described as a *Chaoskampf* battle with the Sea and Leviathan (also called *Rahab*) in several other significant Biblical references as well.[34]

Mount Zaphon/Sapan

Another element of Baal's reign that was touched upon is his mountain abode of Mount Sapan or Saphon (*Zaphon* in Hebrew). As illustrated in the passages above, a plethora of Ugaritic texts link Baal with his "divine mountain, Saphon/Sapan" (KTU 1.101:1-9; 1.100:9; 1.3:3:29), that he is buried there (KTU 1.6:1:15-18), in his sanctuary (KTU 1.3:3:30), and mountain of victory (KTU 1.101:1-

---

[32] Walter C. Kaiser, Jr., *The Ugaritic Pantheon* (dissertation) (Ann Arbor, MI: Brandeis University, 1973), 212.

[33] See also Isaiah 51:9; Ezekiel 32:2; Revelation 12:9, 16, 17.

[34] Psalm 89:9-10; Isaiah 51:9-10; Job 26:12-13. Psalms 18, 29, 24, 29, 65, 74, 77, 89, 93, and 104 all reflect *chaoskampf.* See also Exodus 15, Job 9, 26, 38, and Isaiah 51:14-16; 2 Samuel 22.

4). Earlier Hurrian and Hittite traditions of Baal link Mount Zaphon with another mountain, Namni, both in the northern Syrian ranges.[35]

This linking of the two mountains is of particular importance because as the *Dictionary of Deities and Demons in the Bible* explains, the Psalmist asserts Yahweh's authority as creator and therefore owner of all the heavens and the earth by referring to the mountains of pagan mythology as under the lordship of Yahweh.

> Psalm 89:12
>
> The north (zaphon) and the south (yamin), you have created them; Tabor and Hermon joyously praise your name.

Tabor and Hermon are well-known holy mountains in ANE mythology.[36] But the deliberate linking of *Zaphon* and *Yamin* are most likely Hebrew references to the Saphon and Namni of Ugarit in a symbolic reflection of Tabor and Hermon.

In Isaiah 14:13, Isaiah mocks the arrogance of the king of Babylon by likening him to another mythological figure, Athtar, who sought to take Baal's throne and failed "on the mountain of assembly on the summit of Zaphon [Sapan]."[37]

In the Bible, this Mount Zaphon is subverted by Israel's holy Mount Zion.

---

[35] H. Niehr, "Zaphon", in *Dictionary of Deities and Demons in the Bible*, ed. Karel van der Toorn, Bob Becking and Pieter W. van der Horst, 2nd extensively rev. ed., 927 (Leiden; Boston; Köln; Grand Rapids, MI; Cambridge: Brill; Eerdmans, 1999).

[36] Rami Arav, "Hermon, Mount (Place)," ed. David Noel Freedman, *The Anchor Yale Bible Dictionary* (New York: Doubleday, 1992), 158.

[37] Michael Heiser, "The Mythological Provenance of Isaiah 14:12-15: A Reconsideration of the Ugaritic Material" Liberty University <http://digitalcommons.liberty.edu/lts fac pubs/280>

Psalm 48:1–2

Great is the LORD and greatly to be praised in the city of our God! His holy mountain, beautiful in elevation, is the joy of all the earth, Mount Zion, in the far north [Zaphon], the city of the great King.

Note in this Scripture that the holy Mount Zion is described as being in "the far north," the very location of Mount Sapan, but not in fact the actual location of Israel's Mount Zion. So "the far north" is a theological not a geographical designation of Zion replacing Sapan as the divine mountain par excellence.[38]

Subverting Paganism

The story of deity battling the river, the sea, and the sea dragon Leviathan is clearly a common covenant motif in the Old Testament and its surrounding ancient Near Eastern cultures. The fact that Hebrew Scripture shares common words, concepts, and stories with Ugaritic scripture need not mean that Israel is affirming the same mythology or pantheon of deities. The orthodox Christian need not fear literary similarity between Israel and Canaanite imagination. Common imagination springs from what Old Testament and ancient Near Eastern scholar John Walton calls a "common cognitive environment" of people in a shared space, time, or culture.

Walton suggests "borrowing is not the issue...Likewise this need not concern whose ideas are derivative. There is simply

---

[38] H. Niehr, "Zaphon", in *Dictionary of Deities and Demons in the Bible*, ed. Karel van der Toorn, Bob Becking and Pieter W. van der Horst, 2nd extensively rev. ed., 929 (Leiden; Boston; Köln; Grand Rapids, MI; Cambridge: Brill; Eerdmans, 1999). Also see Job 26:7; 37:22; Ezek. 1:4 where the word "north" is used as a spiritual reference, more allusion to the divine mountain Saphon of Canaanite belief.

common ground across the cognitive environment of the cultures of the ancient world."[39]

The story of a cloud-rider controlling the elements and battling the Sea and Leviathan to establish his sovereignty over other gods with a new world order is not a false "myth." It is a narrative shared between Israel and its pagan neighbors that Jewish authors appropriate, under divine authority of Yahweh, as a metaphor within their own discourse. God uses that cultural connection to subvert those words, concepts, and stories with His own poetic meaning and purpose.

Great fathers of the Faith utilized this same subversive storytelling. Curtis Chang, in his book, *Engaging Unbelief*, explains how Augustine wrote his *City of God* to defend the Christian faith in the Roman Empire in terms of urban historical narrative saturated with references, motifs, and themes from classical Roman authors. He subverted that "City of Man" by revealing the destructive pride lurking behind all human social construction. Aquinas, in his *Summa contra Gentiles*, appealed to the Aristotelian story of knowledge because he was addressing a Muslim culture steeped in Aristotle. But he subverted that cultural narrative by teasing out the ultimate insufficiency of human reason.

Campus evangelist Curtis Chang explains this rhetorical strategy as threefold: "1. Entering the challenger's story, 2. Retelling the story, 3. Capturing that retold tale with the gospel metanarrative."[40] He writes that the challenge of each epoch in history is a contest in storytelling, a challenge to "overturn and

---

[39] John H. Walton, *Ancient Near Eastern Thought and the Old Testament: Introducing the Conceptual World of the Hebrew Bible* (Grand Rapids: Baker, 2006), 21.

[40] Curtis Chang, *Engaging Unbelief: A Captivating Strategy from Augustine to Aquinas* (Downers Grove, IL: InterVarsity Press, 2000), 26.

supplant the inherited story of the epoch with its own metanarrative…The one who can tell the best story, in a very real sense, wins the epoch."[41]

The defense of the gospel in this hostile epoch requires muscular Christians to enter into the narratives of our culture and retell those stories with bold fresh perspectives. I have repeatedly used J. R. R. Tolkien and C. S. Lewis as examples of subversive authors who entered into the genres and mythology of pagan worlds to harness them for Christian imagination. Tolkien's Middle Earth abounded with the mythical Norse characters of wizards, dwarves, elves, giants, trolls, and others. Lewis's Narnia is saturated with a plethora of beasts from assorted pagan mythologies, deliberately subjugated to the Lordship of Aslan.

I am a filmmaker, so I think in terms of movies. We need more storytellers to tell vampire stories with a Christian worldview (*The Addiction*); more zombie stories with a Christian worldview (*I Am Legend*); more demonic stories with Christian redemption (M. Night Shyamalan's *Devil*); more post-apocalyptic thrillers that honor God (*The Book of Eli*); more subversion of adultery (*Fatal Attraction*), fornication (*17 Again*), unbelief (*Paranormal Activity*), paganism (*Apocalypto*), humanistic anti-supernaturalism (*The Last Exorcism*), and our "pro-Choice" culture of death (*The Island*).

I will end with a question and a charge. With two exceptions, why were all these movies that subversively incarnate the Christian worldview made by non-Christians instead of Christians? Rise up, O Christian storytellers and subvert ye the world's imagination!

For additional Biblical, historical and mythical research related to this novel, go to www.ChroniclesoftheNephilim.com under the menu listing, "Scholarly Research" or *Click Here*.

---

[41] Ibid., 27.

If you liked this book, then please help me out by writing an honest review of it on Amazon (<u>click here to write review</u>). That is one of the best ways to say thank you to me as an author. It really does help my exposure and status as an author. It's really easy. In the Customer Reviews section, there is a little box that says "Write a customer review." They guide you easily through the process. Thanks! *— Brian Godawa*

GREAT OFFERS BY BRIAN GODAWA

Get More
Biblical Imagination

**Sign up Online For
The Godawa Chronicles**

www.Godawa.com

Updates and Freebies
of the Books of Brian Godawa
Special Discounts,
Weird Bible Facts!

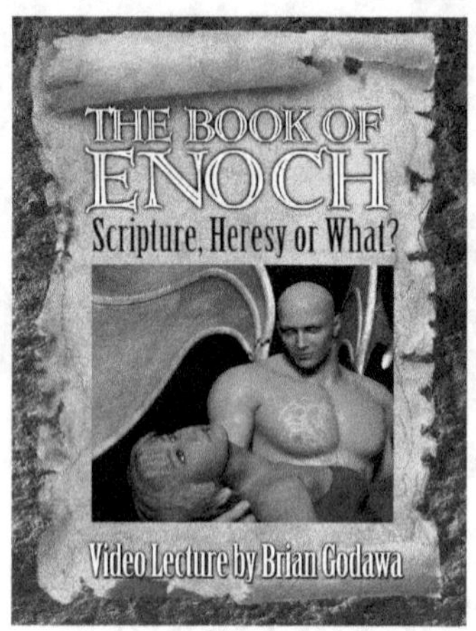

The Book of Enoch: Scripture, Heresy or What?

This lecture by Brian Godawa will be an introduction to the ancient book of 1Enoch, its content, its history, its affirmation in the New Testament, and its acceptance and rejection by the Christian Church. What is the Book of Enoch? Where did it come from? Why isn't it in the Bible? How does the Book of Enoch compare with the Bible?

Available on video.

Chronicles of the Nephilim: The Ancient Biblical Story

Watchers, Nephilim, and the Divine Council of the Sons of God. In this dvd video lecture, Brian Godawa explores the Scriptures behind this transformative storyline that inspired his best-selling Biblical novel series Chronicles of the Nephilim.

Available on video.

To download these lectures and other books and products by Brian Godawa, just go to the STORE at:
www.Godawa.com

How God Captures the Imagination

This book was previously titled *Myth Became Fact: Storytelling, Imagination & Apologetics in the Bible*.

Brian Godawa, Hollywood screenwriter and best-selling novelist, explores the nature of imagination in the Bible. You will learn how God subverts pagan religions by appropriating their imagery and creativity, and redeeming them within a Biblical worldview. Improve your imagination in your approach to glorifying God and defending the faith.

Demonizing the Pagan Gods
God verbally attacked his opponents, pagans and their gods, using sarcasm, mockery, name-calling.

Old Testament Storytelling Apologetics
Israel shared creative images with their pagan neighbors: The sea dragon of chaos and the storm god. The Bible invests them with new meaning.

Biblical Creation and Storytelling
Creation stories in the ancient Near East and the Bible both express a primeval battle of deity to create order out of chaos. But how do they differ?

The Universe in Ancient Imagination
A detailed comparison and contrast of the Biblical picture of the universe with the ancient pagan one. What's the difference?

New Testament Storytelling Apologetics
Paul's sermon to the pagans on Mars Hill is an example of subversion: Communicating the Gospel in terms of a pagan narrative with a view toward replacing their worldview.

Imagination in Prophecy & Apocalypse
God uses imaginative descriptions of future events to deliberately obscure his message while simultaneously showing the true meaning and purpose behind history.

An Apologetic of Biblical Horror
Learn how God uses horror in the Bible as a tool to communicate spiritual, moral and social truth in the context of repentance from sin and redemptive victory over evil.

For More Info
www.Godawa.com

THE IMAGINATION OF GOD

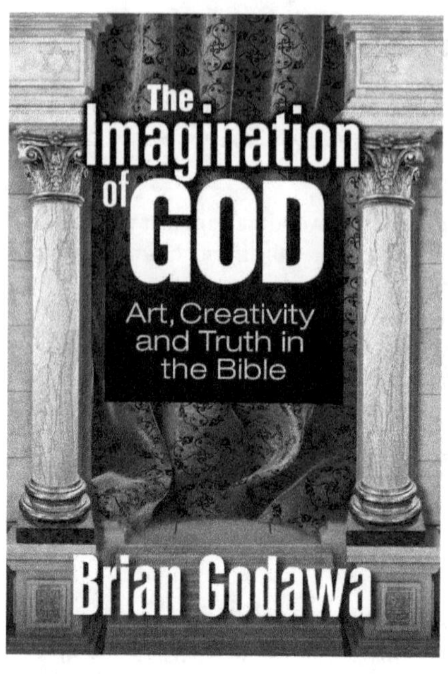

Art, Creativity and Truth in the Bible

In his refreshing and challenging book, Godawa helps you break free from the spiritual suffocation of heady faith. Without negating the importance of reason and doctrine, Godawa challenges you to move from understanding the Bible "literally" to "literarily" by exploring the poetry, parables and metaphors found in God's Word. Weaving historical insight, pop culture and personal narrative throughout, Godawa reveals the importance God places on imagination and creativity in the Scriptures, and provides a Biblical foundation for Christians to pursue imagination, beauty, wonder and mystery in their faith.

This book was previously released with the title, *Word Pictures: Knowing God Through Story and Imagination.*

Endorsements:

"Brian Godawa is that rare breed—a philosopher/artist—who opens our eyes to the aesthetic dimension of spirituality. Cogently argued and fun to read, Godawa shows convincingly that God interacts with us as whole persons, not only through didactic teaching but also through metaphor, symbol, and sacrament."

— Nancy R. Pearcey,
Author, *Total Truth: Liberating Christianity from its Cultural Captivity*

"A spirited and balanced defense of the imagination as a potential conveyer of truth. There is a lot of good literary theory in the book, as well as an autobiographical story line. The thoroughness of research makes the book a triumph of scholarship as well."

— Leland Ryken, Clyde S. Kilby Professor of English, Wheaton College, Illinois
Author, *The Christian Imagination: The Practice of Faith in Literature & Writing.*

For More Info
www.Godawa.com

ABOUT THE AUTHOR

Brian Godawa is the screenwriter for the award-winning feature film, *To End All Wars,* starring Kiefer Sutherland. It was awarded the Commander in Chief Medal of Service, Honor and Pride by the Veterans of Foreign Wars, won the first Heartland Film Festival by storm, and showcased the Cannes Film Festival Cinema for Peace.

He also co-wrote *Alleged*, starring Brian Dennehy as Clarence Darrow and Fred Thompson as William Jennings Bryan. He previously adapted to film the best-selling supernatural thriller novel *The Visitation* by author Frank Peretti for Ralph Winter (*X-Men, Wolverine*), and wrote and directed *Wall of Separation,* a PBS documentary, and *Lines That Divide*, a documentary on stem cell research.

Mr. Godawa's scripts have won multiple awards in respected screenplay competitions, and his articles on movies and philosophy have been published around the world. He has traveled around the United States teaching on movies, worldviews, and culture to colleges, churches and community groups.

His popular book, *Hollywood Worldviews: Watching Films with Wisdom and Discernment* (InterVarsity Press) is used as a textbook in schools around the country. His novel series, the saga *Chronicles of the Nephilim* is in the Top 10 of Biblical Fiction on Amazon and is an imaginative retelling of Biblical stories of the Nephilim giants, the secret plan of the fallen Watchers, and the War of the Seed of the Serpent with the Seed of Eve. The sequel series, *Chronicles of the Apocalypse* tells the story of the Apostle John's book of Revelation, and *Chronicles of the Watchers* recounts true history through the Watcher paradigm.

Find out more about his other books, lecture tapes and dvds for sale at his website **www.godawa.com**.

BLANK PAGE

BLANK PAGE

BLANK PAGE

BLANK PAGE